**Books should be returned on or before the
last date stamped below.**

JUN 02.

31. OCT 06.
24. AUG 07.
09. MAY 08.

04 NOV 09.

08. JUL 10.

08. APR 11.
31. JAN 12.

05. NOV 12. 52

19. DEC 12. N40

04 FEB 13. 48

2 0 MAY 2013

08. JUL 13.

25. FEB 14.

JUN MAR 15.

11. FEB 16.

12. SEP 16.

31. MAY 17.

16. OCT 17.

19. JUN 18.

2 2 FEB 2019

30. OCT 19.

CORONATION ST: KEEPING THE HOME FIRES BURNING

The enthralling saga of life on Coronation Street during World War I

It is 1914 and as childhood pals, workmates and neighbours proudly march off to war, Ena Schofield feels she must do her bit. She grabs a passing lad and asks his name – and so begins a unique correspondence with young Albert Tatlock – but will friendship turn to love?

CORONATION ST:
KEEPING THE
HOME FIRES BURNING

Coronation St: Keeping The Home Fires Burning

by

Daran Little

Magna Large Print Books
Long Preston, North Yorkshire,
BD23 4ND, England.

F

1236786

British Library Cataloguing in Publication Data.

Little, Daran
    Coronation St: Keeping the home fires burning.

    A catalogue record of this book is
    available from the British Library

    ISBN   0-7505-1890-1

First published in Great Britain in 2001 by Granada Media
an imprint of André Deutsch Limited in association with
Granada Media Group

Text Copyright © Granada Media Group Limited 2001

Coronation Street is based on an idea by Tony Warren and is a
Granada Media Production

Cover illustration by arrangement with
Granada Media Group Ltd.

The right of Daran Little to be identified as the author of this
work has been asserted by him in accordance with the
Copyright, Designs and Patents Act, 1988

Published in Large Print 2002 by arrangement with
Granada Media Group Limited

Magna Large Print is an imprint of Library Magna Books Ltd.

Printed and bound in Great Britain by
T.J. (International) Ltd., Cornwall, PL28 8RW

CHAPTER ONE

August 1914

Coronation Street wasn't Ena's normal stamping ground. It was only separated from her home on Inkerman Street by two narrow terraced streets but she was a girl whose world began at Mrs Hawkin's Corner Shop and ended at the public baths. Inkerman Street was a snake-like avenue of two-up two-down brick dwellings, which ran from the dyeworks to the canal towpath. Its steep cobbles acted as stepping stones and urchins in rags, their feet bare, shot down them in converted fruit boxes on wheels. By comparison, Coronation Street was shorter and its houses nestled together on only one side; the other was dominated by a towering cotton mill. Built twenty years after Inkerman Street, the fronts of the Coronation Street houses had boasted bay-windows, and because of this Ena's mother and neighbours considered the residents of the newer street stuck up.

Ena didn't have much cause to venture south towards Coronation Street: the first few years of her life had been spent at her mother's knee, and she went to school at Silk Street Elementary up by the canal. From the age of ten she'd worked a loom at Hardcastle's Factory School. Now she was nearly fifteen, and about to become familiar with Coronation Street: she was to join her father, uncles, aunt and sister in the weaving house at Hardcastle's cotton mill. The houses in the grid-like streets surrounding the mill had been built for its workers and from now on each morning Ena Schofield would run with her fellow clog-footed workers down Coronation Street to clock on. But not today.

To the residents of Weatherfield a bank holiday was a day of enforced unemployment, which led to a lighter pay packet at the end of the week. The only resident of Inkerman Street who genuinely welcomed them was Fred Longsthwaite, the fifty-seven-year-old knocker-upper, employed as a human alarm clock, who rose at three forty-five each day to bang on bedroom windows with his rod to ensure that his neighbours got to work on time. As Ena's father, Thomas, muttered to himself that morning, 'Bank 'olidays are all right for them as can afford 'em.'

His weary wife Mary had nodded in agreement, and sighed at the prospect of carrying out her chores with the house full of people. Monday was wash day, and bank holiday or no bank holiday sheets had to be boiled, pounded, pushed through the mangle, hung out to dry and ironed. She knew from experience that Thomas would lay claim to the table for the best part of the morning as he sucked on his pipe and whittled himself another chessman. He was a fine craftsman, if a slow one, and the pieces he had already spent eighteen months carving stood proudly on the mantelpiece. Mary didn't understand which was which, or the significance of the different sizes and shapes, but she liked the horses.

Thomas had started the carvings as a way of passing the time he'd been accustomed to spend in conversation with his only son. Tom had been his pride and joy, a sturdy, ruddy-looking chap who turned lasses' eyes and was a hearty, chummy fellow. They'd always been good pals, and Thomas had looked upon him more as a friend than a son. When Tom had announced his intention to leave England and seek his fortune in

9

America Thomas's world had dimmed.

Tom's departure had devastated the family: young Ena had mourned the hero she had adored, Mary stared out of the scullery window into the backyard, picturing her lad as the child he had been, while Thomas had refused to let anyone mention his name in the house. In truth, he blamed himself for his son's departure and felt impotent for having brought him into a world that Tom felt had nothing to offer him. He had sailed from Liverpool in the spring of 1912 and it had been three months after his safe arrival that the Schofields were able to lay aside fears that perhaps he had travelled on the ill-fated *Titanic*.

Ena hated the chessmen because they were a daily reminder of Tom's absence. Her elder sister, Alice, didn't mind them so much as she envied Tom having escaped their mean lives. She plotted her own departure, gleefully pointing out to Ena that, as the youngest child, it would be her lot to remain in Weatherfield to care for their parents as they grew older. Ena wasn't bothered by that sort of talk, even when it was meant as a threat: she could think of nothing more comforting than remaining at

No. 14 Inkerman Street, with its dripping tap, draughty bedrooms and damp scullery. It was home.

Ena spent bank-holiday morning helping her mother with the family wash. At lunchtime she crossed the canal and wandered over to Plank Street market where her friend from school days, Minnie Carlton, attempted to drum up trade at her grandfather's foot-ointment and hair-restorer stall. It was a fruitless task: the sight of the old man's bald head and his feet bound in decaying socks never induced confidence in the public. Intelligence didn't feature in Minnie's family genes, and neither she nor the old man ever worked out why sales were always down. Ena, however, was known for her common sense and quick thinking. At school she had looked out for Minnie, and now that they had entered the workforce she still kept a fond eye on the girl. The friendship bemused Mary Schofield: she always maintained that Amy Carlton must have dropped the girl on her head as a baby, and counted it a blessing that Minnie was an only child. But she preferred Minnie to the other girl who was forever hanging round Ena: twig-like Martha Hartley always had a dew-drop hanging off her nose and Mary summed her up as 'shifty and mean-mouthed', saying that she hung on to the drew-drop as she was too mean to give it away.

Martha had joined her two friends at the market and they'd sat beside the canal soaking in the sun for the best part of the afternoon. Ena enjoyed having her around: Martha was a full four years older than her, and it was satisfying to know that an eighteen-year-old wanted to spend time with you. Mary often commented that there had to be something wrong with a girl who had no friends her own age and sought out the company of younger girls, but Ena ignored her. Martha had a bitter outlook on life, which Ena found intriguing as she was a natural optimist and saw the world as a wonderful place. Martha was a worrier, who saw trouble around every corner, while Minnie was a dreamer, who never even saw the corner.

The fourth of August 1914 should have passed like any other bank holiday, but it left a sting in its tail that would alter for ever the lives of Ena, Minnie and Martha, along with those of every other inhabitant in Weather-field. That night, as Ena nestled up against her sister's bony back, and Thomas Schofield's snores echoed around the house, Britain declared war on Germany.

In the morning the news hit the cobbled streets of Weatherfield as the waking workforce made their way to mills and factories. At No. 14 Inkerman Street, Alice was first to hear it: she had overheard gossip as she fed the couple of hens the family kept for their eggs. She rushed indoors. 'We're at war!' she cried.

'You what?' Thomas paused with his breakfast, a slice of bread and jam hanging out of his mouth.

'War, Dad. They're all talkin' about it out there. It's us against Germany.'

Thomas pushed back his chair across the worn lino. He glanced towards his wife, who avoided his gaze, deep in her own thoughts. The losses of the Boer War were still keenly felt and another war in a foreign land was nothing to welcome. She'd joined her friends at shop counters struggling to make sense of an overseas conflict caused by the death of an archduke. None of the women could read so they relied on passing information from mouth to mouth.

Thomas grabbed his cap from its hook behind the parlour door and left the house.

Realising he'd left his snap tin behind, Ena picked it up, along with her own lunch, and skipped after him.

Normally Inkerman Street echoed to the sound of clogs clattering across the cobbles as weavers plodded to work. Today it resounded to the noise of voices as the news was spread and picked over.

The Schofields' neighbour, old Arnold Applegate, himself a veteran of the 1855 Crimean war, held court at the Street corner as he claimed authority on conflict and strategy. Thomas steered clear of the old man, whom he had always considered a fool, and instead joined a group of his drinking partners from the Tripedressers Arms.

'It's 'appened then,' he said, by way of introduction.

'Aye,' said Tommy Flint.

'Aye,' agreed Fred Barnes.

'Aye,' nodded Willie Fletcher.

Standing behind her father, Ena looked around at the clusters of men and women, taking in the unusual sight of inactivity. She knew from experience that the mill hooters would soon be going off and that anyone clocking on after that would be docked a morning's wage, but no one seemed in any

14

hurry to set off to work. The idea of a stationary workforce gave her a rush of excitement, which made her feel defiant and naughty.

The slam of a front door caused heads to turn up Inkerman Street. In the doorway of No. 32, Ernest Clegg brought his heels sharply together, resulting in a click that echoed across the street. Dressed in the smart uniform of a Territorial, he grinned at his neighbours then marched swiftly down the street. The men looked on in open envy, the women with open mouths.

'Where you off to, Ernie, lad?' called a voice.

'I'm reportin' to the Armoury,' came the reply. 'If any of you lads want to, you can follow on.'

He moved down the street like a modern-day Pied Piper, for the sight of his gleaming buttons attracted many men, who threw aside all thoughts of work and marched behind him. Ernest had been a reservist for two years, trained to help in home defence, and had been taunted by his non-military-minded neighbours. Now was his hour, and he was the one to whom they turned for a lead. He wasn't going to let them down. He marched on, his head held high, crossing streets and alleyways while the crowd behind him grew.

Ena put out a hand to touch her father's arm but he didn't notice her. Instead he followed his friends. Caps were thrown high in the air, cheers rang out and someone started up a song. A sharp tingling rushed through Ena's slender body and she gasped at the sight of so many men marching off together – almost every man she knew, from fourteen-year-old Henry Shuttler, with whom she'd sat at school, through to eighty-six-year-old Arnold Applegate. Some women and children joined in the march but Ena shrank back towards her open front door and stumbled into the house. Her mother stood in the hallway, watching the retreating crowd and wiping her hands aggressively on her apron. She couldn't waste time like that: Tuesday was baking day, war or no war.

Named to commemorate the repatriation of brewery son Lieutenant Philip Ridley after the Boer War, the Rover's Return Inn stood at the corner of Rosamund and Coronation Streets. It was a small public house with no frills, a working-man's pub with sawdust on the floor. Women were tolerated but they

16

preferred to drink in the tiny Snug bar. The architect's plans for the pub had included a door directly on the corner of the two streets that would open into the Snug, but this had been overlooked by a corner-cutting builder and the womenfolk grumbled that to reach their sanctum they had to cross the minefield of the Public bar.

The name displayed over the front door was that of James Frederick Corbishley, holder of the pub's licence. It was a grand name for a man of average height, build and looks. Having earned a healthy crust running a grocery shop in neighbouring Salford, Jim had been talked into sinking his savings into buying the pub's licence. It had been his wife, Nellie, short of stature, large of voice, who had seen the potential for climbing the social ladder in running a public house. It might just be a back-street alehouse but she took satisfaction in knowing that she possessed the only zinc bath in the neighbourhood.

'We'll 'ave a nice bit of gammon,' Nellie instructed her housekeeper.

'Creamed 'taters and carrots?' suggested Pearl, sniffing with sinus trouble, the cross she had to bear.

Nellie nodded and turned her attention to

the accounts book. The two women sat together at the living-room table, nursing china tea-cups. Planning the day's movements and meals was something to which they both looked forward, Nellie because she liked to be ordered and Pearl because she was a woman with a hefty appetite.

Life had dealt Pearl Crapper a hard hand. She'd buried empty coffins after her husband and son had been killed in a disaster down the Weatherfield coal mine, and another son, whom she called her late-in-life accident, had been a victim of TB. Nellie had offered Pearl the job of resident housekeeper, but not from generosity of spirit. Pearl worked round the clock, cleaning the pub and the living quarters, cooking, washing, mending and helping out behind the bar.

Pearl shared her bedroom with a woman half her age. Sarah Bridges hailed from Liverpool and was Jim's idea of the perfect barmaid: soft of voice and easy on the eye. She sat with the other two women, sipping tea, but taking no part in the conversation. She had no time for domestic arrangements. 'There's no point in opening up,' she said, draining her cup.

'Oh, no?' asked Nellie.

'All men'll be joining up,' said Sarah.

'Will they?'

'Stands to reason.'

'Well, after they've joined up they'll be thirsty,' said Nellie.

Sarah pulled a face: left to her the pub could stay closed all day.

Pearl kept quiet. Talk of war bothered her.

Beyond the double doors that separated the living quarters from the Public bar, Jim Corbishley pulled himself a glass of best bitter. He enjoyed drinking as much as his customers did and he could see any of them under the table. He swore that the first pint of the day cured the hangover from the night before. He belched loudly and swept a shaking hand across his receding, greasy hair.

Behind him, the cellar door opened and a man in his late twenties carried in a crate of brown-ale bottles. He slid it under the bar, straightened up and pulled himself a pint.

Jim glanced at him with undisguised distaste. Charlie was every inch his son, in looks, mannerisms and attitudes, and as such he was a daily reminder of the ageing process. In his youth Jim had been a womanising rogue, a bare-knuckle champion who had sired three bastards before taking his own father's advice and marrying Nellie, the daughter of a local draper with his own premises. He hadn't intended marriage to hinder his favourite activities but his enthusiasm for such pursuits had waned with his energy after serving behind the shop's counters all hours.

As Jim's sun had set his son's had risen, fast and bright. As soon as he hit fifteen Charlie had launched himself upon the unsuspecting female population of Salford. In 1902 when the family moved to Weatherfield he extricated himself from a couple of difficult entanglements, and started to plough fresh ground. The sight of Charlie's fresh face, guzzling back his pint, intensified his father's hangover.

'Smashin' pint that,' said Charlie, smacking his lips and banging his pot down on the bar.

Jim winced as the clang of pottery against wood reverberated inside his skull.

'Thinkin' I'll go to Armoury in a bit,' said Charlie. 'See what's goin' on.'

'Why? Fancy a spot o' fightin'?'

'Well, it's gotta be better than bein' stuck in this place.'

For once Jim was in agreement with his

son and cursed his luck in being fifty-five. There was no way they'd want him to fight. Charlie would probably go off and have a lark with his pals and Jim would be left to rot with the women and kids.

A week after Charlie Corbishley had taken a stroll across town to join the mass of young men waiting eagerly outside the Armoury, Ena Schofield found herself caught up in a jostling crowd outside the Rover's Return. It was early morning, and Ena had refused to believe her sister when she said that clocking-on time had been delayed an hour as the first wave of volunteers was leaving Weatherfield. She'd risen as usual, eaten her bread and scrape, pulled her shawl around her shoulders and set off down Inkerman Street. Almost at once she'd been caught up in the human sea, her view obstructed by caps and picture hats redeemed from the pawn shop for the occasion.

Children ran between adult legs, darting forward for a better view of the spectacle that promised the impossible: to make this day different from the rest. Weatherfield days always followed the same monotonous inevitability from the bang of the knocker-upper to the throwing out of the drunks from the public houses. It wasn't often that spectacle crossed the cobbles.

Despite her misgivings about the war, Ena couldn't help but feel excited by the electric atmosphere buzzing around her neighbours.

'Ena! Ena!'

She followed the sound of the voice and located Martha, standing across Rosamund Street with her back to the Rover's wall. With the same quick skill she showed at the loom, Ena darted through the crowd and skipped across the Street, her clogs clanging on the metal tram-lines. Martha reached out a hand and pulled her on to the pavement.

'It's so exciting, in't it?'

'I guess.' Ena shrugged and cast an eye around the street. There was certainly a party atmosphere. Someone had hung bunting from the lamp-posts and the Union Flag flew from several windows. A woman, who Ena knew worked at the public baths, stood on the other side of the Street proudly holding a framed likeness of the King. Her solemn expression made Ena want to laugh.

Martha grabbed Ena's arm and shrilled, 'I can hear a band!'

The crowd fell silent as the first notes of a bugle and the beat of a drum echoed down Rosamund Street. Then, as a body, the onlookers cheered as if their lives depended upon it. Martha's voice threatened to deafen Ena, and she stepped back, away from the kerb. People pressed forward and took her place, the men waving their caps wildly in the air.

Behind her, the door to the Rover's Return opened, and she watched as a group of people walked out on to Coronation Street. The focus was on a tall man in an ill-fitting uniform. A well-dressed woman, clad in black as if already in mourning, held a handkerchief to her eyes to hide the tears that betrayed her feelings. An older man with a worn face, set in a hard expression, slapped the tall man on the shoulders, a blow that seemed to propel him away from the door. Another woman, a toothless old biddy with her hair dragged into a bun, seemed to be taking her cue from the well-dressed woman but wailed loudly. The new recruit stood to attention, saluted, and marched towards Ena and the cheering crowds.

As he came close to her Ena was aware of his blue eyes staring straight at her. She felt uncomfortable and blushed. He laughed, then pushed his way through the crowd.

Rather than be seen crying in public

Nellie Corbishley retired into the pub but Pearl Crapper, always one for spectacle and ceremony, rushed after Charlie, determined to watch him and his fellow soldiers march away.

Left alone outside the Rover's front door, Jim lit his pipe and leant heavily against the brickwork. The young, fit men went to war, the old, useless men stayed behind.

Next to the Rover's Return stood the first of the seven terraced houses that made up Coronation Street. As Jim watched the banners and flags waving, the front door of No. 1 opened and another group came out on to the cobbles. As before, one was in uniform, but there the similarities between the Corbishleys and their nearest neighbours ended. The uniformed lad, nineteen but small and slight for his age, was Albert Tatlock, a quiet boy who, to Jim's certain knowledge, had never taken a drink at the Rover's. Jim gave him the once over and decided he'd probably never taken a drink anywhere. He looked insipid and pathetic as he clung to his kit-bag.

Jim nodded to his neighbours and went back to sucking his pipe. He wasn't interested in those who never crossed his threshold.

'Well, I'd best be off then,' said Albert.

'Remember, lad, you can only do your best. No one, not even God himself, can ask more from you,' said Tommy Osbourne, Albert's uncle by marriage and tenant of No. 1 Coronation Street. His thick accent made Tommy stand out as a first-generation Russian immigrant.

His wife, Albert's maternal aunt, Mary, patted her nephew's arm and kissed his smooth cheek.

'Take care of yourself. You'll be home soon. They say it'll be over by Christmas.'

'Hanukkah even,' said Tommy, with a smile.

'I'll write when I can,' promised Albert.

'You know where we live,' said Mary.

Albert shook hands with his uncle, who drew him close in an embrace, then kissed his aunt. The couple stepped back and Albert was faced with his younger brother Alfred. Both boys had the same, under-nourished build and if Albert looked less than his age, his sixteen-year-old brother seemed no more than thirteen. Since their parents had died Albert had taken care of his brother, working long hours in a mill to pay for their lodgings in Rosamund Street.

Albert had been one of the first to volunteer upon the declaration of war and they had relinquished their one-roomed home in favour of Alf staying with Aunt Mary on Coronation Street.

Albert tried to ignore the tears he saw forming in his brother's eyes and concentrated on being bluff and cheery. He slapped Alf's shoulder and told him to do as he was told and not to worry, that he'd see him again soon. Alf bit his lip and nodded. Neither brother was good at expressing their feelings, yet they had grown to depend upon each other. Without Albert around Alf didn't know what he was going to do.

'Hey, Albert!'

Albert turned towards the voice and gave a wave as he recognised his best friend Dinky Low. Dinky sprinted down Coronation Street and stopped next to the Tatlock brothers. At nearly six foot he towered over his friends and Albert noticed with envy that his uniform actually fitted.

'Isn't it all just grand?' Dinky asked, his voice dancing.

'Aye,' mumbled Albert.

'Are we for the off, then?'

'Aye.'

Dinky nodded towards Tommy and Mary

and gave them a cheery wave. 'Take care of yourselves, Mr and Mrs Osbourne. Don't you worry about Albert – I'll make sure he kills his share of Jerries.'

The onlookers laughed. Everyone liked Dinky. He was a good-looking lad, with charm and a love of life.

The two friends waved and set off past Jim Corbishley towards Rosamund Street.

Ena watched Dinky as he came towards her. She felt her heartbeat quicken and bit back a sigh. She knew him by sight, as did all the girls, and he had once passed the time of day with her in a queue for tripe, but she was certain he wouldn't remember that. She had no idea who the short chap was. The pair paused, close by her, and Dinky lit a cigarette. Their conversation drifted over to her.

'Madge wanted to wave me off,' said Dinky, 'but she's a terrible weeper so we said our goodbyes in her front parlour. Her mother had made Eccles cakes.'

'I like Eccles cakes.'

'I've got a couple in my kit. We'll share them later.'

'Champion,' said Albert.

'She's going to write to me every day, she says.'

'I've to write to me auntie,' said Albert.

'No, that won't do,' cried Dinky. 'You're a soldier going off to war – you've got to have a lass writing to you. It's tradition.'

'And me auntie won't do?'

Dinky laughed at his friend's troubled face. 'No. It has to be a girl.' He smiled at Albert then his eyes fell on Ena.

She blushed when she saw that Dinky was looking at her, and turned away but his voice arrested her. 'Excuse me...'

'He remembers me!' she thought, but she didn't want to be associated with tripe.

He beckoned Ena to join him and her feet moved quickly to his side. She took no notice of the blushing Albert. 'Hello, I hope you don't mind, but my friend and I are just about to go off and I wondered if you could help us.' Ena wallowed in Dinky's charm.

'If I can I'd be glad to.' She made an effort to sound her consonants.

'Well, it's my friend here. I wonder if you'd agree to write to him. He's not got anyone else and it would mean a lot to him to hear from his home town.'

Albert noticed Ena's face fall. It was always the same: the lasses fell at Dinky's feet but didn't want anything to do with him.

Ena regained her composure. She had been brought up to help her fellow man and if anyone needed help the poor blighter who stood next to Dinky did. 'Of course I'll write. What's his name?' she asked, still looking at Dinky.

'Albert Tatlock,' answered Albert. 'Private. Lancashire Fusiliers, Weatherfield Division.'

Ena smiled at him and nodded. 'How do, Albert? I'm Ena Schofield.'

She stood on the pavement as Albert and Dinky pushed their way through the crowd and joined the tail end of the marching column. She watched as best she could until they were out of sight. Actually, she watched Dinky because she could easily see his head above the crowds. She assumed Albert was marching alongside him but he was so short it was as if the onlookers had eaten him up. She uttered a quiet prayer: 'God bless you, lads, and bring you home safely. God bless you, Dinky Low. God bless you, Albert Tatlock.'

CHAPTER TWO

November 1914

Ena Schofield and Mary Makepiece shared a bond that had united them in friendship since their first day at Silk Street Elementary: they had been born on the same day, 14 November 1899, within ten minutes of each other. Mary was triumphant that she had arrived first, but school chums had always made more of the fact Ena had been born with the caul covering her face and therefore, as everyone knew, would never drown.

Not that many people drowned in Weatherfield unless they were the sort who drank too much ale and stumbled into the sinister waters of the canal. The only running water in the local homes was cold and dripped from the scullery tap into an enamel sink. Those who practised weekly bathing, like Ena, carried the iron bath from its hanging place in the backyard into the kitchen and filled it with water heated on

31

the range. Every two months or so Ena, and like-minded people, visited the public baths on Nelson Street where for twopence a large tub of clean water was made available for five minutes.

Ena and Mary celebrated their birthday differently, in accordance with their appearance and character. Petite and sullen, Mary was used to grabbing attention with the same ferocity she pounced upon bread and jam. Ena, large-boned and inquisitive, had been reared in a loving environment and was well aware of her worth within the home and the community. She had been nurtured while Mary had been weaned at ten months in favour of her mother's next born. She had been scratching around for attention ever since.

At her home inside No. 11 Coronation Street, Mary woke on the morning of her fifteenth birthday with no feeling in her legs. She groaned and delved under the threadbare blanket to pull her sister Susie's flaxen hair. The youngster squealed in her sleep and shifted herself enough for Mary to free her legs. Susie had a habit of drifting down the bed and turning ninety degrees in the middle of the night. Her mother, Ivy Makepiece, thought it a wonder she didn't suffocate.

Mary shared a bed with her sisters, eight-year-old Susie, twenty-year-old Vi, and Lil, who had robbed her of her mother's nipple fourteen years before. Upon waking, her mind was occupied with three thoughts: the first that it was her birthday, the second that it was a Saturday, so there was no work, and the third that it was Vi's wedding day. The latter meant the most to her: there would be one less body to take up the bed space, one less person to share the toilet, and more elbow room at the table. She leant over snoring Lilian and pinched her elder sister's shoulder.

'Wake up, Vi! Yer gerrin' 'itched today.'

Three alleys away, Ena Schofield was also the first in her bed to wake up. Week day or weekend she always woke at five thirty in anticipation of the knocker-upper's rap at the window. Her sister Alice lay huddled beneath the bedclothes and Ena lay in silence, her breath steaming white in the cold air.

Downstairs she could hear her mother stoking the dying embers of the range fire. Mary Schofield was always the last to bed and the first up each morning. As a child

Ena had once tried to stay awake all night in an attempt to discover if her mother ever went to bed. The experiment had failed. She'd fallen asleep, and woke at the usual hour to find that Mary had carefully tucked the eiderdown around her.

Ena savoured her birthday lie-in, her eyes darting around the bedroom as the light from the gas lamp outside the house shone through the curtains and illuminated the pieces of furniture with which Ena had grown up. The bedstead was old and brass. She knew it was old because it had belonged to her maternal grandmother's parents. The mattress was lumpy and un-comfortable; Ena thought it was probably as old as the bed. Rag rugs covered the bare floorboards, giving some protection against the draughts that whistled around the house. Beside the bed, on Ena's side, stood a wooden chair. It served two purposes: first as a ledge upon which Ena placed her candle each night, second as a chair, on the rare occasions when the family had a party. Then, it was carried downstairs and re-united with its siblings at the kitchen table. A chest of drawers, painted yellow by Ena's brother, faced the bed. It was three drawers high: the first drawer contained Ena's clothes, the second Alice's, and the third was missing, a constant reminder of the ferocity of the previous winter when the price of coal had shot up and the family had had to burn any spare wood. Over the bed hung a sampler Ena had completed at Sunday School when she was nine. The tiny cross-stitch letters read, 'Thou, Lord, Seeth Me', and served as a constant reminder to Ena that her every action was known to God. By exchanging letters with Albert Tatlock she hoped she was doing her bit in helping to keep up morale on the Front line.

14 August 1914

Hollingworth Camp
Littleborough

Dear Miss Schofield
First off, I hope this letter finds you as it leaves me. You were very kind to say you would write me. I hope you still wish to. I have a friend in Inkerman Street and know of your mother who I believe was friendly with my own dear mother who passed on eight years since. If this is the case you might tell your mother that I am Emmeline Tatlock's eldest.

We have not left Lancashire as yet, although we keep on packing up our kits. I share a tent with Dinky, my friend who you met when we left Weatherfield, and a few other chaps. We are all from Weatherfield and are called Pals. They are a good sort. A number were at school with me and some I know from working in the mill. I am certain many will be known to you too. We get up at 5 o'clock and do plenty of exercises and marching with full kit. This is not something I am fond of and envy Dinky his long back as he carries his kit with ease.

After noon we do mending, of which I am well used, having looked for both myself and my brother Alf since our mother passed on. Today a gang of us ran down to the lake and swam. It was cold but our spirits were high. We just want to get on with the business of teaching the Germans a lesson. Each morning I wake and wonder if it is today we leave for Southampton.

Well, I must close. Give my regards to your family and do ask your mother if she remembers mine.

Yours respectfully

Albert Tatlock

18 August 1914

Dear Mr Tatlock

Thank you for the letter which I received today. My father once went on a works picnic to Hollingworth and I believe it is a very fine place.

I asked my mother if she knew of your mother and she says they were at school together and worked at Cartwright's Mill before they were married. She says your mother had a beautiful laugh. Fancy them knowing each other. She (my mother that is) is very pleased that I am to write to you. She wanted me to say that she is not one for letter-writing but that I should pass on her kindest regards to you. My father also sends his best.

What can I tell you? Life carries on much as before. There was great excitement as you all left and father says more lads are volunteering each day, but not in the same great numbers. There are many lads who have not volunteered and there has been some upset over this. I attend the Mission of Glad Tidings on Victoria Street and on Sunday we had a sermon telling us it was our duty to take up arms against tyranny. I find this confusing as Jesus tells us not to kill. I asked my father about this and he said sometimes man had to kill in order for the Good News to be spread. He recalled the story of the Crusades in the Middle Ages. I think history is interesting, do you?

Do be careful at Southampton. I had a cousin who visited Fleetwood and nearly drowned.

God bless you

Your friend,

Miss E Schofield (Ena)

No. 11 Coronation Street was a scene of chaos. Since TB had claimed her husband, Alfred, Ivy Makepiece had struggled to bring up seven children. Mission do-gooders had offered to place her boys in institutions, leaving her with her four daughters but Ivy had refused to break up the family and had taken in washing and mending to make ends meet. Six years on she still had her family, but they had grown into an unruly mob, bickering, fighting for attention, and each plotting their own place in life. Vi, the eldest, was very much her mother's child, short in stature but loud in voice. The boys, Frank and Ralph, separated by only ten months, operated like a couple of mobsters within the crowded house. They dispensed discipline to their younger siblings and laid down rules and regulations regarding behaviour. Young Will, at ten, suffered most from this regime. Like his brothers, he had a strong stubborn streak but while Frank and Ralph ignored their rules Will was governed by them and the thick leather belt that hung from the mantelpiece was no longer known as 'Dad's belt' but as 'Will's belt'.

In Ivy's eyes Mary and Lil were a couple of lazy sluts who would never amount to much at work or in life. The apple of her eye was her youngest child, Susie, who was resented by the rest of the family: to them she would ever be the whining, attention-seeking brat who always got her own way.

As she'd expected, Mary had to make do with a new pair of woollen stockings for her birthday present. Funds were always low, even with five wages coming in. As soon as Vi had started at Hardcastle's in the loom room, Ivy had given up taking in washing and relied upon her daughter's income. Ralph and Frank gave most of their wages to her but held back enough to drown their sorrows each night at the Rover's. Mary and Lil always handed her their wage packets unopened, and in return each received a handful of pennies to live off. Although they grumbled about this state of affairs to each other none of the Makepiece girls ever dared to voice objection to their mother. Each could remember the not-so-distant past when worry and hunger had caused Ivy to lash out with the belt in blind anger.

Mary accepted her stockings with gratitude, aware that this year her birthday was viewed as an annoying interruption in a landmark day. Unfortunately, bride-to-be Vi knew that her mother saw her wedding in the same light. During the morning of 14 November Ivy Makepiece's mind was on other things. As well as her daughter marrying and moving out of the family home, her two elder sons were going, and not to a warm bed at No. 7 Mawdsley Street, like Vi, but to some unknown barrack. Ralph and Frank were to march off to war directly after their sister's wedding reception. Furthermore Vi wasn't just saying goodbye to her brothers: her groom-to-be, Jack Todd, was going with them.

'Mary, get yer arse out of that chair and make yer brothers some tea,' shouted Ivy, through a mouthful of pins. She glared up at her eldest daughter. 'Keep still!'

Standing on the kitchen table Vi looked down at her mother as she pulled at the skirt of her wedding dress in a last-minute attempt to stop the hem trailing.

Mary eased herself up from her chair and lifted the kettle from its place on the range. She swilled it around and then announced, 'There's no water in it.'

'Then fill it!' shouted the exasperated Ivy

Mary sighed and plodded into the scullery. To reach the tap she had to step over Will, who sat cross-legged in the doorway working black polish into the family's boots. She grabbed her skirt in her hand as she trod over him and hissed, 'Yer not lookin' up my skirt, yer little pervert.'

Will stuck out his pointed tongue and spat on a boot.

As she filled the kettle Mary glanced out of the scullery window on to the cluttered backyard and watched as a young woman came through the opening where the back gate had once hung. Mary sighed and shouted into the kitchen, 'Mam, Betty Cog's 'ere again.'

Ivy stood up from her hemming, leaving Vi standing on the table, and scuttled into the scullery, jumping over Will. She pulled open the back door just as Betty Cog reached it. 'I told you not to come round 'ere again,' she hissed at the girl.

Betty flinched but remained were she stood. 'I wanna talk to Ralph,' she said.

''E don't wanna talk to you,' snarled Ivy.

''E's gonna 'ave to. Me dad sez 'e's fetchin' the bobbies if 'e don't.'

Ivy glared at the girl and cursed her son's stupidity in getting her pregnant.

'You can't prove that's my Ralph's bairn in there,' she said, prodding Betty's protruding stomach.

'You know it's 'is,' said Betty. 'Everyone knows it's 'is. I ain't bin wi' no one other than yer Ralph and I never wanted to go wi' 'im then.'

'Oh, don't start on that story again,' snapped Ivy. 'Everyone knows you're just a little tart who couldn't get 'er knickers down fast enough when my Ralph come sniffin' around.'

Betty bit her lip. There was no point in arguing with Ivy Makepiece. She was known throughout the district as a malicious old cow who'd even poisoned her own mother when she thought she was in the way. Betty remembered how Ralph had laughed as he'd ripped off her clothes, slapped her when she'd protested, savaged her breasts with his teeth and pounded into her with a fierceness that had left her bloodied in the back alley just yards away from where she stood. She'd been the prettiest girl in the neighbourhood, and now she was ruined. The light had been extinguished from her eyes, her growing stomach a testament to her robbed virginity. She was fourteen and, unless she could persuade Ralph to marry her, her life was ruined.

'Please, Mrs Makepiece, I just want to talk to 'im. Me dad's that set on gerrin' the bobbies to 'im an' I don't wanna get 'im into trouble.'

'Then do us all a service an' find some other bugger to blame that on,' spat Ivy, and slammed the back door in the girl's face.

Betty's face crumpled and she ran back to her own home, directly opposite the back of No. 11 Coronation Street.

When Ivy returned to her task, after smacking Ralph around the head and warning him that Archie Cog meant business, Vi was still standing on the table. 'They'll send you back to gaol,' she warned him, as she stabbed pins into Vi's dress, being all too aware of his thieving habits in the past.

'They won't,' said Ralph lazily, as he sprawled across the easy chair. 'Betty won't let them. She's mad about me.'

'Is that why you 'ad to rape 'er to get yer way wi' 'er?' asked Ivy, who had believed Betty's story – she knew her son too well.

Ralph snorted. 'She wanted it as much as I did. Not my fault the silly tart got 'erself pregnant.'

'I've finished yer boots,' said Will, bringing them over to his brother, who glanced at them and sneered, 'Call them finished?'

'What's wrong wi' 'em?' demanded Will.

'They need more elbow grease.'

'But I can't do 'em no more. I got Vi's shoes to do and me mam's an' I gotta get ready for weddin',' protested Will.

'Tough. I need me boots shinin' for when I march off wi' the lads.'

'Mam,' appealed Will, 'do I 'ave to?'

'Do as yer brother sez an' stop mitherin' me,' said Ivy. Will glared at Ralph and trudged back to the scullery. He slumped down in the doorway again in time to glance quickly up Mary's dress as she returned to the kitchen.

'It teks forever to fill that kettle,' she grumbled.

'Just be grateful the tap's in the 'ouse,' said

44

Ivy. 'When I were yer age we 'ad a tap in the street an' I 'ad to go down four flights of stairs to get to it.'

Mary placed the kettle upon the range. A drop of water splashed on to the hot surface and hissed. 'I'd best get ready,' she said, and wiped her hands down her apron. She looked enviously at Vi standing on the table. 'Wish I was gettin' married,' she thought to herself. 'Anythin' to get out of this midden.'

Ena Schofield enjoyed her birthday morning. She had received a book on the life of the Apostle Luke and a bag of her favourite hazelnuts. Mary Schofield always tried to make birthdays special and spread the best cloth over the table. Ena appreciated the gesture, knowing it was the hardest thing in the house to wash. Any food spilt on it had to be pummelled out by Mary's raw hands in the sink against the washboard. The cloth only saw daylight on birthdays and at Christmas. Otherwise it sat in a drawer in the sideboard or on a shelf in the pawn shop if it had been a bad week for finances.

''Ow do it feel to be fifteen, then?' asked Thomas, sucking on his pipe.

'You ask me that every year, whatever age I am,' said Ena, with a smile.

'I can't remember that far back, you see,' said Thomas. 'Yer brain slows down as you get older. You'll find that out soon enough.'

'Not me,' said Ena smiling, 'I'm gonna work on me brain, mek it sharper as I get older.'

Thomas laughed. 'I've never 'eard such rot.'

Alice, annoyed that it wasn't her birthday, agreed with her father. 'All you've got to look forward to is more work and then gerrin' wed an' 'avin' bairns.'

Ena laughed. 'I'll 'ave to find someone to marry me first.'

'What about that chap who's bin writin' to you?' asked Alice playfully. 'Plannin' on marrin' 'im after war?'

Ena gave her sister a brief smile. She was getting fed up with Alice's snide comments about her letter-writing. She and Albert had only exchanged two letters but in Alice's narrow mind that constituted a romance. 'I've told you before, me and Albert Tatlock are friends an' that's all there is to it.'

'At least our Ena's got 'erself a fella,' said Thomas. Like the rest of Ena's family and friends, he believed Albert was her boyfriend. Otherwise why should she be writing to him? 'I don't see many lads queuing up to tek you out.'

Alice sniffed. 'What do I want wi' lads?'

'Nah, lass, I'm not gonna tell yer that. If yer don't know by now, chances are you never will,' and Thomas cackled as Alice flounced out of the room.

'Thomas,' cautioned his wife, 'stop teasing the girl.' She put down her mending and rubbed her tired eyes, then blinked and smiled at Ena. 'What 'ave you got planned today, love?'

'Mary Makepiece's sister's gerrin' wed at the Mission,' said Ena. 'I thought I'd go and watch.'

'Is that Vi?' asked Mary with interest. 'She's marrying Daisy Todd's lad, isn't she? The shifty-lookin' boy.'

'Oh, Mam,' said Ena, 'it's not 'is fault 'e looks like that. There's not many lads who get kicked in the face by a donkey.'

The groom – he of the kicked face – posed uncomfortably with his new bride on the Mission steps. The photographer had been his mother's wedding present, and the man's presence, with his tripod and boxes, caused more stir among the guests than anything else.

'Bit much, ain't it?' asked one of Vi's

cousins, ''avin' a picture took of yer wed-din'.'

'Oh, yes,' agreed her mother. 'It won't catch on – these things never do.'

Daisy Todd had been able to pay for just the one photograph and as soon as it had been taken the wedding party headed across Coronation Street to the reception at the Rover's Return.

Ivy marched ahead of the bridal party, intent on making sure that the wedding tea had been laid out to her specifications. Daisy attempted to keep up with her, but lacked Ivy's determination to get to the pub first and soon fell back to walk alongside her new daughter-in-law.

Nellie Corbishley had laid out the sand-wiches and cakes in the Select bar of the Rover's. Her housekeeper, Pearl Crapper, had prepared the buffet while Nellie had concentrated on the place settings. It was to be a quiet gathering, just immediate family and friends. More like a wake than a wed-ding, mused Nellie.

Ivy barged into the bar, which was separated from the Public bar by a glass-panelled door. She took in the scene and sniffed in approval. It was as it should be.

Pearl, who had known Ivy since they'd both moved into Coronation Street on the day it had been built, smiled at her. 'Was it a good service?' she asked.

'It were a weddin',' replied Ivy drily. 'They both turned up.'

'That's summat,' said Pearl.

'Aye.'

Ivy moved over to the food table and picked up a sandwich. She sniffed it and raised an eyebrow in surprise. 'Fish?'

'Potted,' said Pearl.

Ivy took a bite. 'Tasty.'

'Oh, it's very nice,' agreed Pearl. 'I bought a load in before the war.'

'Where from?' asked Ivy with a raise of her voice.

'Thwaite's,' said Pearl.

'You what!' Ivy spat the sandwich on to the floor.

'Really!' objected Nellie, stepping forward and screwing up her nose.

'You tryin' to poison me,' demanded Ivy, 'givin' me paste from Thwaite's?'

'But it's fine,' said Pearl. 'I've bin usin' it for weeks.'

'Poisoner!' screamed Ivy. 'Crippen!'

The sound of her mother's screeching greeted Vi as she and Jack entered the pub, closely followed by the guests.

'What's to do?' Jack asked of his new mother-in-law.

'I'll tell you what's to do,' bellowed Ivy, lifting a hand and pointing at Pearl. 'That witch is tryin' to poison us all.'

Pearl flushed and opened her mouth to protest but Ivy carried on: 'She's made sandwiches wi' paste from Thwaite's!'

The onlookers drew breath sharply and stared at Pearl, who clutched at her apron and said, 'We've 'ad it stored for weeks. I've 'ad it meself.'

She cursed herself for having told Ivy the source of the potted fish. She should 'ave said it had come from Edwards', the fish-monger, and no one would have been any the wiser. Why hadn't she thought first?

At the other end of the terrace, at No.15 Coronation Street, the cause of Ivy's wrath swept out the floor of his shop, unaware of the commotion. Cedric Thwaite had run the shop at the junction of Coronation and Viaduct Streets since it had first opened for business in August 1902. He had always been a loner and a religious fanatic, preaching from the pulpit at the Mission of Glad Tidings and running weekly Bible-study classes. His greatest ally over the years had been Mission caretaker Gladys Arkwright, and many of the congregation had anticipated a matrimonial union of the couple. The local gossips noted every meeting between the pair as Gladys cooked and kept house for Cedric unaware that she had been cast in the role of scarlet woman. A widow in her forties, she felt no attraction to Cedric, ten years her junior, and looked upon him purely as someone whose company she enjoyed. He was a good God-fearing man, she was a good Christian widow. There was nothing else in their relationship.

But that wasn't how others saw it, and matters came to a head in the spring of 1904 when, during Cedric's sermon on sexual continence, Ivy Makepiece had stood up and denounced him, saying everyone knew he'd been stoking Gladys's boiler for months. A Mission investigation had uncovered Cedric's secret drinking and he had been removed from the preaching circuit. His friendship with Gladys had been irreparably damaged, and over the ten years since Ivy's outburst the pair had done little more than nod to each other when they passed in the street. Besides, Cedric had no need for Gladys to continue cooking his meals: in the summer of 1912 he had taken a wife. Lottie Hofner had spoken little English when she married Cedric after the briefest of courtships in Blackpool. He had moved her straight into the shop where the neighbours were suddenly confronted with their new shopkeeper: a German.

Lottie was a timid woman who, even in her homeland, had kept herself to herself. She occupied her spare time by producing pieces of fine needlework. She wasn't a gossip, was always well thought-of by those around her, and was a good, conscientious wife. She submitted to her husband in all things, and was frustrated only by her failure to present him with a child. Four miscarriages in two years had left her feeling useless as a wife, without the closeness of love to communicate her desperation.

Lottie had never understood the strange ways of her neighbours. As Ivy Makepiece said, 'You 'ave to be born round 'ere to live round 'ere.' If Lottie had been born in York-shire or London she would have felt just as alienated in Weatherfield but she had the added drawback that English wasn't her native tongue. Despite being a quick learner she still reverted to German in times of stress or confusion. When this happened in the shop, it reminded the customers that she could never be accepted in the Street.

As soon as war was declared Lottie and Cedric became aware of the anti-German hostility aimed at them. Non-regulars shifted allegiance to local shops owned by Anglo-Saxon faces with Anglo-Saxon accents. Now, two months into the war, lack of custom was hitting the shop. Only Gladys Arkwright and a handful of customers remained faithful to Thwaite's. Everyone else believed that Germans couldn't be trusted. Ivy Makepiece spoke for many when she said to her cronies in the Rover's Snug, 'She could be a spy, writin' down all we say in that shop. For all we know she could be poisonin' all the food so we all drop down dead.'

Gladys told Cedric not to take any notice, that Ivy and her friends were just stupid old women who lived for gossip and specu-lation, but the empty till mocked Cedric and he knew the situation would come to a climax in one way or another.

While Ivy screamed murder at her daugh-ter's wedding reception, Cedric waited in his spotless shop for custom that never came. In the shop's backroom Lottie baked his favourite treacle pudding but even the thought of its stodgy stickiness failed to raise his spirits. If trade didn't improve soon he'd have to sell up. It was as simple as that.

Vi's wedding reception was a short one, and three p.m. sharp the bride joined the small crowd that stood along Rosamund Street and waved to her husband of three and a quarter hours. Jack Todd had exchanged his wedding suit for his new uniform and was flanked by his new brothers-in-law as the soldiers marched towards the station. Vi and her family kept step with their men, rushing along the pavement with the rest of the waving masses. Young Will darted in and out of legs with glee, knowing his days of being belted had come to an end. He was now the man of the house. Ivy watched her sons march off with pride. 'Go, lads,' her thoughts urged them. 'Go and kill the bastards.'

As he marched along, Frank Makepiece spoke out of the side of his mouth to mournful Jack: 'I can't believe you didn't tek 'er back for a quick one after the service.'

'It didn't seem right,' said Jack.

Ralph laughed at the older man's stupidity. 'What's the point of marryin' and not gerrin' a poke in?'

'Eh up,' warned Frank. 'Talkin' about pokin'...'

Ralph followed his brother's gaze to where Betty Cog was scampering along Mawdsley Street, waving her hands in the air and urging the body of men to stop.

'Bloody 'ell,' he hissed, in alarm.

Frank laughed at his brother's discomfort and turned to smile sweetly at Betty as she flung herself through the crowd. "Ello, Betty, love, come to kiss 'im goodbye, 'ave yer?' He leered at the distraught girl.

Betty took no notice of him as she tried to push her way through to reach Ralph. 'You can't go!' she wailed. 'You can't leave me like this!'

Ralph kept his eyes straight ahead, concentrating on marching in time. Betty pushed past Frank and Jack to throw her arms around him. 'Gerroff!' he hissed.

'Ralph, please!'

'Gerraway from me, yer stupid bitch.'

He tried to shake himself free of her but Betty clung to him. He looked around for the sergeant, who was escorting the new recruits to their barracks, a seasoned soldier, but he was at the head of the column and could offer no help. Instead Ralph turned to a trusted familiar figure. 'Mam!' he shouted into the crowd. 'Do summat!'

Ivy Makepiece had already decided to take action and, snarling viciously, loomed out of the crowd to grab Betty's hair. The girl screamed in pain as Ivy tugged her backwards. Ralph marched on, his eyes straight ahead.

After attending the wedding service of her friend's sister, Ena had spent the rest of the day at home with her family. Martha Hartley had called round to wish her a happy birthday and inflict her runny nose and chesty cough upon the Schofields. Thomas had never taken to Martha whom he deemed an unpleasant creature. He liked women to be docile, ready with warming food and affection, rounded, homely creatures. The only things rounded about Martha were the spectacles that perched on her bony nose. She was a ferret of a woman, with ashen skin and beady eyes. Thomas felt sorry for women like Martha: even when there wasn't a war on they struggled to find a man interested in them. But feeling sorry for her wasn't enough to keep Thomas in Martha's company: he soon made his excuses and joined his pals at the Tripe-dressers Arms.

As well as bringing birthday wishes Martha came with her usual supply of gossip. 'Did you 'ear about Mary Makepiece's sister's weddin' tea?' she asked.

'What?' asked Ena.

''Er mother threw all the food away cos it 'ad been bought at Thwaite's.'

'Why did she do that?'

'Cos 'e's married to a German.'

'You've lost me,' said Ena, cracking a hazelnut.

'Don't you know nothin'?' Martha sniffed. 'Thwaite's married a German spy an' she tried to kill the whole of Coronation Street by poisonin' the food for the weddin'. Germans know about that sort o' thing.'

'Rot,' snorted Ena.

'It's true,' said Alice, joining in the conversation gleefully. There was nothing she liked better than gossip. 'There were a butcher in Prestwich, a *German* butcher, who went mad one night with 'is cleaver and cut the 'eads off three of 'is neighbours.'

Martha gasped and clutched at her throat.

Ena shook her head in disbelief. 'You two would believe anythin' you 'eard. I'm glad I don't peddle tittle-tattle.'

'I don't peddle it either,' said Mary, getting up from her chair to clear the table.

'But I still won't shop at Thwaite's.'

Alice jeered at Ena, who took no notice. Instead she rose to help her mother, and asked, 'Why wouldn't you shop there?'

'Because it's unpatriotic. I'm sure Thwaite's wife is just like the rest of us but she's a German and this country 'appens to be at war wi' Germany. It wouldn't be right to give a German my money.' She slid a penny off the mantelpiece and showed it to Ena. 'Who's 'ead is on that?'

'The King's,' said Ena.

'Aye, not the Kaiser's.'

As Ena lay in bed that night, going over the events of the day, her conscience troubled her. All her life she had followed her mother's lead, but the knowledge that Mary would not frequent a German-owned shop disturbed her. Ena believed that all men were cast in the image of God. All men, no matter what their nationality. That being so she couldn't condone the boycotting of a business based purely upon national pride. It startled Ena to discover that she disagreed with her mother. Perhaps this was what it meant to grow up.

Back in Coronation Street Ivy Makepiece's

conscience was pricking her too. As her remaining children trundled off to bed, she sat in her kitchen, disturbed by the alien silence that surrounded her. She resented the fact that her boys had been sent off to fight for their country. She didn't understand why there was a war and wasn't sure who was fighting who. All she knew was that Germany had started it and that Britain was going to finish it ... before Christmas. All her life Ivy had felt the need to hit out at things. When her husband had died she'd lashed out at the children, heaping the blame for his death upon Mary, who had brought TB into the house. When the family had been faced with starvation, she had hit out at her mother, who had an insatiable appetite. The old girl ate so much that Ralph had been forced to steal to feed her. He'd been sent away to an institution for three years, and Ivy had lashed out at her mother: she had soaked fly-paper to extract the arsenic from it, and had administered it to the old woman over two months until she dropped dead. Now, with her boys taken from her, Ivy needed to blame someone, and it didn't take long for her to decide upon whom she should vent her rage.

It didn't take long either to round up a

lynch mob. It never did in Weatherfield, where a crowd could be rallied at the drop of a hat. As Ivy went from door to door down Coronation Street the tension was heightened as parents who had given their sons, and wives their young husbands, joined her cause.

The sound of shattering glass was the first warning Cedric Thwaite received. He ran from his living room into the shop in time to see burly Harry Popplewell from No. 7 climb through the broken window and smash the lock on the shop door. Cedric stood rooted to the spot before the sea of angry faces staring at him from out of the night's darkness.

'What are you doing?' he demanded. 'I have no money–'

'We don't want yer money!' snarled Harry. He advanced, grabbed the shopkeeper by his lapels and head-butted him.

Cedric gave a cry of pain and tasted blood, as around him his neighbours and customers crowded into the shop.

Ivy pushed her way through, determined to lead the mob.

'Where's yer German whore?' she demanded.

Cedric groaned but turned his head

towards the door that led to the living quarters.

With a war cry, Ivy ran towards the door, closely followed by her female neighbours. Cedric opened his mouth to warn Lottie, but was silenced by Harry Popplewell's fist. The blow smashed into his face, knocking him out. His body fell back limp, and Harry dragged him out of the shop. As the mob set upon him, Gladys Arkwright appeared in the doorway of her cosy vestry at the Mission in her nightgown, her grey hair falling upon her shoulders. She raised her hands to her face and screamed.

Lottie's screams were muffled by the women who fell upon her in her bedroom and dragged her out of bed. Ivy Makepiece spat in her face and stamped on her spectacles before kicking her in the stomach. Harry's wife, one-eyed Clara Popplewell, grabbed Lottie's hair, pulled her out of the bedroom and kicked her down the stairs. Her head smashed against the skirting-board at the bottom of the stairwell and her blood smeared the plaster on the wall. The women carried her into the Street to where their children danced around Cedric, aiming stones at his beaten body. The menfolk had given up on Cedric and now occupied themselves with grabbing as much off the shop's shelves as they could carry.

Gladys watched in horror as her neighbours set upon Lottie like a pack of hungry lionesses, clawing at her, kicking and punching. Finally she found her feet and ran towards them, begging them to stop, telling them that what they were doing was wicked. Ivy spun around and glared at Gladys through hate-filled eyes. 'Stay out of this,' she warned.

'Stop – please stop,' begged the caretaker, sobbing through her words.

Ivy found half a brick lying on the pavement, grasped it and hurled it at Gladys's head. Gladys stared blindly at her neighbour then sank to her knees. Ivy turned her back on her and sent her makeshift weapon down upon German flesh. As she did so she laughed hysterically.

By the time the police arrived, the Street was deserted, apart from Gladys and the motionless shopkeepers. Cedric was taken to the Infirmary where, when he regained consciousness, he was informed that his wife had been interned in a camp for aliens on the Isle of Man for her own safety. It was left to Gladys to break the news to him that the attack had left Lottie blind and deaf.

'I don't understand,' Gladys said to God in prayer. 'I don't understand.'

On the morning after the attack Ivy took her place in the congregation at the Mission of Glad Tidings without a flicker of regret on her face. She took the hymn book Gladys offered her without comment, and Gladys, her head still spinning from the blow Ivy had inflicted, bit her tongue and reminded herself of the passage from St Mark's gospel in which a teacher of the law had asked Jesus which was the most important commandment. 'Love your neighbour as yourself,' Jesus had replied.

Gladys took her place at the harmonium, ready to play for her neighbours.

CHAPTER THREE

March 1915

Weatherfield was enjoying an early hot spell and the residents of Coronation Street benefited from a halt in building the extension to Earnshaw's mill. The new chimney would not block the early sun from the Street's backyards this spring.

For most, Sunday was the only day of relative inactivity. No one worked on the Lord's Day or did much more than sit on hard pews and bend their knees at the Mission of Glad Tidings. Before the war, uniformed musicians had brought colour to the park's bandstand while couples ambled around the grounds. Elsewhere housewives picked over exotic goods brought to the Plank Lane market by travellers, and the men, freed from the restrictions of work, propped up bars while children played with makeshift toys in the back-streets.

Much of this still went on now, although the bandstands were empty and money was scarce so travellers hardly ever called. Women still cooked Sunday dinners, though, and men swallowed pints of ale, and children would always play.

Coming out of the autumn and winter months of war, the glow of the sun was a warming change as it licked its way into the grey corners of Weatherfield, like the backyards of Coronation Street. They were so small that there was little room to move in them but the back door steps were a favoured spot to sit and catch the sun.

Sixteen-year-old Alf Tatlock sat with his back to the open scullery door, shelling peas. He popped each pod and then drew his finger down inside it, flicking each moist pea into the basin he supported between his legs. It was a satisfying process, and he was in no rush to complete it. Inside the house his aunt Mary bustled about the kitchen cooking the Sunday dinner. From time to time she darted, humming to herself, into the scullery for a knife or to run water into a pan to heat on the range.

On the other side of the wall that separated Alf's yard from the Hewitts', at No. 3 Coronation Street, a boy of the same age also sat in the sun. Thomas Hewitt had grown up with Alf. They'd sat together at

Silk Street Elementary and had progressed to Hardcastle's factory school at eight as part-timers. Two years later they'd joined Hardcastle's as full-timers, leaving school-days behind them. For the past six years they had been members of the workforce at the mill, running errands and darting in and out of looms retrieving stray bobbins. They weren't the best of friends but they were mates, thrown together by circumstances and shared experiences.

'What you doin', Tatters?' called Thomas from his backyard.

'Shellin' peas,' called back Alf cheerfully. ''Ow about you?'

'Polishin' me boots.'

'You can do mine after,' said Alf.

'No fear. I've got our Flo's to do next. You've never seen a lass wi' such big feet as our Flo.'

Alf grinned to himself. Flo was Thomas's sister. She was the younger but only by nine months and was almost the same size. Thomas wasn't a great hulking lad but even so Flo, with her long lanky limbs and awkward features, wished she had been dainty.

'If you don't shurrup you'll get one of me big feet in yer big mouth,' Alfred heard Flo say to her brother on the other side of the wall.

''Ow do, Flo,' he called.

''Ow do,' she replied.

'What you doin'?'

'She's doin' nowt,' said Thomas. 'She's a lazy mare, that's what she is.'

'I'm relaxin',' replied Flo smugly. 'I'm still gerrin' over those measles.'

'Now she's spotty as well as 'avin' big feet,' called Thomas.

'Shurrup,' said Flo.

Alf whistled to himself as he continued to shell the peas, and Thomas joined in. They continued in harmony until Flo interrupted them. 'Are you goin' to the Bijou next Saturday, then, Alfie?'

'Next Saturday?'

'Aye. You must 'ave 'eard. Nancy Miller's comin'.'

Alf pulled a face. When it came to music-hall acts none was bigger than Nancy Miller, except perhaps Marie Lloyd, but she seldom ventured off the London circuits.

'We're goin',' called Flo. 'Do you fancy it?'

'I dunno. I'll think on.'

'Go on, Tatters. Come wi' us. You know our Flo fancies you.'

Alf flushed as he heard Flo squeal with

annoyance. Judging by the thud and the cry Thomas gave, she had thrown one of her big shoes at him. At sixteen he had never had a girlfriend, never even been kissed. He was a shy boy, only comfortable with lasses he'd grown up with, and he didn't look upon them as any different from his male friends. As his aunt Mary fondly put it, he was a late developer. In that respect he was in awe of Thomas Hewitt, who was already shaving and had caught the eye of some of the girls in the weaving shed.

The girls who worked in the various weaving sheds at Hardcastle's and the other mills across Weatherfield, Manchester and the North-west of England found a new topic of conversation when posters went up urging them to take on factory work. Many factories were running short of workers as the men who traditionally manned the machines had volunteered to fight overseas. Women were being asked to take their places to ensure that the wheels of industry didn't grind to a halt.

Over the dinner table at 14 Inkerman Street, Ena and Alice Schofield broached the subject from different viewpoints.

'I wouldn't want to be doin' 'eavy work,'

said Ena. 'Operatin' looms might not be everyone's cup o' tea but it suits me fine.'

'You've no ambition,' said Alice. 'You'll be operatin' looms till they bury you. You know what you are, our Ena, you're a right stick-in-the-mud.'

Thomas Schofield raised an eyebrow in amusement. 'And what are you, our Alice? I suppose you're one of them modern girls. You'll be chainin' yerself to railin's next.'

'Why shouldn't she?' challenged his wife. 'I carried a placard outside town hall in 1911 and I don't care who knows it.'

''Ear 'ear,' rallied Alice. She enjoyed a moment of rare solidarity with her mother, which was spoilt by what Mary said next.

'Mind, I'm wi' our Ena. There's women's work an' there's men's work. If all those boys 'adn't gone marchin' off they'd never even think of askin' lasses to work those 'ulkin' great machines.'

Thomas laughed. 'What 'ulkin' great machines? When did you ever set foot inside a factory?'

'Never,' replied Mary sharply, 'and that's my point. Women work at mill, men work at factory.'

'Some men work at mill,' said Alice.

'Aye, that's cos weavin's an age-old skill.

Any fool can pull a lever and fiddle wi'
switches.'

'So long as they're men,' added Thomas
slyly.

'Aye,' said Mary. 'Most fools tend to be
men.'

Ena and Alice both broke into delighted
laughter, and Thomas took the ribbing in
his good-humoured way. 'You girls should
be careful you don't grow to be as sharp as
yer mam,' he said. 'Men don't like sassy
women.'

'That's true,' said Mary drily. 'I 'ad to force
yer father to marry me.' She looked up from
her dinner plate and caught her husband's
eye. He winked at her and she blushed. Ena
smiled at them both. She was never happier
than when she was with her parents. She'd
happily follow in her mother's footsteps.
Another four or five years operating looms,
then she'd marry a good man, have children,
keep his house, and he'd always be master of
the house as her father was master of theirs.
The differences between the sexes were as
plain to Ena as buttons on a coat. She knew
her place, and it wasn't taking a man's job in
a factory. Such thoughts reminded her of
Albert, and the correspondence they shared.

A few streets and alleys away, Flo Hewitt took a different view from Ena on factory work. She was heartily sick of trudging across to Hardcastle's and spending ten hours of each day watching her loom, beside a grate-like window that looked directly down on to the rooftop of her family home. The deafening roar of the machines as bobbins darted and twisted, combined with the same faces she'd grown up with, had prompted her to grasp the opportunity that had suddenly opened up.

'Barker's are takin' on,' she said. 'I fancy workin' there. They've got a canteen.'

''Ave they now?' said Gertie Hewitt, raising an eyebrow. 'That's fancy.'

Since the age of seven Flo had looked upon Gertie as her mother. She was actually her aunt, who had married her widowed brother-in-law less than six months after her sister's death. She had moved into No. 3 and taken on the role of mother to Thomas and Flo. In 1909 Samuel Hewitt had died of TB, three months before Gertie gave birth to her daughter, Molly, who was now nearly six. On his father's death Thomas had been elevated to man of the household and chief bread-winner. A boy starting full time at Hardcastle's was automatically paid more than any woman in the weaving sheds and, tall and broad for his age, Thomas Hewitt had been treated as a man from the age of thirteen.

Gertie was as proud of Thomas and Flo as if they were her own children: Thomas with his handsome features, his high brow and confident laugh, and Flo's delicate English-rose beauty. She had fine, slender bones and, before the war, had attracted the eye of many young men. The war was a constant source of irritation to Gertie. At sixteen Thomas was too young to serve in the forces and Gertie prayed on bended knees at the Mission Hall each Sunday that the conflict would be over before he was faced with the prospect of taking up arms. Thomas tried to push the war to the back of his mind: he had no desire to shirk his duty but wasn't keen on the idea of killing men.

'I've 'eard tell it's better money at Barker's too,' continued Flo.

'Perhaps we'd all best start there,' said Gertie lightly. ''Eaven knows, we could do wi' the extra.'

'They only want young women,' said Flo.

Gertie sighed and looked down at her time-ravaged hands. She'd been a young woman once, before household chores, mill work and life had aged her. She was thirty-one years old now, well into middle age. 'If you fancy it, you take a job at Barker's,' she said. 'There's no reason why we all 'ave to slave away at 'Ardcastle's.'

'I 'oped you'd say that,' said Flo joyfully, 'I'll pop down tomorrow and see what's what.'

'Check yer hours, though, and don't let them fob you off wi' dangerous work. I've 'eard tell some o' them machines are lethal.'

Gertie watched Thomas as he helped Molly spoon up the last of her peas. He looked worried and the wave had gone out of his sandy hair. 'You're quiet,' she said.

He looked up and forced a smile.

'Summat on yer mind?' she asked carefully. Thomas was like his father – easily frightened into a corner by direct questions.

Thomas shrugged. 'Not really. Just thinkin' that everyone seems to be doin' their bit for the war 'cept me.'

'Well, you're doin' your bit 'ere, bringin' in money so we can 'ave food on the table and coal in the grate. Them's important things, you know.'

'Aye,' said Thomas. She was right, but he still felt as if he should be doing more.

Having won approval to change jobs, Flo

decided to change the subject. 'You'll come to see Nancy Miller, won't you?' she asked her stepmother.

Gertie shook her head. 'My days sat in gaiety theatres are well and truly over. You two go and 'ave a laugh.'

'Don't fret,' said Flo happily. 'We'll 'ave a grand old time, won't we, Tommy?'

'Aye,' said Thomas. ''Appen we will.'

The rest of the week sped past for Flo Hewitt. First thing Monday morning she handed in her notice at Hardcastle's, giving it to a disgruntled foreman who grumbled that she was the sixth girl to give notice in an hour. In her humblest voice she told him she thought it her duty to do factory work.

'That's what they all say,' he said. 'Funny 'ow they never mention the better pay an' shorter hours.'

She'd left the mill on Wednesday and had started on Thursday morning at Barker's. It was a large factory built only a couple of years before the outbreak of war. Everything was whitewashed and the equipment all shiny: such a difference from the Victorian mill she was used to. She'd been placed in charge of a lever and been instructed to turn it sharply and continuously to the left. As she turned, a drill bored into a sheet of smooth metal, making a perfect circle the size of a penny. She had no idea what the metal or the hole were used for but the process delighted her and that night she could talk of nothing else at home.

At the end of the week she was still excited about her new job and friends, and sailed through Saturday's shift with the prospect of the evening's show foremost in her thoughts.

Weatherfield's one and only playhouse, the Bijou, was situated opposite Hardcastle's warehouse on Rosamund Street. It was a huge, imposing building with a mock-classical front. Pillars of stone supported ledges that bore finely carved statues. On one side of the big entrance doors stood Comedy, in the shape of a guffawing clown, and on the other Tragedy, a mournful-looking figure, weeping into a cloak. Inside, the audience stood upon a scarlet carpet, which swept majestically up a winding staircase leading to the expensive circle seats, which were hardly ever occupied as most could afford only the cheap seats downstairs. At the foot of the stall seats was the orchestra pit with its ornate piano.

The stage area was launched from the middle of a proscenium arch, decorated with carved cherubs, elaborate trees and plants. The heavy stage curtains had been in position since the playhouse opened in 1886. They had never been washed and the deep red material had turned grey. They had to be winched back slowly by stagehands to avoid clouds of dust being jerked out on to the audience.

The shows put on at the Bijou were mainly second-rate music-hall performances with either comics and singers on their way down the ladder, but every now and again someone who had once been 'a name' trod the Weatherfield boards. Those who could remember their former glory greeted them nostalgically and enthusiastically. Those too young to have known them often booed them off the stage. The prospect of 'a name' who was still at the peak of success playing the Bijou caused a sensation Weatherfield had not experienced since the pit disaster of 1910.

Nancy Miller was a sensation, the toast of music-hall royalty, a woman who dressed as a man to sing to her audiences. She had so impressed them that she set the fashion for the gentlemen of London. There wasn't any danger in the men of Weatherfield hoping to copy her outfits – they only had one pair of trousers each. However, she was a star and it seemed to Ena Schofield, as she pushed her way along through the crowds swarming towards the Bijou, that the whole of Weatherfield had turned out to see her.

Ena had hoped her mother would join her at the playhouse but Mary had insisted that she was too old to sit still for hours while others sang to her and attempted to make her laugh. Ena knew that Mary would have loved to go but couldn't justify spending the shilling entrance fee on herself. Instead she had set off with her sister Alice but had ended up linking arms with Minnie Carlton, who saved her money to go to the Bijou once a month. Sitting in the glow of the stage lights, with handsome men serenading her and beautiful women dancing for her, transported Minnie to a world where it didn't matter that she was clumsy, tongue-tied and stupid.

'Isn't it excitin', Ena?' she said, her cheeks flushed.

'All this fuss just to see a woman dressed as a man,' said Ena, attempting to sound disapproving as she felt she ought, but unable to keep the excitement out of her voice.

'I'm sure no one would rush to see me dressed in owt but me Sunday best,' she said.

'I dunno,' said a man behind her. 'I'd pay to see you out of it.'

Ena flushed and turned to see who had made the lewd remark. It was a man she knew to be a drinking pal of her father's. He gave her a suggestive wink. She shuddered and pushed further into the crowd with Minnie.

'There's Martha,' said Minnie, recognising her friend's straw hat. She called out and Martha turned to wave.

'Who's she's with?' asked Ena, craning her neck.

'Oh, I think it's that girl who's started work wi' 'er at Barker's. Martha said she was comin' wi' 'er and 'er brother.'

'Might 'ave known there'd be a fella involved,' said Ena drily.

She looked around the area where Martha stood and noticed the tall handsome lad near her chatting to a fair bonny girl. Ena took them for the friend and her brother. 'Very nice,' said Ena, despite herself. It made a change to see a good-looking lad around the place. So many were out of the country.

Martha shared Ena's opinion of Thomas Hewitt. From the moment she'd first met him, calling for Flo in Coronation Street, Martha hadn't been able to drag her eyes off the lad. Noticing her brother's discomfort under Martha's stare, Flo wished that she'd not invited her new workmate.

'Do you like toffees?' Martha asked Thomas, allowing the crowd to press her up against him. She longed to reach out and touch the buttons on his jacket but somehow she controlled herself.

'I dunno,' said Thomas, aware that he was flushing. He was used to the attention of girls but none had ever been as obvious as Martha.

'I like toffees. If they're sellin' any inside I'll buy some. We can share.'

'Right.' He smiled politely and was glad to reach the box-office counter where a sour-faced woman sat under a misleading sign that read 'Welcome to the Pleasure Palace'.

'Two back stalls, please,' said Thomas, handing over a selection of coins.

'Oh, Thomas,' squealed Martha with delight, 'you shouldn't! Folk'll talk.'

Thomas stared at her in confusion. 'I shouldn't what?'

'Pay for me.'

'I'm not,' he said, shortly. 'I'm gerrin' tickets for me and our Flo.'

Martha tried not to sound too dejected as she forced a laugh and muttered, 'Silly me.'

Thomas grabbed his tickets and strode off with Flo, leaving Martha hunting about in her pockets for her money. 'Just one please.' Her eyes darted to the entrance in time to see Thomas's back disappearing into the theatre. ''Urry up,' said the man behind her.

'All right, wait yer sweat,' Martha snapped back.

The air inside the Bijou was thick with stale smoke but this was replaced half-way through the first half of the show with the smell of fresh tobacco. Another smell mingled with it and assaulted Ena's nostrils: the theatre was so crowded that it was impossible to escape the pungent odour of sweat that rose up from the audience. Like most of her ilk, Ena had bought a ticket for the back stalls, where the floor climbed slowly up the wall and where the tallest eyed the ceiling warily. The ceiling was the floor of the circle above and many recalled an incident in Sunderland where a balcony had come crushing down on to the unsuspecting audience below. Ena never worried about such things, her life was in God's hands, and when it was her time, it was her time. Her sister Alice, however, feared life itself and would not dream of sitting beneath a balcony. She paid extra to sit in the front stalls, where Ena knew she'd be full of complaints that the orchestra was too loud.

Ena sat between Minnie and a lad she vaguely recognised. He looked familiar but she was certain she'd never met him. Who he was and why she knew him bothered her throughout the first half of the show. He was a feeble-looking chap and didn't understand the lewd jokes the second-rate comic shouted. While older men roared with laughter until tears rolled down their faces Ena's neighbour looked puzzled. When the audience fell quiet to listen to a girl in a long frock singing about her lost love Ena noticed the lad's eyes moisten.

During the interval the auditorium buzzed with excitement. Nancy Miller was to close the whole show and there were only a couple of acts on before she was due to come on. Some stood up to stretch their legs but most stayed sitting where they were and chatted to their neighbours.

'Enjoyin' the show?' Ena asked the lad cautiously. She didn't normally talk to strangers.

'Oh ... yes. Yes, thank you,' he answered.

'That comic weren't much to write 'ome about,' she said, and then gasped. 'You're Albert Tatlock's brother,' she said. The jigsaw piece had fallen into place.

'Yes,' said the boy, turned to her and smiled. 'Do you know him?'

'I write to 'im, my name's Ena Schofield.'

The lad opened his eyes in wonder. 'You're Miss Schofield? Albert's told me about you. He does enjoy gettin' your letters. They cheer 'im up no end.'

'Fancy us sittin' 'ere together,' said Ena, with a smile. 'And 'im so far away.'

'It seems odd without 'im,' agreed Alf.

'You must miss 'im,' said Ena kindly. 'Me mam told me 'ow yer folks died and that 'e's brung you up.'

'Aye.' Alf fell quiet.

'I'll write to 'im tonight,' said Ena, 'tell 'im I saw you.'

''E'd like that,' said Alf.

On the other side of the auditorium, Thomas Hewitt was contemplating going home. He leant close to his sister and whispered in her ear, 'Swap places or I'll kill 'er.'

Flo sighed and looked past her brother to

where Martha sat sucking a toffee and purposely rubbing her shoulder against Thomas's. 'What'll she think if we swap?' she whispered back.

'I don't care,' said Thomas. 'If you don't I'm goin' 'ome. I can't take any more.'

Flo nodded and stood up. Thomas followed suit.

'What's goin' on?' asked Martha in alarm.

The siblings squeezed past and took each other's seat.

'Thomas wanted more leg room,' lied Flo.

Martha glanced to where Thomas was happily adjusting to his new seat. The leg room looked exactly the same.

Flo gave her friend a false smile and screwed up her nose as if to say, 'Men!'

Martha half smiled back and sighed. She sucked at her toffee and then a pleasant thought entered her head. He'd moved because he was worried about controlling his urges. He must have felt he had to put some distance between them. She squirmed in her seat and sniffed contentedly. She was going to enjoy being Flo's friend and intended to see as much of Thomas as she could.

The second half of the show flew by: there was another comic, a trick-bicycle act and a woman who danced on her toes in a frilly dress. Then came the announcement they'd all been waiting for. 'Ladies and gentlemen ... The Bijou, Weatherfield, is proud to present the London Idol ... Miss Nancy Miller!'

Ena, Minnie, Alfred, Martha, Thomas and Flo joined in the enthusiastic applause as the curtains rose and a figure stood spotlighted on the stage: a handsome figure, in a tight serviceman's uniform, with the peaked cap at a jaunty angle.

The applause died away as the soldier coughed into a gloved hand, the signal for the orchestra to start up, and suddenly the theatre was filled with the confident, strong singing voice of the world's best male impersonator.

'Oh, I think she's wonderful,' said Minnie.

'Sssh.' Ena urged her friend to silence.

Nancy Miller sang songs known to the audience and encouraged them to join in with her after the first couple of verses. They were chirpy numbers, with witty choruses designed to titillate and make the innocent girls titter. It was a fine act, and the audience were firmly on her side. After leading them in five numbers she took to the centre stage and then shouted, 'Ladies and gentlemen, it gives me the greatest pleasure to introduce to you the ladies of the chorus.'

One by one twenty young ladies walked on to the stage, each wearing a flimsy dress, showing off bare shoulders and legs. Ena felt she ought to close her eyes and feel disgusted at the sight, but the girls looked so pretty. As she sat there every inch of her body, except her hands and face, covered with dull-coloured thick material Ena gazed jealously at the girls in their bright costumes, with their hair tumbling about their shoulders.

The showgirls linked arms and danced from the back of the stage towards the audience, raising their legs and swaying their hips seductively. Ena noted the men around her leaning forward. Apart from Alf Tatlock, who seemed to shrink back further into the safety of his seat.

'Right, lads,' shouted Nancy Miller. 'I'll let you into a little secret. All these lovely ladies have one thing in common. They all love soldiers, isn't that right, girls?'

They nodded in agreement and giggled coyly.

Nancy Miller peered into the audience. 'Only I can't see any soldiers out there,' she said. 'What a pity.'

One of the showgirls rushed to her side and pointed into the wings excitedly. Nancy Miller followed her gaze, then threw out her arms. 'Oh, ladies and gentlemen, I stand corrected. We have a soldier among us.'

The audience all looked to where she pointed and watched as a stiff-looking army officer marched on to the stage. He came to a halt in front of Nancy and saluted. She saluted back and winked at the audience. 'At last, a soldier!'

At her signal the showgirls squealed and fell upon him, petting him. The man continued to stand to attention, his face bright red.

Nancy allowed the audience to laugh, then held out her hands for silence.

'Gents, lads ... now's your chance. All it takes is a step up to the stage. Here you can sign up and have a kiss.'

Ena gasped. She had thought the officer and the girls part of the act, but it was a set-up. Why else would someone as grand and important as Nancy Miller come to Weatherfield? They were all being used.

Some rows in front of Ena a man stood up and waved his cap.

'I'll 'ave a kiss,' he yelled.

'And you'd be very welcome,' shouted Nancy, 'but first sign on to fight for your king.'

The man hesitated.

'Don't you want to fight for your king? For your country?' urged Nancy, her tone inviting the audience to take her side.

'Course he does!' shouted another man. 'I do!'

'Then come on up, sir, grasp the pen with one hand and a pretty girl with the other.'

There was a roar of approval from the audience as the man pushed his way out of the row and ran down the aisle towards the stage. He leapt on to the boards and Nancy Miller pointed him towards the Army officer, who now sat at a table with sheets of paper and a pen in front of him. The man was directed to sign his name. Hands were shaken and then, to the delight of the crowd, one of the girls planted a kiss on his lips.

'That's all it takes, gents, just come forward. Don't be shy. Don't be a coward.' Nancy pointed at a man in the front row. 'You, sir, how old are you?'

'Eighteen,' stuttered the man.

'Are you married?'

'No.'

'Then why aren't you in uniform?' she demanded. 'Are you with this young lady?'

'Yes,' the man replied.

Nancy smiled at the girl. 'You want him to be a hero, don't you?'

'Y-yes,' said the girl feebly.

'You heard her, sir, come on, shoulders back, chest out. Just a few steps and you'll be a hero in her eyes.'

Nancy leant forward and held out her hand to the man. He looked at his companion, unsure what to do. She gave a half-smile and a shrug.

'Go on, lad,' urged an older man. 'It'll mck a man o' you.'

The boy rose to his feet, cast a look at his girl, then stepped forward. The audience's cheers rang in his ears.

'Come on, lads. Now's the time. The Hun's rising up. We can squash him!' Nancy ground the heel of her boot into the stage. She nodded into the orchestra pit, and the brass section rose to play.

Nancy played the stage as if it were an instrument. She strode up and down, pointing to men in the audience, beckoning them to come forward. The showgirls joined her, moving down off the stage to flounce into the audience, seeking out young men, who stared nervously about them. One by one they were pulled forward, petted and cajoled into mounting the stage and signing their names.

A spotlight was aimed on Nancy as she belted out a patriotic song. Stagehands perched above her on the lighting rig high above the stage and let loose streamers that floated down, glittering as they caught the light.

Gesturing for the men to come forward, Nancy carried on singing, her voice reaching the furthest corners of the theatre.

Ena was aware that Alf was shifting uncomfortably in his chair. She leant back and, without turning to him, placed a calming hand on his sleeve. 'Yer too young,' she hissed, out of the side of her mouth.

'I feel I should go up,' he said.

'Yer too young,' she repeated, and swallowed hard. She wanted the doors to open, for them all to rush out into the night, and wished she hadn't come. In the morning she'd describe the scene to Gladys Arkwright at the Mission Hall. She'd say it was like watching Satan himself and his demons luring the lost souls into Hell. She looked around her with frightened eyes, saw young men waving their caps as they rushed forward blindly. Others were more reluctant and were pulled out of their seats by show-girls or, even worse, by their neighbours.

Minnie sank into her seat and put out a hand to Ena, seeking reassurance.

'It's all right, lass,' said Ena. 'We'll go soon.'

'It's not normally like this,' Minnie said in bewilderment. 'Normally we 'ave a sing-song at the end.'

Flo Hewitt saw the chorus-girl make eye-contact with Thomas and gasped when she realised what was about to happen. The girl ignored other men seated in front of Thomas and made a bee-line for him. Away from the stage lights her dress looked cheap and moth-eaten. Stage makeup exaggerated her eyes and lips, and Flo thought she looked common. The girl smiled brightly at Thomas. 'My, you're a strappin' fella,' she said. 'Don't you want a kiss?'

'No, he doesn't,' said Flo sharply, before Thomas could open his mouth.

The girl ignored her and carried on smiling at Thomas. 'Why don't you come up on the stage wi' me?'

'Leave us alone,' shouted Flo, above the din.

The girl put forward her hand to grasp Thomas's but Flo landed a slap on the girl's wrist. 'Watch it,' the showgirl snarled.

'Just leave us alone,' pleaded Flo.

'Yer boyfriend is 'e?'

'My brother.'

''E can mek 'is own mind up, darlin',' said the girl, fixing her eyes on Thomas's square jaw.

''E can't sign up,' said Flo. ''E's too young. 'E's only sixteen. It's against the law.'

The girl shrugged.

''E looks older. Easily pass for nineteen, couldn't you … soldier?'

Thomas entered into the debate, turning to Flo in uncertainty.

'She's right, I could lie.'

'No! Thomas Hewitt, you can't! You're needed at 'ome.'

''Is country needs 'im, darlin',' said the girl.

'I think it's romantic,' said Martha, to anyone who was listening.

'Shurrup,' hissed Flo, turning on her friend.

The girl saw her chance, leant forward quickly and planted an open-mouthed kiss firmly on Thomas's lips. As she drew back her head he stared at her in alarm. He'd never been kissed by any girl outside his family and the stirring he was feeling made him giddy. 'That was for free,' breathed the girl. 'If you want another it'll cost you yer signature.'

To Flo's alarm Thomas rose from his seat, his hands fumbling for his cap. 'What are you doing?' she demanded. 'Sit down.'

Thomas stared at the smiling chorus girl, mesmerised by her laughing eyes.

'I ought to sign up, Flo,' he said. 'It's me duty.'

'It's not,' shouted Flo, panic in her voice. She looked around for someone to help her but the audience were caught up in the wave of patriotism and those nearby were cheering Thomas on. He pushed past Flo so she stood up and clung to him, tears in her eyes. 'Please, Thomas, think of Gertie, think of Molly. We need you.'

The showgirl continued to smile, never losing cyc contact with her victim. She stepped backwards, inviting Thomas to follow her, and he did, under her spell. Flo felt useless. There was no stopping him, he was going to mount the stage, sign his name and be rewarded with another kiss from the temptress.

Martha sucked her toffee joyfully, thrilling

to the drama of the evening. She wished she was a lad and could take part in the spectacle.

Flo stood beside her seat as Thomas followed the girl down to the stage. He did not turn back to his sister.

From her seat across the auditorium, Ena saw the tall young man leap on to the stage and the girl push him towards the front of the queue. She saw him write his name without hesitation and the girl drag him willingly into the wings, out of sight of the audience.

Her neighbour had also seen. He turned to Ena and whispered fearfully, 'That's my mate Thomas 'Ewitt. 'E lives next door. We're same age.'

''E looks older,' commented Ena.

''E is, but only by two months. 'Appen I should go too.'

'No, lad. You go 'ome and talk it over wi' yer auntie. If you feel same in mornin' then get yerself down to the Armoury. Do it the proper way, not like this. All swank and show-off.'

Ena smiled at the boy, and was relieved to see the chorus-girls edging back towards the stage, their job done.

Flo Hewitt let herself sadly into the family home. It already felt empty without Thomas. She found Gertie darning socks by the light of the fire and a solitary gaslamp.

'Where's our Thomas?' asked Gertie, realising from Flo's face that something was very wrong. ''E's not got drunk again, 'as 'e?'

'No.' Flo gulped. The only way to say it was just to spit it out quickly. ''E's signed up.'

''E can't 'ave done. 'E's only sixteen.'

''E lied. I tried to stop him...' Flo burst into tears and fell into a chair.

'Where is 'e?' asked Gertie, her voice rising with alarm.

'They took 'em off, out o' the theatre. I don't know where 'e is.'

Gertie dropped the sock into her lap and stared into the glowing coals in the grate. Flo looked up from crying and stared at her stepmother. She'd never seen her so still.

''E wouldn't listen to me...' she said quietly.

''E's 'is father's son all right,' muttered Gertie.

'Perhaps we can go to see someone,' said Flo hopefully, 'tell 'em there's bin a mistake, that 'e's just a boy.'

Gertie gave a hollow laugh. ''E's not a boy no more, lass, 'e's a soldier.'

Flo left her chair and sank to her knees in front of the range. She burst into fresh tears and allowed Gertie's comforting hands to soothe her. Then she sought out Gertie's soft lap and gave herself over to the sobs that racked her body. Gertie stroked Flo's hair as tears ran down her own cheeks. Thomas was gone.

CHAPTER FOUR

October 1915

The oak-panelled vestry was as warm and
snug a place as Ena had ever known. The
furniture edging the room was large and
ornate, cheap copies of Empire-inspired
pieces: a dresser decorated with wooden
bull elephants, plant-holders with elaborate
latticework. Every inch of available wall
space was taken up by richly coloured
samplers extolling Christian virtues, and
sepia photographs of stern, forbidding
figures. The room was overcrowded with
knick-knacks, a bewildering contrast with
the other residences in the area. Each piece
of furniture and ornament in the tiny room
had been crammed in not for practicality
but out of sentiment. Her belongings were
all that Mission caretaker Gladys Arkwright
had left to remind her of her childhood in
the Lancashire town of Oldham. She had
been the youngest daughter of a successful
doctor, but a frowned-upon marriage to

impoverished lay preacher Samuel Arkwright had left her isolated from her family
with only her dowry of furniture to serve as
a reminder of better times. Furniture that
her elder sisters had rejected. Gladys had
been happy to relinquish her old lifestyle for
the love of a man who had died of con-
sumption a year and two days after their
wedding.

That had been twenty-one years ago and
now, Gladys was content to live in her one-
roomed vestry, her home since December
1902 and her instalment as caretaker at the
Mission of Glad Tidings. Although the
Mission's front door opened on to bustling
Victoria Street, the vestry – at the back of
the hall – was numbered No. 16 in Coronation Street. Gladys's position at the
Mission set her apart from her neighbours,
as did her clearly defined speech, fine
manners and literacy. She had only a small
circle of friends and generally kept herself to
herself. At times of evangelical fervour she
could be found standing outside the doors
to the Rover's Return urging drinkers to
repent and sign the Pledge. The drive to
temperance had been a prominent part of
Mission activity since the turn of the
century. Most signed the Pledge to give up

the demon drink with the full intention of honouring the commitment all their lives, but many back-slid within weeks, if not days. A recurring sermon on the Mission circuit held alcohol responsible for all broken commandments.

'The man who covets finds strength through alcohol to steal and gain another man's belongings.'

'The foul-mouthed idolater brings curses upon his intoxicated head when he takes the name of the Lord God Almighty in vain.'

'The adulterer stares at his own reflection in the bottom of a glass.'

Like all God-fearing folk, Ena had signed the Pledge at an early age. So early that she had never tasted alcohol in her life. The subject of alcohol divided her home: her father, brother and elder sister indulged while Ena and her mother did not.

Mary Schofield had attended local missions all her life and when the Glad Tidings had opened she had transferred from the Salvation Mission on Booth Street with some of its other members to create the new congregation. Singing hymns provided Mary with an escape from the humdrum household chores that dominated her life. Each Sunday Mary and Ena attended the eighty thirty meeting at the Mission and, when possible, Ena returned at four o'clock for the Bible-study group. Both were members of the ladies' group, which organised picnics and outings for the small number of pauper children they could afford to help with their limited funds. While Mary Schofield's loud, off-key voice joined the congregation in worship her daughter would sit at the front of the hall, pounding the keys of the ancient harmonium, with Gladys turning the pages of the music. Gladys had played the instrument until arthritis had left her fingers stiff and deformed. When her pupil Ena had taken on the task so admirably Gladys was able to limit her playing to special occasions. As well as being Gladys's pupil, Ena soon became her confidante and one of her most trusted friends. Thomas Schofield was disturbed that his daughter spent all her free time in the fifty-three-year-old widow's home, and felt that Ena should mix more with people of her own age. Little did he know that one of the main attractions of the vestry was not Gladys's homemade gingerbread but the presence of her nineteen-year-old nephew

Phil Moss was a squat, broad-chested lad

with rosy cheeks and a squint, and was the love of Ena's life. Both were regular visitors to the vestry and, to Gladys's delight, had shown more than a passing interest in each other. At the start of the war Phil had volunteered for active service, but his civilian job as a groom had led to him being stationed at an army camp just outside Bolton where he had charge of the company's horses. Being so close to home he visited his favourite aunt often. With a sparkle in her eye, Gladys always made certain that Ena was around when he called.

The threesome sat around Gladys's laden tea-table and conversation turned to Ena's impending birthday.

'I remember my seventeenth birthday,' said Gladys fondly. 'Father gave me a leather writing case.'

'I'll be lucky to get a pencil,' said Ena wryly. 'There's cutbacks at Hardcastle's, you know. Management say the war's forcing up the price of coal and that there'll be cuts in wages just to keep the machinery going. Mother's already started to put aside what she can.'

Gladys sucked in air through the gaps in her teeth. 'It's a crying shame.'

'Aye,' agreed Ena.

Gladys looked across at her nephew. She knew that something was troubling him, and as he hadn't unburdened himself to her yet she felt it was time to probe. 'Something on your mind, Phil?'

He started at the mention of his name and looked sharply at her.

'Sorry?'

'Don't be, lad. You seem preoccupied.' Gladys looked keenly at him and then asked, 'Have you received orders to move on?'

Phil lowered his eyes and nodded.

'Oh...' Ena gasped.

'When?' asked Gladys, putting down her bone-china teacup.

'We're moving out over the next few days. Majority of chaps are leaving tomorrow, I'm bringing the horses the following day. We're off to France.'

'You'll miss my birthday,' Ena flushed. It was the first thing she had thought, and now she wished she'd kept her mouth shut. She felt selfish and insensitive.

'I've brought you a present,' said Phil, reaching into his tunic pocket.

'Oh, I didn't mean–' began Ena.

'I know ... but I wanted you to have it.' He produced a small scarlet box.

At the sight of the box Ena's eyes rushed to meet his. 'Phil...' she said, but the words died on her lips.

He opened the box to reveal a silver ring with a cluster of what looked like glass forming a crescent on its top.

She gasped and stared at it. She had never seen anything so beautiful.

'This was my mother's,' said Phil. 'My father gave it to her when he asked her to marry him. It has five diamonds.'

Ena was speechless and her eyes remained locked upon the ring.

Phil took the ring out of the box and held it out to Ena. 'Would you do me the honour of agreeing to become my wife, Ena?'

Gladys squealed in delight and bit into a linen napkin. She looked from Phil's earnest face to Ena's shocked one and nudged her young friend's arm. Ena opened her mouth and stammered, 'Oh ... Phil ... are you sure?'

'Positive. I've thought it through and through and you're the girl for me. I've known it since I first saw you in this very room. You're kind and generous, selfless and beautiful and I want to spend the rest of my life with you.'

Ena burst into tears. No one had ever said anything so wonderful to her. Phil looked at his aunt in concern, but she smiled encouragingly at him and inclined her head, prompting him to comfort his sobbing sweetheart. He rose clumsily from the table and moved to Ena's side. As he placed his arm around her she turned into his neck and said, 'I'd love to marry you, Phil.'

Across the cobbles of Coronation Street, at No. 9, a nineteen-year-old girl's thoughts had also turned to love. Alice Buck was the prettiest girl on the Street and the only daughter of mill-workers Ned and Sarah. The whole family worked at Hardcastle's mill, including Alice's brothers, Joe and Larry, and it had been at the mill that Alice had fallen for Vic Piggott.

The youngsters had all grown up together – the Bucks at No. 10, Vic and his twin brother Robert at No. 13 – but it had only been in the early summer of 1915, when Alice had been given a work station near Vic, that she fell for him. With the war in its sixth month most of the young and able men of the area had volunteered or been pushed into joining up by critical family and peers. Alice's brothers were both serving overseas, but the Piggott twins had remained in Coronation Street and attracted the attention of local girls.

Although identical in appearance, the twins differed greatly in personality. Vic had always taken his cue from his brother and when Robert had decided war wasn't for him Vic had stayed at No. 13 with only the slightest twinge of regret. The boys' father, trade unionist Fred, had grown used to the cutting remarks aimed at him in the mill or the pub. He agreed with them and, in the privacy of his own home, he took his belt to his sons to beat some patriotism into them.

Each beating left Vic prepared to volunteer but Robert was as stubborn as his father and each welt left upon his skin fuelled his determination to remain in England. That determination was shaken on the morning of 9 May when newspapers carried the story of the sinking of the luxury liner *Lusitania*. Travelling from New York to Liverpool, the liner had been torpedoed by a German submarine and many lives had been lost.

Like the rest of the country, the Piggotts had been enraged by the sinking and as the reported death toll rose to settle at 1,978, Vic voiced his opinion that he and his brother should fight back against such an inhuman monster as the Kaiser. Although shaken by the sinking, Robert remained adamant that war was not for them, and under cover of night confessed to his twin why he was so against the idea.

The boys lay side by side in the bed they had shared since infancy.

'Do you remember going to the fair last Empire Day?' Robert asked.

'Of course,' said Vic. It had been one of the year's highlights. Travelling players had gathered on Plank Lane and entertained the residents of Weatherfield with tombolas, side-shows, freaks of nature and rides.

'Well ... you took Nancy Wallis on the swing boats and I went off to buy toffee apples and later you couldn't find me.'

'Yes?' Vic remembered it well: he'd tried to run his fingers across Nancy's ample bosom and had been slapped away.

'I didn't tell you at the time but I reckon I ought to now,' said Robert, his voice cutting into the stillness of the room. 'I went to see that gypsy woman, to have my fortune told.'

Vic raised his head and stared at his brother, the candlelight reflecting in his clear blue eyes. 'You didn't!'

The boys' mother, Emma, had stressed the evils of the occult, and had always grouped fortune-tellers with witches and demons. The idea that his brother had

visited one fired Vic with horrified excitement.

'What was it like?' he asked.

'She was sat at a table with a black cloth
on it that sparkled. She was very, very old, at
least a hundred, and she had hair growing
out of her chin.'

'Like Grandma Peel?'

'Yes, just like her.'

Vic shuddered. Their maternal grandmother had always filled the boys with
terror when she grabbed their smooth faces
and rubbed her own rough cheeks against
them.

'What did she say?'

'Well...' Robert sighed, knowing that now
he'd started he would have to tell the whole
tale. 'She knew about us being twins and
she told me stuff that only we know about.
Our secrets.'

Vic closed his eyes tight. 'Go on,' he
whispered.

'She knew we weren't in the army, and she
said that was good, that we shouldn't enlist,
no matter what anyone said or did, that we
should remain in England.'

'Why?' asked Vic, his own heart beating in
time with Robert's.

'She said that if we ventured overseas we

would both … die.'

Vic groaned. He'd known what Robert was going to say before he said it. The flash of light and scream of agony that had been his recurring nightmare over the past months flared up inside his head, and his lips quivered.

Neither spoke of the matter again until a letter arrived from Liverpool in September. Letters were seldom delivered to Coronation Street and the sight of the postmaster stopped to knock at the front door of No. 13 was much commented upon by the locals. Emma had rubbed the flour from her hands and taken the letter in alarm. She spent half an hour fingering the envelope and tracing the lettering before placing it on the kitchen table where it remained to haunt her throughout the day. She had burnt the day's bread and broken a plate before the arrival at midday of her family for dinner.

As soon as the men entered the house Emma rushed to them. 'There's been a letter,' she cried, pointing into the kitchen.

Fred shared his wife's alarm but Robert pushed ahead of his parents and picked it up. 'It's from Liverpool,' he said, and opened it.

Emma clutched at her apron and stared at

her son. He scanned the letter, then looked up, his face grave. 'Mother, you should sit down. I'm afraid it's bad news.'

Emma sank into a chair. She'd known it would be. Why else would a letter be delivered to her home?

'It's from Lizzie, writing for Auntie Mary.' Like Emma, her sister could not write. 'Lizzie says they know now for sure that Barney's dead. He'd been serving in the engine room of the *Lusitania*. She says Auntie Mary kept up hope that he was alive, maybe having been rescued and taken to hospital in Ireland, but one of his shipmates has been to see them and says he saw Barney drown.'

Emma groaned and slumped on to the table. Fred stared at his wife awkwardly, unsure how to react. Vic pushed past him and grasped his mother's hand. He knew what the news meant to her. Barney had been the youngest of her family, the thirteen-year-old godson she had loved as if he were her own. She had travelled to Liverpool to stand beside her sister and wave Barney off when he'd started working as an engine boy on the luxury liner *Mauretania*. She'd been so proud to know that her Barney was working just feet away from where millionaires were eating off gilt plates. Now cheeky-faced Barney was dead, murdered by an enemy with whom he had had no fight.

Vic stared at his brother, knowing they shared the same thought. Robert caught his gaze and nodded. 'Mother ... you should go to visit Auntie Mary. She'll need you.'

'I'm needed here,' murmured Emma.

'No, you're not. We can manage.'

By the time the afternoon hooter sounded to call the workers back to the mill, a bag had been packed and Emma sent on her way west. With their mother out of the way, and unable to stop them, Vic and Robert spent the afternoon at the Armoury, volunteering to fight for their country.

Emma Piggott had been mortified by the news that her beloved boys were to be shipped out to France in three weeks' time. She did not share her neighbours' attitude towards war: she saw the amateur soldiers as nothing but machine-gun fodder. Her views were not welcomed by the local women who preferred to see their husbands and sons as gallant heroes.

In the Corner Shop, Cedric Thwaite continued to serve the community but did so with the utmost reserve: he was civil to those who had turned so savagely on him and his wife but he no longer asked after their health or took an interest in their lives. He was biding his time until he could rid himself of the albatross the shop had become.

When Emma was cornered by Sarah Buck, the one-time arbitrator of rows, she stood back and waited for the screeching to finish. 'My boys have been over there for nigh on a year without a scratch or a graze. They're having a great time,' said Sarah, with pride.

'Your boys are a couple of insensitive oafs who probably find dossing down in tents a damn sight more comfortable than living at home!' shouted Emma, pulling her shawl tightly round her shoulders.

'You old cow!' screamed Sarah. 'Just cos you mollycoddle your two wet fish–'

'I do nothin' of the sort!'

'Yes, you do. Why else 'ave they waited so long before takin' King's shillin'? Cos they're a couple of mummy's boys.'

Emma flushed, as she always did when defending her sons. 'They never joined up cos they know what I know. That war's a terrible thing, where men get killed.'

'Men get killed down pits and in mills every day o' week. Don't stop 'em workin', do it?' Sarah's brand of logic was peculiar to herself.

'Aye, in accidents. I'm talkin' ruddy great guns and cannons!'

'You're talkin' rot. I know my boys are all right. Know why?' Sarah stepped closer and rammed her fat face into Emma's thin one. 'Cos they can 'andle themselves. Cos they're men and not wet fish like your two!'

Emma flinched as Sarah spat the word 'fish' in her face – unlike Sarah she tended to shy away from confrontations. The upset that crossed her face was enough for Sarah Buck: grabbing her purchases she made for the door, calling out to Cedric that she'd settle her account at the end of the week.

Cedric chalked up the two shillings' worth in his book and, as if not having witnessed the attack on her, calmly asked Emma what she required.

Later that day, as she stood peeling potatoes at her enamel sink, Sarah told the story to her daughter Alice. 'That'll teach her to go round scaremongerin'. She's like a chicken that's 'ad its 'ead chopped off, runnin' around flappin' its wings and gettin' into a state. Do them lads of 'ers some good to do some fightin', make proper men of 'em.'

Alice stared out of the window into the backyard and said, 'I think Vic Piggott's lovely.'

Her mother snorted and dug her peeling knife into a potato. 'These spuds 'ave got more eyes in 'em than all the needles in loom room put together. Which one's Vic? They both look same to me.'

'Vic's the quiet one. He thinks a lot.'

'Probably got nowt inside that 'ead of his. 'appen she dropped him when he were a bairn. I saw 'er tryin' to catch a ball o' string once, all fingers and thumbs. Oh, yes, if anyone dropped kiddies I bet Emma Piggott 'as.'

''E's got plenty goin' on inside 'is 'ead,' said Alice in defiance. 'I've seen 'im readin' paper durin' break. The other lads play football or smoke but Vic sits there readin'. Gettin' knowledge.'

Sarah shuddered at the word. 'Knowledge? What does 'e want wi' that? 'E's nowt but a loom boy an' a slow one at that.'

''E's gonna mek summat o' 'imself one day is Vic Piggott.'

'Oh, aye?' Sarah eyed her daughter. 'You're smitten, ain't you? I should o' guessed. I were just the same at yer age. Blond curly 'air and blue eyes, and I forgot meself and let yer dad 'ave his way.'

Alice frowned. 'Me dad's got no 'air.'

'Aye, that's worryin' about you lot, that is.' Sarah drained the potato peelings, scooped them up in her fat red hands and threw them into the slop bucket that stood beside the sink. 'Don't waste yer time on wet fish like Vic Piggott. Get yerself a man wi' some life in 'is bones. Pretty ones are all right to look at but it's in bed where you want some action. You want to get yerself down to abattoir. There's some great 'ulkin' sods down there. Grab yerself one before they all sign up for war.'

Alice flushed and pushed a stray strand of hair away from her face. 'There's more to a man than what 'e's like in bed,' she said, before her voice was drowned by Sarah's loud cackle. She smarted as her mother supported her large frame against the sink, her shoulders shaking in laughter.

'Oh, Alice love,' said Sarah, wiping a tear from her eye, 'you've got a lot to learn.'

Only one house separated Alice's home from Vic's but as far as she was concerned they were an ocean apart. As the number of available young men had dwindled, Alice and her friends had seen the folly in maintaining childhood friendships when trying to catch themselves a sweetheart. Robert Piggott, with his mixture of good looks and charismatic personality, had caught the eye of a number of local girls – or, at least, those who didn't despise him for not being in uniform. Vic, while blessed with the same good looks, confused many of them by having an unusually quiet nature and appearing to live in his own secret world. Alice found this quality attractive and sought out his company, much to his disquiet.

While awaiting call-up orders the Piggott brothers continued to work at Hardcastle's mill and endure the taunts of workmates who had been kept in the dark as to the boys' new military careers. When he started work one morning Vic found a feather laid across the handle of his loom. He stared at it, then lifted it to his face. It was a goose feather, silky and as white as snow. Laughter broke out around him when he was seen handling the instrument of humiliation and torment. He had been given a white feather because he was a coward. Now he knew exactly what they thought of him.

'Stop laughing!' screamed Alice, struggling to be heard above the noise. 'He's not a coward! He's enlisted!'

No one took any notice of the indignant girl but Vic turned towards her, touched by her defence. The concern in her eyes surprised him and he threw the feather on to the floor where it joined the ends of cotton and discarded bobbins. She smiled at him, and he turned back to his loom to start work. That night Alice lay in bed looking out of her bedroom window and hoped that Vic would find the courage to ask her to walk out with him.

As Ena Schofield broke the news of her engagement to her startled family over breakfast, two telegrams arrived at No. 13 Coronation Street giving the Piggott boys twenty-four hours' call-up notice. In Inkerman Street, a delighted Mary Schofield hugged her daughter and wished her well, while in Coronation Street Emma Piggott burst into tears and had to be comforted by her sons, who both recalled the fortune-teller's prediction. Ena linked arms with her friends Minnie and Martha and chatted in excitement about becoming Mrs Phil Moss, while Vic and Robert walked to work across the cobbles of Coronation Street in silence.

Alice picked up on Vic's mood straight away: he was always quiet but today seemed distant too. At dinner-time he had broken five threads and owed the company more in damages than he'd earned in wages. She caught up with him as he hung around waiting for his brother and father to appear from the third floor. 'Are you all right?' she asked.

Vic sighed, glad of the chance to talk to someone. We 'ave to go to Southampton tomorrer. Then it's on to France.'

Although the news was not unexpected, it still shocked Alice. She'd only just started to get to know Vic, and it would ruin everything if he left so soon. 'That's awful,' she said.

'Aye, but that's the way of it.'

As Robert appeared on the stairwell, Vic tipped his cap to Alice and left the building, the wooden soles of his shoes thumping against the cobbles. Alice watched the two fair-haired brothers disappear around the corner into Coronation Street and dug her hands into her apron pockets. Unable to stomach the thought of the dinner her mother would have ready for her she sank into the shadows and sobbed into her dress.

Phil Moss had arranged to call at No. 14 Inkerman Street on the eve of his departure to meet his future in-laws. Mary rushed about the house in preparation for his arrival, thanking God that she hadn't got round to taking the mantelpiece clock and their best clothes to the pawn shop that week. She brushed fluff off her husband's suit as he fiddled with his shirt collar and complained, 'I don't see why I 'ave to wear me suit. I'm sure lad won't mind what I look like. It's our Ena he wants to wed, not me.'

'First impressions count. I don't want 'im goin' back to 'is folks tellin' 'em our Ena lives in a midden and 'er father 'asn't the grace to wash be'ind 'is ears to meet 'is future son-in-law.'

'I don't see what all the fuss is about,' said Alice, siding with her father.

'That's cos yer nose 'as been put out cos yonder fella wants to marry our Ena and not you,' said Mary.

'Aye, our Alice. And you're the eldest too. You wanna get yerself out there – you don't want to end up old and dried up like yer auntie Aggie,' said Thomas, wincing at the thought of his sister who, still single at the age of thirty-five, knew she'd remain a spinster for the rest of her life.

Alice glared at her father but her retort remained unspoken for they all heard a loud, sharp knock at the front door. In a community where neighbours walked in and out of each other's homes at will, a knock represented the postman, the rent man or a gentleman caller.

Ena ran down the stairs and into the hall. She was wearing her Sunday best dress, blue with tiny white flowers. She paused at the door to smooth her long hair down her back and glanced over shoulder to her excited mother, who nodded encouragement. She opened the door and Phil blundered in, shuffling from one foot to the other and blushing at the sight of his fiancée. 'How do, Ena.'

'How do, Phil.'

Ena made way for him and introduced him to the three members of her family. He shook hands and was invited to take his place at the table, at which point Mary dragged her daughters into the scullery and left Phil with Thomas Schofield.

Having been told what to say and how to say it, Thomas was keen to get his prepared speech out of the way as soon as possible. 'You want our Ena as yer wife?'

'Yes. I do that,' said Phil earnestly.

'She's a grand girl, a great 'elp to 'er mother.'

'I'm sure she is. My aunt, Miss Arkwright, says she's a credit to yerself and Mrs Schofield.'

'A credit?' The compliment distracted Thomas from his train of thought but he nodded. 'Yes, she is a credit. The man who weds our Ena will be a very lucky man. You're a very lucky man, Mr Moss.'

'I think I am that.'

'Ena's told 'er mother that she likes you a great deal, Mr Moss, but I speak plain and I need to mek certain you can take care of her. What are your intentions?'

Phil took a deep breath and fiddled nervously with his shirt cuffs.

'I earn a decent wage. I'm honest and 'ardworking, an' I don't owe a penny or a farthin' to no one. I'm not a big drinker...'

'I'm glad to 'ear it,' murmured Thomas.

'...but I 'aven't taken the Pledge either. I believe a man's entitled to a little beverage on occasion...'

Thomas nodded in agreement.

'When the war's over,' continued Phil, 'I intend to make a good 'ome for Ena. I'm not an extravagant man, Mr Schofield, and

I 'ave no politics either. I'm better with 'orses than wi' most people but I reckon I'll make Ena a good 'usband.'

Thomas looked at the boy's serious face, then slapped him hard on the shoulder. 'Aye, lad, I reckon you will. You'll do for me.'

In the scullery, Mary straightened up from listening at the key-hole and pushed the door open. Ena rushed in and threw her arms around her father's neck.

'Oh, Father, thank you,' she said, blushing.

'Right, I'm 'ungry,' declared Thomas gruffly. 'Where's this tea I've been promised? Young Phil 'ere'll be goin' 'ome telling 'is folk we're a right stingy lot! It were same wi' the wife's lot.'

'Thomas Schofield!' expostulated the offended Mary. ''Ow can you say such a thing?'

Ena grinned at Phil and squeezed his hand underneath the table. She was very happy.

Alice Buck was very sad. The sun was long set and Coronation Street was cast in darkness, lit only by the solitary gas-lamp outside the Corner Shop. She slipped out of the front door of No. 9 and pulled her shawl

121

around her slender shoulders, gasping at the cold night air. Despite the hour Weatherfield was as noisy as it was in daytime. The engines in the mills were kept running throughout the night to keep the huge buildings from becoming too cold to operate the looms and, with more than the Piggotts enlisting in the morning, the local public houses echoed with the songs of rowdy youngsters having drinks bought for them by generous elders.

At the Rover's, Vic felt sick as his father pressed another pint on him. He'd hardly crossed the pub's threshold before and the beer swilling around inside him made his stomach lurch. Robert was having better luck in downing his ale but his speech was slurred as he grasped his father's arm and joined him in a song.

In the Snug Ivy Makepiece, the toothless old crone from No. 11, leant across the bar to see who was making such a racket.

'It's one of them Piggott brats,' she reported back to her companion, Sarah Buck. 'I 'eard they're off tomorrer.'

'That'll shut their mother up,' said Sarah. 'She can't go on about machine-gun fodder when 'er own lads are on front line.'

Ivy, who had two sons fighting in the

Front, nodded. 'She wants to watch 'er mouth sayin' wicked things like that, or she'll get a fist in it.'

Sarah slurped at her drink and wiped the back of her hand across her mouth.

'She thinks she's summat she ain't. I saw her yesterday mornin' emptyin' her piss pot. I said to 'er, "Blue, is it? Or is it same colour as rest of us pee?" You should've seen 'er face!'

Ivy cackled into her glass. 'Don't mek me laugh or I'll piddle meself.'

''Ere,' said Sarah, suddenly serious, 'where's Bulgaria?'

'You what?'

'Bulgaria. It's a place.'

'Sounds like it's out Yorkshire way,' said Ivy.

'No, it can't be cos they were sayin' down the market that Britain's declared war on it. Britain can't declare war on some place in Yorkshire, can it?'

'Why not? It 'appened in Civil War, when we chopped old 'Enry the Eighth's 'ead off.'

It was past ten o'clock when Alice saw the blond-headed figure lurch out of the pub, supporting himself against the brickwork. She stepped out of the shadows and put out a hand to him. 'Vic ... Vic, it's me, Alice.'

The boy looked up and smiled, and she knew she had to kiss him.

''Ello, Alice... I don't feel too good.'

She took hold of him, he leant on her, and she stumbled under his weight. Bracing herself against the wall she walked him towards Rosamund Street. 'I don't live down 'ere,' he said, pointing behind them. 'Our 'ouse is down there, next to shop.'

'We're goin' back way,' said Alice, determined.

'Are we?'

'Aye.'

Alice continued on her way, stumbling in the dark until she had her prey propped up against the wall behind the Rover's. The air was thick with the smell of stale beer and rubbish, but Alice took no notice as she pressed her lips to his. Reflexes rather than passion made him respond and, driven by her basic instincts, Alice grappled with his braces. His trousers dropped to the cobbles.

Ten minutes later Vic Piggott opened his bedroom door and called goodnight to his father. He pulled down his braces, stepped out of his trousers and pulled his shirt over his shoulders before he fell into bed. 'It's freezin'!' he complained to his brother. 'I thought you'd 'ave warmed it up for me.'

'I've only just got in meself,' murmured Robert.

'How come? You left pub ages ago.'

'I know, but I met Alice Buck outside Rover's and she dragged me round the back. Gave me a right seein' to.'

'Alice Buck?' asked Vic.

Robert grunted.

'I always thought she were easy,' said Vic, in a quiet, regretful voice. He could tell from the change in Robert's breathing that he was already asleep. Vic stared out of the bedroom window, to where huge chimneys rose into the sky, billowing out clouds of smoke that would settle upon the buildings below in flurries of soot. It was the brothers' last night in England, and Vic couldn't shake off the fortune-teller's prophecy that swam through his head: 'Leave England and die'.

CHAPTER FIVE

Christmas 1915

As the workers left Hardcastle's mill, the murmur of disenchanted voices threatened to match the clatter of the wooden clogs as they trundled home. It was the end of the working week, Friday 24 December, Christmas Eve. The complaining had started at dinner-time when someone in the main loom shed had realised that as Christmas Day fell on a Saturday the workforce would not be getting a day off work because they'd be off anyway. Fred Piggott, union representative for the weavers, had been cajoled into mounting the wooden stairs that separated the crowded, ear-shattering loom and weaving rooms from the foreman's hut, which towered above the work stations. The foreman had listened in silence to Fred's complaint. Fred pointed out that if Christmas Day had fallen on a weekday the mill would have closed as usual and the workers would have had a day's holiday. Fred

127

reckoned that as it fell on a Saturday the workers were being done out of a day off. The foreman's response had been predictable: the workers should count themselves lucky that they didn't have to work weekends, Christmas or no Christmas.

After reporting back to the workforce Fred had suggested a strike but the very word sent alarm around the loom sheds. In 1911 Fred had brought the mill to a standstill after the bosses had refused his demands for a minimum wage of one pound for a fifty-five-hour week. The strike was called to coincide with action across the whole of Weatherfield and lasted for weeks, culminating in a riot when police attempted to break up a protest. Some of Hardcastle's workers had been injured in the uproar, including Clara Popplewell, from No. 7 Coronation Street, who had lost an eye after being clubbed in the face by a policeman. The workers had returned to work victorious, but with the memory of those hardships and injuries, no one was willing to strike over losing a day's holiday.

Fred was a large, lumbering man with outsize hands and a ginger moustache. Husband of Emma and father of twins Robert and Vic, he looked out from his bedroom window at No. 13 Coronation Street straight on to the weaving room at Hardcastle's. The mill occupied every aspect of his life, with union meetings in the Rover's Select bar taking up much of his free time. At home he was a virtual stranger, leaving first thing in the mornings and only returning for his dinner before heading out again to the Rover's for the rest of the evening. Even when he had no meeting to attend he preferred the smoky atmosphere and masculine company to sitting with Emma or talking to the boys.

Since their births eighteen years previously, he had abandoned fatherly duties, and watched the twins grow up from afar. The Piggott men lived by unwritten rules. The twins understood that their father's role as unionist set him a cut above the rest of the workers and that those he represented had first call on his time. They weren't bothered that he was seldom around: they looked to each other for company and their mother for guidance. Fred was aware that Emma mollycoddled their sons, but did not interfere. Theirs was a passionless marriage, and Fred could no longer remember why he had married Emma. He felt he had little to complain about – Emma was house-proud, a competent cook, and never nagged him. In fact, she hardly ever spoke to him.

Fred came into his own sitting in the Rover's with his workmates, playing dominoes, drinking best and smoking Woodbines. He was a man's man, married to a woman devoted to her sons. As he left the mill on Christmas Eve he stood in the shadows of the huge Victorian building to light a fag and watch the workers rushing home, jacket collars and shawls pulled close to protect them against the night air. At the far end of Coronation Street light escaped from the hallway of his house, and he knew his dinner would be waiting. Tripe and onions with potatoes and onion sauce. He spat a thread of tobacco on to the pavement, hacked a cough and crossed the street, heading straight for the Rover's.

Inside No. 13, Emma Piggott pushed Fred's dinner further on to the hot surface of the range, then glanced around her tidy kitchen: the wooden table she scrubbed each morning, the sideboard with what pieces of crockery she had on display, the brass oil lamps shining from dedicated elbow-grease. A 1912 calendar, with a painting of Lake Windermere, still hung from the wall as Emma was attached to the

130

picture. It was a practical room. Practical and empty. Emma sighed and lowered herself into one of the pair of easy-chairs that sat at each side of the range. It had been three months since the twins had marched off to fight, the longest months of Emma's life. It seemed to her that all the fun and light had left the house with them. It had ceased to be her home.

Jim Corbishley placed a pint pot on the bar in front of Fred and took the offered money. 'Good 'ealth an' 'appy Christmas,' said Fred, before savouring his first taste.

''Appy Christmas,' replied his friend Harry Popplewell.

'I don't see what there is to be 'appy about,' complained Jim. 'It don't seem like Christmas much in 'ere.'

Fred and Harry looked about them. Jim was right: there they were, Christmas Eve, and they were the only customers.

'It's times like Christmas you want yer young fellas in, knockin' 'em back and startin' fights,' sighed Jim.

'Aye,' replied Harry wistfully, 'ye're not wrong there.'

'I dunno 'ow long I can keep openin' up,' said Jim. 'The wife's all for closin' and us

131

goin' to 'elp 'er brother at his place in Chester.'

'I thought you 'ated 'er brother.' Fred leant on the bar.

'I do that, but even so there's more old folks round 'is way. Least his pub feels like a pub, not a flamin' morgue.'

The pub door clattered open and the men spun round. The bowed shape of Ivy Makepiece appeared in the doorway and they watched as she plodded through the bar to the empty Snug. As their eyes followed her Ivy bristled.

'What you lookin' at?' she demanded.

'Nowt,' muttered Jim, as his customers turned their backs on her.

Ivy gave him a long, hard stare then pushed her way into the tiny Snug. 'Landlord!' she called, rapping a coin on the bar top.

Jim sighed and wandered over to her. 'Yes, missus.'

'This fire's not lit,' she complained. 'It's as cold as a bat's titty in 'ere.'

'Sorry, but we're savin' fuel. You'll 'ave to open the door and sit there. You'll soon warm up.'

'I'm doin' nowt of the sort. Oh, you'd like that, wouldn't you, Jim Corbishley? You'd love it if I sat in the draught and caught me death and were taken before the year were out.'

'Don't be stupid, missus. Why on earth–'

'Oh, so I'm stupid now, am I?' interrupted Ivy, glaring out at Jim under the fringe of her shawl, which framed her wrinkled face.

'Nay...'

'I suppose my money's not good enough for you. I don't think it's much to ask, just a fire for a body to warm 'er bones while she sups a stout.'

'Is a stout what you want, missus?' asked Jim, escaping to fetch a brown bottle from the back of the bar counter.

'I did,' said Ivy, 'before I set foot in this ice-box. You ought to be ashamed, Jim Corbishley. This used to be a good pub.'

'It still is,' shouted Fred from the Public.

'Aye,' agreed Harry.

Ivy chose to ignore them. Instead she took the bottle Jim offered her and marched with it into the Public. She threw pennies over the counter to Jim and plumped herself down on a stool.

'You can't sit there,' warned Fred. 'You belong in the Snug.'

'Is someone sat 'ere?' asked Ivy, looking around at the empty pub.

'Women stay in the Snug,' said Fred, slowly, as if speaking to a child or a dog.

'I know,' replied Ivy, just as slowly. 'But it's too cold in there and there's a fire in the grate in 'ere.'

'But this bar's for men,' said Fred.

'Look,' said Ivy, breathing out deeply, 'it's Christmas Eve. Are you sayin' I'm not welcome in the inn? That I 'ave to sup in that freezin' 'ole when there's plenty of room in 'ere for me? Where's yer Christian charity?'

Fred and Harry looked at Jim for guidance, and were disappointed when the landlord merely shrugged and turned away. It made no difference to him where the woman drank her brew. He fingered the coins in his hand and stopped short. 'You've only paid Snug prices.'

'Aye,' said Ivy, attacking her bottle. 'I'm not payin' Public prices just cos you're too stingy to light a fire. An extra 'alfpenny might be nowt to you but it means the world to an 'ard-workin' widder whose sons are off fightin' for king and country.'

Jim's shoulders dropped in defeat and he threw the coins into the money drawer. Some Christmas this was going to be.

Ena Schofield looked forward to Christmas. Ever since she had seen her first Christmas greetings card with its snow-covered scene she had longed for snow to cover the bleak cobbles on Inkerman Street, but any snow that fell in Weatherfield quickly turned to a grey mush. As a child the delights of Christmas for her had been a handful of nuts and an orange at the bottom of a stocking, with a doll or a toy instrument poking from the top. Then the gifts had been overshadowed by the knowledge that Christmas was Christ's birthday, and as she developed her relationship with the Trinity this fact became pivotal to her. There was the added bonus that everyone seemed happier at Christmas: it was a time for laughter and that was to be cherished.

'Second Christmas of war,' commented Mary Schofield, as she placed the dinner on the table.

'Aye,' said Alice morosely. 'I wonder how many more there'll be.'

'I reckon it'll all be over in the next sixth months,' said Thomas.

Ena carried in the plates and smiled at her father. 'Do you really? It would be smashin' if it were.'

'You only want war over so yer Phil'll

come back an' marry you,' said Alice.

'An' why shouldn't she want that?' asked Mary, annoyed by her elder daughter's sniping. 'I must say I can't think of a better thing to wish for.'

Ena blushed. 'I weren't just thinkin' about meself,' she said. 'It seems so strange without all the lads around the place. Empty.'

'More room to breathe,' said Alice, holding up her plate as Mary spooned vegetable stew on to it.

'Since when 'ave you bin one for breathin'?' asked Thomas. 'You do talk a load of rubbish, our Alice. You wanna do yerself a favour. When war's over an' all the lads come back you'd do best to keep yer mouth shut. Otherwise you don't stand a chance of gerrin' a fella.'

Alice bit her lip. She hated it when her father teased her and she hated Ena for always being in the right.

'What you doin' tonight, then?' Mary asked Alice.

Alice noticed that she hadn't asked Ena that question. They all knew what Ena would be doing: the same as she did every Christmas Eve. She'd be off Bible-bashing somewhere. 'I'm goin' to visit my friend,' she said.

'Oh,' Mary raised her eyebrows. 'Which friend is that?'

'Alice Buck.'

'Who?'

'Alice. I were wi' 'er at school. We've been next to each other on looms for three weeks now. She lives in Coronation Street.'

'Buck...' mused Thomas. 'Is that Ned Buck's lass? 'Im who makes cheap coffins on the side, an' his wife does the layin' out?'

'Yes, that's right.'

Thomas chortled. 'You mek some rum friends.'

'There's nowt rum about Alice Buck,' said Alice hotly. 'She can't 'elp it if 'er parents muck about wi' dead folk.'

Alice Buck was feeling particularly rum as she perched on the cold lavatory seat in the water-closet at the bottom of her yard. All the terraced houses had these closets, or 'cludgies' as they were known, and they made Coronation Street a desirable place to live. In the old part of Weatherfield, on the other side of the viaduct, one lavatory had to service three households. Since moving into No. 9 Coronation Street in 1910, the Buck family had taken their exclusive closet for granted. Now, though, the younger family members complained about the sub-zero temperature, in the closet between September and March.

Alice shivered and got up from the seat. She lowered her candle into the lavatory bowl and peered down into it. Sighing, she straightened and pulled the chain to flush it. It was as she'd expected. Nothing.

Inside No. 9, Sarah Buck coughed up a yellow strand of phlegm into her red-raw hand and wiped it on her apron. Coughs and catarrh were common Christmas ailments, arriving with more regularity than a full stocking. 'There's more 'taters,' she announced.

Ned Buck grimaced at the thought of stomaching more of his wife's cooking. One helping of whatever it was she served up was always enough for him. Before he married Sarah, Ned had been a man who enjoyed his food and had been classed as a large man. Now, twenty years later, he was as lean as a greyhound, while Sarah, who finished up his leavings, was as plump as a Christmas pudding.

'Not for me,' he said. Whatever mysteries Sarah performed when turning ordinary-looking food into the foul-tasting concoctions she served up were beyond him. He envied his two sons their rations of bully-beef on the front.

Sarah stared longingly at Alice's untouched plate. 'She ain't eaten proper in days.'

'Aye,' agreed Ned, amazed that it had taken his daughter nineteen years to reach the same conclusion regarding her mother's cooking.

The back door opened and shut, and Alice wandered back into the house. She joined her parents at the table and pushed away her plate.

'What's to do?' asked concerned Sarah.

'I'm not 'ungry,' said Alice.

'Oh...' said Sarah, her eyes on her daughter's dinner. Alice slid the plate across to her and Sarah tucked in. Ned turned away in disgust as gravy ran down her chin.

The two Alices – Buck and Schofield – met, as planned, on a bench in North Cross Park. The bench bore a plaque, declaring it to be dedicated to the memory of 'Hetty McClure, a friend of the birds'. Mary Schofield had once explained that Hetty had been a miserable vagrant who had lost three fingers after getting caught in a loom as a young girl. She had been one of the 'characters' of Weatherfield, always seen sleeping under the stars, begging for food and drunkenly cursing anyone who crossed her path. The bench had been placed there after her death by an unknown benefactor and the meaning of the plaque remained a mystery to everyone. Nobody could recall seeing Hetty with any birds. Whoever Hetty had been, her bench offered one of the finest views in Weatherfield. It stood on a mound that dipped down to a duck pond, beyond which the bandstand glistened in summer.

There was no sun to illuminate the bandstand now as the women sat huddled against the winter chill. They had known each other by sight for much of their lives, had shared a classroom as children and worked in the same mill for the past five years, but it had only been in the past few weeks that a friendship had grown between them. It had started when Alice Buck had broken her third bobbin in a morning. Alice Schofield, who never broke bobbins, had taken the blame and had saved her work-mate a whole morning's pay. Ena would have been surprised to hear of her sister's Christian act – Alice had never done anyone a good turn in her life. She thought only of herself, pitying those who put others first. That day, though, there had been something heart-wrenching about the look in Alice's eye, which had made her speak out. Afterwards Alice Buck had offered thanks and promptly burst into tears. So it was that domineering, strident Alice Schofield became her confidante.

The news that Alice shared with her friend was sensational rather than shocking: pregnancies among unmarried girls were not uncommon and lately a number of local girls had found themselves put in that state by departing sweethearts. Secretly Alice Schofield condemned her workmate for her lax morals but until now she had kept Alice's secret to herself, not that she had anyone to whom she could pass on snippets of gossip. Unlike her sister Ena, Alice Schofield was a solitary young woman who had never sought the company of others.

Alice Buck had grown up with a group of friends and would have loved to discuss an unwanted pregnancy with them, if it wasn't hers. She shifted on the bench and sighed. Her baby wasn't unwanted anyway. She loved Vic Piggott, and the knowledge that she was expecting his child filled her with butterflies, fluttering around her heart and into her throat. If only they had married before he'd gone overseas. If only there was a wedding-ring on her finger. Then she could happily have faced her parents.

Alice Schofield promised her friend she wouldn't tell a soul about the baby. She lied. Just twenty minutes after leaving Alice at the park gates she announced to her family that she knew a secret. She was annoyed that no one seemed interested in questioning her. Instead they fussed over making paper-chains to decorate the kitchen in readiness for Christmas morning. Ena giggled as she darned a hole in her best stocking. The thought of her stocking hanging over the range flooded her mind with childhood memories and transported her into a world of crackling fires and warm embraces.

'I *do* know a secret,' repeated Alice impatiently.

'Good for you,' said Thomas, licking the gum on a paper-chain.

'Of course, I couldn't possibly tell you,' said Alice, as mysteriously as she could.

'Good,' replied Thomas.

Alice stamped her foot in annoyance and glared at her family. The cosy scene made her feel even more of an outsider than usual.

'My friend Alice Buck's just told me she's pregnant ... and she's not married.'

Mary looked up from the chains and sighed deeply. 'The poor girl,' she said.

'Poor girl to have such a friend,' said Thomas, looking in disgust at his eldest daughter.

'I dunno why you're lookin' at me like that,' complained Alice. 'I'm not the one who's gonna 'ave a bairn.'

Ena looked at the troubled faces of her parents. Like them she knew Alice Buck by sight: a pretty little thing with a waist as big as a twig, and clear blue eyes that twinkled in a face full of promise. A girl who's life would never be the same again.

For Ena Christmas Day started with carols, when she dragged her friends Martha Hartley and Minnie Carlton out of their beds and made them stand outside the rent offices on Edward Street, singing and collecting pennies for the Mission of Glad Tidings children's party. However, the good cheer that had prompted Martha to volunteer her services the day before had vanished by eight o'clock as she stamped her feet in an effort to keep warm.

'Yer singin' flat,' observed Ena.

'I feel flat,' muttered Martha, 'stood 'ere singin' to no one cos no one's stupid enough to be out in this cold so early on Christmas mornin'.'

'Oh, give over complainin',' said Ena, thrusting the tin under the nose of an unsuspecting mill-worker returning from the night shift.

'I like Christmas,' said Minnie. 'It reminds me...'

'Of what?' asked Martha.

'Nice things.'

'I know what you mean,' said Ena. 'Folk feel better towards each other at Christmas. It's a time for givin', for charity.'

Martha looked uncomfortable. She was aware of her own shortcomings and knew that she wasn't the most charitable girl in the world. She opened her mouth and joined in the singing. Ena watched her friend out of the corner of her eye and smiled to herself. When it came to charity Martha ran rings around her sister Alice, who would be pulling the bedclothes around her and dreaming of her Christmas dinner.

'Come on, girls, "Hark the Herald Angels",' prompted Ena, jingling the coins in her tin.

There wasn't much Christmas charity on offer at No. 9 Coronation Street. Ned Buck watched as his wife cremated the chicken he had bought off Plank Lane market. He'd wrung the bird's neck two days beforehand and had let its blood drip from its beak into a cup to strengthen the gravy, and Sarah had plucked it, saving the feathers to fill a cushion. Now the burnt bird sat in a roasting tin surrounded by blackened bullets, which had started off as potatoes. Ned longed to skip dinner so that he could delve into the bag of chocolates with which Alice had presented him that morning.

Thoughts of Alice made Ned frown. The girl wasn't her usual cheerful self and that bothered him. It was bad enough not having the boys crashing around the house without Alice going sour-faced on him.

Christmas Day was one of the few days of the year when the front parlour received an airing. It was the best room in the house, kept for entertaining visiting relatives or laying out the dead. With Ned working a sideline as a coffin-maker it was normally filled with coffins in various stages of completion but he'd made an effort to shift all the panels, lids and handles out of the way.

145

Without all the clutter the room seemed empty, with just a horsehair sofa, a sideboard and a couple of tables in it.

Alice sat on the floor and laid a fire in the empty grate. It was a Buck tradition to drink tea in the parlour after Christmas lunch, and Alice had grown up watching her precious brother Larry lay the fire. It had become a rite of passage for each child to take on the job. Normally the only fire in the house was the one in the kitchen range and Sarah worked hard to ensure it never went. The children steered clear of the range, which made the Christmas parlour fire magical.

Alice didn't feel magical as she placed pieces of coal upon a bed of kindling. Her troubles weighed on her mind and she was sad to know that her mood had cast a shadow over Ned's Christmas. She'd seen the concern in his eyes as he'd watched her creep around the house, heard his sighs as she'd left a room. Sarah hadn't noticed anything but she seldom did. She used her poor eyesight as an excuse but in reality she couldn't be bothered with anything that threatened to cause a storm in her ordered life. Food was important to Sarah Buck, and everything else came second.

Alice watched the flames take hold and watched them lick the nuggets of coal. She knew she couldn't hold off telling her parents much longer. She was a slight girl and her father at least was certain to notice a growing stomach. She could only guess at how they would react but one thing she was sure of: it would have been different if she had a ring on her finger. If not a wedding-ring then at least a commitment ring. She knew Vic would stand by her. He was good on the inside as well as on the outside. He'd be delighted by the news. Maybe the army would let him come home and see her. All she had to do was to tell him and everything would be all right.

After Christmas dinner with her family, Ena had spent the afternoon at the Mission of Glad Tidings. She had handed over the three shillings that three hours of carol singing had produced, and had helped Gladys Arkwright to set out the wooden chairs for the Christmas service. Lay preacher Sid Hayes had spoken about the wise men bearing gifts and how important Jesus's own gift to mankind had been.

After the congregation had departed, Gladys had encouraged those she knew

147

were lonely to remain for tea and cake in the vestry. Ena stayed to help look after the guests, offering mince pies and fruit cake to the toothless widows and the young woman who had left her native Yorkshire to live in an alien county on the promise of marriage to a man now at war.

'Loneliness is a terrible thing,' said Gladys, as she stood at her stove making hot chocolate.

'It's good of you to open yer 'ome,' said Ena.

Gladys looked at her friend and shook her head. 'No, lass, you don't understand,' she said. 'These poor things aren't the only lonely ones. If they weren't here for me to fuss over I'd be staring into the fire remembering the old days too.'

'No, you wouldn't,' said Ena. 'I wouldn't leave you alone on Christmas Day.'

Gladys squeezed her arm.

'Besides, Phil would never forgive me if I left his old auntie to fend for herself.'

'Less of the "old",' said Gladys. Her eye darted to the mantelpiece where Phil's last postcard stood next to the clock. He'd sent it from the trenches and had attempted to draw a bunch of holly on the card. He was no artist. Ena followed her gaze and smiled.

148

She had received an almost identical one. Neither woman had any idea of exactly where Phil Moss would be that Christmas – if he'd have a special dinner, if the shooting would stop for the day. Both knew it made no sense to dwell on the unknown.

Emma Piggott had spent a lonely day at No. 13 while Fred drank with his pals in the Rover's. He'd emerged for his dinner nearly an hour late, after Emma had eaten hers. He'd ploughed through the dried-up meat and vegetables without comment, swilled it all down with a bottle of brown ale brought from the pub, belched loudly and then marched back to the Rover's. Not so much as a 'thank you' or 'Happy Christmas' had escaped his lips. Emma had had a little weep then sat down to think about her sons. She imagined them cold and miserable in some God-forsaken place, longing to be back in their comfortable home. For the umpteenth time she cursed herself for being unable to read and write, and silently composed letters to them in her head. Later she'd ask Gladys Arkwright to transcribe them for her.

The knock on the front door startled her and she darted into the hall like a frightened hen. 'Who is it?' she called.

'Alice Buck,' came the reply.

Emma frowned. She wasn't used to neighbours calling. 'What do you want?' she demanded, through the safety of the front door.

'I need to talk to you ... please.'

Cautiously Emma opened the door and peered out. She made out Alice's delicate features beneath the shawl that swamped her. 'Can I come in?' asked Alice.

'What do you want?' asked Emma again.

Alice stepped forward and Emma drew back automatically into the hallway, but kept her hand resting on the door. She watched the girl shuffle in and stared at her face. She looked like a frightened child.

Having built up her courage to come this far, Alice felt her legs weaken as she looked at Emma's unwelcoming face. 'Mrs Piggott ... I – I need yer 'elp,' she blurted out.

Emma viewed her with suspicion. She'd never spoken more than two words to her in the five years the Bucks had lived on the Street. Alice had always seemed a sly, troublesome child, the product of an unruly family, and Emma had always been pleased that her sons had steered clear of forming friendships with the local children. She could think of no way in which she could help the girl.

Alice gulped. This was harder than she had anticipated. 'I need to know how to send a letter to your Vic.'

Emma stared at her, and sweat broke out on her palms. There was only one reason for a girl to *need* to write to a boy. Her stomach lurched as she asked, 'Why?'

Alice held the older woman's gaze and said, 'I'm pregnant.'

The force of the slap took her by surprise and she staggered backwards out of the hallway. Emma advanced on her, shaking in fury and slapped her again.

Alice stumbled out of the house, and fell on to the cobbles.

Across the road, the door to the Mission vestry opened and Gladys Arkwright showed out her visitor. Before she could thank Gladys for her hospitality, Ena's eyes fell upon Alice and she gave a cry.

Emma stood over Alice. 'You little liar!' she screamed, giving no heed to the two women staring at her across the street.

'I'm not lyin',' cried Alice, as she tried to get up.

Ena left Gladys in the doorway and rushed over to Alice.

'It's nowt to do wi' my Vic, you little whore,' Emma spat.

Alice allowed Ena to help her to her feet and stared defiantly at Emma. 'It is. 'E's the only one I've bin with. It's 'is baby in my belly.'

Ena gasped and watched in horror as Emma advanced, her hand out ready to hit Alice again, but this time Alice was ready and darted out of her way.

'I need to tell 'im,' she said. ''E needs to know.'

''E'll know nothin' of this,' hissed Emma. 'You're a dirty little liar an' yer not layin' the blame on my doorstep.'

Ena pulled Alice away from Emma and down the Street. Gladys crossed from the vestry and placed a hand on Emma's arm but Emma shook herself free and glared at her. 'What do you want?' she demanded.

'Nothing,' replied Gladys. 'You should go inside.'

Emma turned and ran back into the safety of her home. She slammed the door behind her and slid down it to the floor. Her head fell into her hands and she started to sob. It couldn't be true. Her Vic would never sully himself in such a way, not with a common tart, a stupid little slut like Alice Buck. Tears flooded down her cheeks as she crouched on the hall floor and the sobs racked her.

Outside, in the street, Ena hugged Alice to her as she walked her home.

'Do you want to talk about it?' ventured Ena.

'There's nowt to talk about,' said Alice.

'Are you pregnant?' asked Ena in awe.

'Yes.'

Ena fell silent. She didn't know what to say. She glanced around for support from Gladys but when the older woman caught her eye she shook her head.

'She's best left,' said Gladys.

'But surely...' began Ena.

Gladys pushed Alice towards her front door and squeezed her shoulders. ''Ave you told yer mother?' she asked.

'Not yet.'

'Go on, lass. She'll not kill you.'

Ena watched Gladys push open the door to No. 9 and guide Alice inside. There was much she didn't understand. Her mother had warned her about being alone with men, and she knew that pregnancy resulted in childbirth. She'd lived long enough in the back-streets of Weatherfield to know that not every child born had a father, and she'd once questioned her mother about the muffled groans and moans that infiltrated her bedroom at night from the next-door house. She had been told she would understand when she got married. She sighed. If her father was right and the war ended in 1916 then Phil would come home and she'd learn what all the mystery was about. Until then she'd just have to wait.

CHAPTER SIX

July 1916

Ned Buck was convinced that his drinking
pals at the Rover's Return were laughing at
him behind his back. He knew that in their
place he'd be having a dig and saw no
reason to believe that they didn't feel the
same.

His daughter was pregnant. She'd been
given a good seeing to. She hadn't crossed
her legs. She was a strumpet. A whore. A
tart. She was every father's worst nightmare.
She'd brought disgrace upon Ned and his
household. An unmarried scrubber with
one in the oven. It would have been different if he'd been the father of the lad who
had put her that way. Lads were lads. Good
for him. Sowing his oats. Getting his leg
over. Having a fumble. It was only natural.
He wouldn't be a lad if he'd passed up a
chance like that. But he wasn't the father of
the lad, he was the father of the girl. That's
why they were laughing behind his back.

That's why they were all talking about him. That's why he'd disowned the girl.

When Alice had broken the news of her pregnancy Ned had withdrawn from the situation, as though ignoring it, it might go away. He felt bitter disappointment that Alice had allowed herself to be caught out. He remembered the bonny little girl he'd bounced upon his knee, dimples in her cheeks. His little flower. His Alice. Nineteen years on and the baby he'd held for the first time in his trembling hands had turned into a woman he didn't understand. Hadn't she been brought up to know the difference between right and wrong? At first he'd blamed the Piggotts. He'd known Fred Piggott for years, worked with him and drunk beside him. It was hard to fall out with a mucker over something their children had done and his hostility towards the man had fallen away after the briefest exchange in the Rover's.

'Rum do,' Fred had said.

'Aye,' he'd said.

'I'll mek sure me lad stands by 'er.'

'Aye.'

'Not worth us fallin' out, mind. Leave that to the women.'

'Aye.'

The matter had been sorted and laid to rest there and then and the hysterics were left to the women. Infuriated by Emma's treatment of her daughter, Sarah maintained a hostile attitude towards her neighbour, while Emma had refused to discuss it with her and insisted that her son would never sully himself with a common trollop like Alice Buck. Her silence inflamed Sarah's fury and at every opportunity she berated Emma in public. Alice found herself caught in the middle of the barrage.

At home Alice became a shadow, avoiding her father, who had made it clear that he wanted nothing to do with her. Sarah acted as a buffer between the two, preparing separate meals for them and dwelling in two worlds. In one she was the dutiful wife, never mentioning Alice or her condition. In the other she was a concerned mother, coping single-handedly with her frightened child.

Ivy Makepiece kept her eye firmly on the weights as Tommy Foyle measured out baking powder on his scales. 'Well, missus,' he said cheerfully, 'satisfied?'

'Aye.' Ivy nodded.

Tommy tipped the contents of the scales

into a piece of brown paper and twisted the ends together. 'Owt else you want?' he asked.

'Two eggs, biggest you've got,' she said. She watched him lean across to his eggs. She had to admit he was a marked improvement on Cedric Thwaite. He'd taken over the shop just before the Christmas after the Thwaites' departure. A native of Leeds, the young man enjoyed flirting with the female customers and drinking with the men. There was nothing of the lay preacher about him. He'd served his time in the army, and had been invalided out before the war, after being wounded in India. The trophies he'd brought back with him intrigued the neighbours he invited into the back room. A tiger's skin covered the lino, silk hung from the walls and he burned exotic-smelling sticks, which glowed when lit. Tommy had made himself popular with the locals by offering limited credit to each of the closest households, which Cedric had always refused. Tommy took the stance that in times of a national crisis everyone had to be given a helping hand. Besides, it encouraged the customers to spend more than they would if they'd been paying immediately in cash.

Ivy took the eggs and put them in her basket. 'Chalk it down for me, will you?' she asked.

Tommy tapped his nose and produced the credit ledger from beneath the shop counter.

Ivy attempted to read its contents but gave up. For a start the book was upside down and, anyway, she was illiterate. It was frustrating because she'd have loved to know how much the likes of Gertie Hewitt at No. 3 owed for their groceries.

The ping of the shop bell alerted Ivy to fresh custom and she straightened up. Gathering her basket up she glanced at the new shopper. It was Emma Piggott. Ivy gave a nod in recognition. After Tommy had closed the ledger she began to leave but changed her mind when Sarah Buck pushed the shop door open.

'Was there anything else, Mrs Makepiece?' asked Tommy.

'I'm not sure. I need to think,' said Ivy, eyeing the new arrivals with delight. The prospect of a cat fight was never far off when warring mothers clashed. 'You can serve Mrs Piggott,' she said.

'Yes, Mrs Piggott?' said Tommy cheerfully. 'What would you like?'

'Some sugar,' said Emma quietly.

'By 'eck,' Sarah's voice boomed into the shop. 'She talks. Go run and tell 'em at the *Evenin' News*, Emma Piggott's got a tongue in 'er 'ead.'

Emma attempted to ignore her neighbour and dug into her purse for the pennies she needed. 'Oh, and look, she's payin' cash. That's posh for you,' said Sarah pulling a face, 'Ivy, when were last time you 'ad pennies in yer purse to spend on sugar?'

'Oh, I can't think that far back, Sarah,' said Ivy, who loved being included in someone else's fight.

'Must be from havin' two lads in army sendin' their pay 'ome to their mother,' continued Sarah, 'them not 'avin' owt else to spend their money on. Course, if Em-the-rake 'ere would open 'er gob enough to tell one of 'em they've got my Alice up the duff then the money could be put to better use.'

Emma took the sugar from Tommy and, her head low and eyes on the floor, she scurried towards the door.

Ivy sighed in disappointment. 'I thought you were gonna belt 'er one,' she said.

'I couldn't be bothered, she's that skinny I could flatten 'er wi' a sneeze. To tell truth

I'm sick of the whole mess. You'd think she'd want to be part of it all. I mean, look at you with that Betty Cog's bastard across the way from your backin'.'

'What's Betty Cog to me?' demanded Ivy angrily.

'Everyone knows that's your Ralph's bastard. I'm just sayin' you must feel summat for the brat, it bein' yer grandson an' all.'

Ivy flushed. 'I'll ask you not to go round spreadin' such talk. That Betty Cog's got nowt on our Ralph. She's just a common little tart like another I could mention.'

'Are you meanin' my Alice?' challenged Sarah, her voice rising in anger.

'She is up duff, you can't say she isn't. I've got four daughters and none of my girls 'ave ever bin in such a way. They've bin brought up proper.'

'They've bin dragged up more like,' screeched Sarah, advancing on Ivy, who stood her ground and laughed in her neighbour's face.

'My girls 'ave never brought disgrace on me.'

'They 'aven't but yer sons 'ave. Poor Betty Cog. It was inhuman what your Ralph did to the girl. I bet 'e picked up those ways from his days inside.'

Ivy could tolerate any slur upon her daughters but at the slightest hint of an attack on her precious Ralph she saw red. Reaching into her basket she grabbed an egg, threw it hard in Sarah's startled face and darted out of the shop, cackling.

Gladys Arkwright always started reading a newspaper at the obituary section just in case someone she knew had passed on. If the deceased had ever attended the Mission she'd make a point of paying her respects and suggesting to the bereaved that they might like to hold the funeral service at the Mission of Glad Tidings. She offered a rate she knew undercut that of St Mary's Parish Church.

The paper she read while Ena Schofield made a pot of tea was disappointingly low on local deaths so she introduced an alternative topic of conversation. 'They're looking for women to take on factory work, I see.'

'Are they?' Ena put a match to the single gas ring that was Gladys's cooker.

'Do you fancy it? It would make a change from working the looms at Hardcastle's.'

Ena pulled a face. 'I like it at 'Ardcastle's. It's 'ard work but I've never bin one to shy away from that.'

162

'Oh, I know,' said Gladys. 'You're like me in that way.' She carried on reading.

'I'm not sayin' I wouldn't like a change,' said Ena. 'It can get very tirin' watchin' out for yer bobbins.'

'It could be more pay,' suggested Gladys.

'Do you reckon?'

'Well, if they're looking for girls to take on the jobs left by men they're bound to pay men's wages.'

Ena considered. 'Extra money would come in handy. I could save it for when Phil comes 'ome. Then we could 'ave a few nice bits and bobs after we're wed.'

'That's a thought,' agreed Gladys. 'Mind, there's a few pieces I've decided to give you. I've far too much clutter.'

Ena smiled indulgently. She missed Phil terribly and wished his letters would come with the regularity of Albert's. He wasn't a natural letter-writer, though, and she told herself to be grateful for the scribbled notes she did receive. 'It's his birthday next month,' she said. 'I don't know what to buy him only I've got to send it off soon or 'e'll never get it.'

'Oh, I know,' said Gladys. 'I've a tin of milk put aside but I wanted to knit him something cosy as well.'

'I'm not one for knittin',' said Ena sadly. 'Me mother says it's on account of me fingers bein' so fat.'

'Are they fat?' asked Gladys, peering through her spectacles at Ena's hands.

Ena self-consciously hid them from view.

'Get 'im some toffees. He likes toffees,' suggested Gladys.

'Not very special, though, is it?'

'Well, make the toffees yourself and put them in a nice box with a bow on it. I reckon that'll go down a treat.'

Ena smiled at the thought of Phil receiving it, opening it and showing his chums the toffees his girl had made. It gave her a warm feeling inside. 'I've not made toffee before. Is it as 'ard as parkin?'

'Oh, no. When we've had our tea I'll fetch my book and we'll have a look.'

Ena smiled her thanks and told herself once again how lucky she was.

Sarah Buck regarded Alice's stomach with concern. The girl was still operating looms in Hardcastle's weaving shed but Sarah had watched the lump in her stomach drop lower and knew her time would come soon. It had been an easy pregnancy – the only difficulty had been orchestrating movements within No. 9 so that Alice and her father didn't meet. Ned had no idea that Alice was near the end of her pregnancy. The last time he had laid eyes on her had been six months before, when she still retained her girlish figure, and when there was still fire in her eyes. Now they were bleak, as she worried about what the future held for her and her child.

With Ned spending his days at work or in the Rover's Return, it was relatively easy for Alice to receive visitors at No.9. Since witnessing her encounter with Emma Piggott, Ena Schofield had been a regular caller, replacing her sister Alice as the pregnant girl's ally.

Sarah had been surprised by Ena's interest in Alice. She knew her to be one of the Bible-thumping brigade, always preaching against the so-called evils of drink. That sort were meant to frown upon the likes of Alice, condemn her to eternal damnation, not call round with home-made toffees.

For her part, Ena had surprised herself over her friendship with Alice. Gladys had commented that the war was changing attitudes and Ena felt this must be the explanation. After hearing of Alice's love for Vic Piggott, and seeing her desperation to

be close to him on the eve of his embark-
ation, Ena felt it served no purpose to
condemn her. These were strange times.
Men were scarce and Ena understood about
love. She'd never had to face the question
herself but if Phil had pressed her before he
went overseas Ena admitted she might have
given in to him out of love. These thoughts
she kept to herself.

While Ena visited Alice, listening to her
complaints of discomfort and delighting to
watch her stomach roll as the baby turned,
Ned remained cut off from his daughter.
The regulars at the Rover's bowed to his
wishes and never mentioned or asked after
her. He walked along five corridors to avoid
passing her at Hardcastle's and Sarah feared
his temper enough not to bring Alice into
any conversation. It was, Sarah told Nellie
Corbishley one day, as if Ned believed his
daughter was dead.

The news spread throughout Weatherfield.
The literate few were pressed to scan news-
print for details, which were then passed on
by word of mouth. Twenty six divisions of
Kitchener's army had been ordered out of
the trenches and into battle in fields of mud
in France. The first reports were of a great

victory: thousands of the Hun were dead.

Ivy Makepiece, as proud as any mother could be, pinned a Union Flag in her parlour window and bellowed out a drunken rendition of 'God Save the King' in the middle of the Street. Jim Corbishley offered half-price bitter for any man who had a son fighting overseas. There was talk in Coronation Street that the war had been won. The Weatherfield Pals had done their bit and now they'd be coming home.

The Rover's piano was wheeled from its home in the Select bar to the Public, and Harry Popplewell from No. 7 pounded the ivories as Ivy and her cronies led the sing-song into the night. Nellie Corbishley turned a blind eye to the cavorting and felt proud to know that her own Charlie would have been one of the thousands of lads shouting for victory as they charged out of their muddy makeshift homes.

'Pack up yer troubles in yer old kit-bag,
And smile, boys, smile.
Pack up yer troubles in yer old kit-bag,
Smile, boys, that's the style.
What's the use of worryin',
It never was worth while...'

Clara Popplewell stood upon a bar stool and lifted her skirts as she sang along to her husband's piano-playing. Fred Piggott gazed upon her thick legs and envied Harry the chance to snuggle up to such a well-covered woman at night. His own Emma was little more than bone these days, nibbling food like a mouse and constantly worrying about her boys. Fred smiled at the thought of his sons, allowing himself a moment's indulgence with the thought they would soon be home.

Barmaid Sarah Bridges kept the tankards flowing with Newton & Ridley's best bitter and was delighted when her boss suggested she drowned out Clara's warbling with her own song. 'Come on, Sarah,' he called, 'give us a tune.'

'Go on wi' you,' she said, laughing.

'What do you say, lads?' asked Jim. 'Let's 'ear it for our own little song bird.'

As the men started clapping and cheering Clara stepped down from her stool with a sour look on her face. 'Ain't I good enough for yer?' She pouted, her one good eye glinting dangerously.

'Ye're good enough for me,' cried Fred Piggott, making to grab her from behind.

Clara gave a delighted screech as he pulled

her towards him and nestled into her plump neck. 'By 'eck, Fred,' said his victim's husband, 'if you fancy 'er you must be drunk!'

Clara pulled a face at her husband and pushed Fred's face into her ample cleavage.

There was a roar of approval from the regulars although Nellie Corbishley turned away in disgust.

Clara cackled and took a swig of ale, before red-faced, delighted Fred emerged from her sweaty bosom. 'You don't get many o' them to the pound,' he muttered.

Sarah stepped confidently on to the Rover's bar, her smart black shoes kicking pint pots out of the way. She lifted her skirt and nodded to Harry. He thumped the keys and she started to dance, clicking her heels and toes on the bar top. As she danced she swayed her hips and gestured to the men who watched open-mouthed.

''Ello! 'Ello! Who's yer lady-friend,
Who's the little girlie by yer side?'

The show was brought to an abrupt halt by the arrival of Archie Edwards, the local policeman. Facing the pub's doors, Sarah came to a faltering stop when she saw him in the doorway looking grim. The customers followed her gaze.

'What's to do, Archie?' asked Jim.

The policeman walked into the bar, and the women in the Snug craned their necks to see what the fuss was about.

'I see yer all celebratin',' said Archie.

'That's right, we're not doin' any 'arm,' said Jim in defence.

'I'm not sayin' you are but I reckon you'll want to stop soon enough,' said Archie.

Whatever's to do?' demanded Ivy, from the Snug. 'Spit it out, man.'

'Word's just come through to the station,' said Archie, looking around at his neighbours and friends, men of his father's age whom he'd known all his life. 'There's bin plenty of casualties in France. Worse yet.'

'What are you sayin', lad?' asked Jim, the confidence ebbing from his voice.

Archie swallowed before answering. 'The Weatherfield battalion were 'it 'ard. Reports are still comin' in but I don't reckon we've got owt to celebrate.'

A silence descended. Sarah jumped down from the bar and fiddled nervously with a drying-up cloth.

Ivy pushed her way through the men to reach Archie. She thumped him in the chest and glared up at him. 'I've known you all yer life, Archie Edwards. Tell me what ye're thinkin'.'

Archie avoided Ivy's eyes and shifted uncomfortably under the gaze of those around him. 'I ... I reckon there's plenty in 'ere who'll be gerrin' telegrams in the next few weeks... I'm sorry.'

Nellie put out her hand to steady herself behind the bar but fell into a dead faint. Sarah bent down to attend to her while Jim hung his head in sorrow. 'I reckon you'd all best go 'ome,' he said.

The first telegram arrived six days after Archie's prophetic words. It was delivered by hand to No. 11 Coronation Street and sent Ivy Makepiece screaming into the Street.

Vi Todd rushed along the cobbles to reach her mother as she collapsed, pulling at her hair in anguish. Doors flew open as the womenfolk investigated the disruption. Workers at Hardcastle's mill were distracted from their looms and hung out of the windows to gaze at the scene below. The telegram boy fled the scene, dreading his next visit to Jubilee Terrace where he had two telegrams to deliver next door to each other.

'Not my Ralph,' cried Ivy. 'Not Ralph!'

Susie Makepiece stood in the open doorway of No. 11, her eyes wide with fright as she watched her mother pull clumps of hair from her own head. Vi attempted to hug Ivy to her but was pushed violently across the cobbles.

''Elp me,' she cried. 'Please someone 'elp me!'

Ivy threw herself down on the cobbles and started to bang her head on them. 'Not my Ralph!'

Gertie Hewitt from No. 3 strode across to reach Ivy, grabbed her hair and pulled her head off the ground. Blood was smeared across her brow.

'Come on, Ivy,' she shouted. 'That's enough. Ye're frightenin' bairns.'

Ivy lashed out at her neighbour. 'My Ralph's dead!' she screamed.

'I know, I know...' Gertie was unable to say any more. Would the telegram boy call at her house tomorrow with news of Thomas?

Ivy started to scream again so Gertie slapped her hard across the face. Vi looked at her with tears in her eyes. 'Mrs 'Ewitt,' she said, 'what are we gonna do?'

Gertie's own eyes filled with tears as she looked into Vi's frightened face. 'I dunno, love.'

Like her neighbours, Sarah Buck had run to her front door to investigate Ivy Makepiece's screams, and now her thoughts rushed to the fate of her own sons, Larry and Jim. She had no idea if they were safe or even alive.

'Mam...' The cry came from Alice in the scullery and Sarah turned in alarm at the tone of her voice.

As soon as she saw her daughter's face Sarah knew that the time she'd been dreading for months was upon her. She'd lost count of the number of babies she'd delivered as an amateur midwife but never had she been called upon to deliver one of her own.

'Mam ... I'm all wet. It 'urts!'

Sarah rushed to her daughter, pushing her rolled-up sleeves further up her substantial forearms. 'Nowt to panic over, love, it's perfectly normal.'

'Mam, what's 'appenin'?' cried Alice.

'Yer 'avin' a baby, love,' was all Sarah could think of to say.

Ten minutes later Alice lay on her own bed in her tiny bedroom at the back of the house, and spasms of pain washed over her. Sarah tried calm reassuring words as she checked to see how far on Alice was. She heard the front door open and shut and prayed it wasn't Ned returning for his tea.

'Alice ... Mrs Buck...'

Sarah sighed with relief. 'Up 'ere, Ena, love, our Alice 'as started.'

Alice whimpered as Ena tore up the wooden stairs and burst into the bedroom.

'Oh, Alice, love,' she cried, kneeling down beside the bed. What can I do to 'elp?' she asked Sarah.

'Just stay 'ere and try and tek 'er mind off it. I've got summat to see to downstairs.' Reluctantly Sarah left her daughter and rushed down the stairs. She glanced at the clock and cursed: Ned would be home for his tea any minute. She calculated it would take him less than ten minutes to pick at her offering and then he'd be down to the Rover's.

Right on cue Ned slammed into the house. Upstairs, Alice heard his arrival and clamped her mouth shut. Downstairs Sarah scurried to the range and dished up a plateful of mutton stew. She laid it on the table and sat, looking at the meal with worried eyes. 'Did you 'ear that banshee screamin' 'er 'ead off earlier?' Ned asked, as he threw his bait box on to an easy chair and dropped his jacket on the floor.

'It were Ivy Makepiece.'

'I know, I saw 'er.'

'She just 'eard 'er Ralph's bin killed.'

Ned took in the news and nodded sadly. 'Shame that. 'E were a good lad.' He grimaced at the sight of the fatty stew in front of him. He sighed and half-heartedly picked up his spoon. 'Stew again,' he muttered.

'Aye, best I could do,' said Sarah apologetically.

'No matter,' said Ned. Whatever she served up would be disgusting. He started to spoon the food into his mouth then noticed Sarah wasn't eating. 'You not 'avin' any?' he asked in surprise.

'I'll eat later. That business wi' Ivy Makepiece 'as upset me.'

Ned pulled a face. Stew and upset women. Not a good combination. He took a couple more mouthfuls then pushed away his plate. 'Think I'll go down Rover's,' he said.

'Aye. Off you go, then.'

'Right.'

Two minutes later Sarah was back upstairs, attempting to calm her daughter.

Ena held her friend's hand and, following

175

Sarah's barked instructions, kept talking to her to provide some distraction from the pain. Alice gripped Ena's hand and opened her mouth in a silent scream. Sarah urged her to make her cries heard but Alice was terrified that Ned might hear. Ena knew of Sarah's reputation as a good midwife but had never been present at a birth before, and found it terrifying. Everyone knew of women who had died in childbirth, of babies born dead or horribly deformed. Alice was such a frail girl and Ena couldn't see how the huge lump in her stomach could possibly come out of her.

Sarah prayed the baby would come before Ned rolled home from the Rover's. He wasn't likely to enter Alice's bedroom but if for some reason he did she dreaded to think what his reaction would be at the sight. As the hours ticked by Alice's physical strength ebbed and Sarah feared she wouldn't have it in her to push the baby out.

'Come on, Alice, love, ye're nearly there,' she said, forcing encouragement into her voice.

'You're doin' real good, Alice,' said Ena. 'Not long and you'll 'ave a beautiful baby.'

Alice clutched the sheets, her hair plastered to her face with sweat, her eyes tight shut and her face contorted as her body was racked by a strong contraction. As it died away she opened her mouth and sobbed, 'I can't do it ... I can't.'

Ena glanced at Sarah's worried face.

'Course you can,' said Sarah.

Tears rolled down Alice's face.

'Is there nothin' you can do?' asked Ena in concern. 'She's a wreck.'

'Do you think I don't know that?' said Sarah sharply. ''Ave you any idea what this is doin' to me? Sat 'ere watchin' 'er?'

Ena squeezed Alice's hand and bent down to whisper to her. 'You're doin' so well, Alice. You'll be 'oldin' yer baby soon.'

Sarah rubbed her weary eyes. She wished she could believe what Ena was saying.

The front door slammed and Sarah heard Ned kick off his boots. She glanced nervously at Ena. 'What time do you 'ave to go 'ome?' she asked.

'I'm stayin' put so long as I'm needed,' said Ena.

Sarah smiled in gratitude. 'I'll 'ave to go and see to me old man. I'll get word to yer mam,' she said.

Ena watched Sarah leave the room then turned back to her friend. It was going to be a long night.

Ben Buck was born at six fifteen on Thursday 13 July 1916. Ena let herself out of No. 9 Coronation Street and decided to call upon Gladys at the Mission with the news before rushing to work. It was while she was knocking on the vestry door that the telegram boy cycled along the cobbles and came to a halt outside the Corner Shop. He checked the address on the telegram in his hand and rapped the knocker on the door of No. 13. Ena watched him from across the street.

'What are you looking at?' asked Gladys, as she opened the door.

'Telegram for the Piggotts,' said Ena in hushed tones.

Gladys's hands flew to her face. 'No!'

Fred Piggott opened the door and received the telegram. He rubbed the envelope between his fingers, as if by doing so he could work out the contents without opening it.

He called back into the house, 'We've got a telegram.' There was no dread in his voice: he might just as well have been announcing the arrival of a pound of sausages. Then Gladys heard a cry. Emma. She pushed past Ena and rushed to where Fred stood in the doorway, watching his wife.

'Go to her, man,' urged Gladys.

'What?' Fred stared at her, not comprehending.

Without waiting to be invited, Gladys rushed into the Piggotts' kitchen. 'Let's sit you down, Emma,' she said.

'There's a telegram,' Emma wailed.

'I know, but neither of us know what it says yet, do we?' Gladys tried to sound cheerful as she manoeuvred Emma on to a chair.

Fred walked back into the house, leaving the front door wide open.

Across the way Ena could see the whole scene. She saw Gladys remove the telegram from Fred's hand.

'Do you want to open it?' she asked, holding it out to Emma.

'No!'

'Shall I?'

Neither Fred nor Emma attempted to stop her, so Gladys ripped open the envelope and drew out the telegram. She scanned the contents and felt sick, but with both Piggotts staring at her anxiously she knew she had to put them out of their misery.

'They're dead, aren't they?' demanded Emma.

'Well...'

'Aren't they?' Emma.

'Yes.'

'Both of 'em?' asked Fred, in disbelief.

'Yes.'

Gladys looked at them. 'I'm so sorry,' she said, 'so sorry.'

Neither Emma nor Fred moved or spoke, so Gladys laid the telegram on the table, next to the bread-board, and walked out of the room. In the hallway she glanced back but there'd been no movement behind her. She left the house, pulling the front door shut after her.

Over by the vestry Ena was sobbing. The emotions of the night and morning rushed over her uncontrollably. She'd seen the wonder of childbirth, held a newborn babe in her arms, watched him seek out the nipple, and now she'd watched a mother being told her sons were dead. One of them had been the father of the new baby, a child he would never see or hold. The waste of it all swamped her and in her head she cried out, 'Why, God? Why let it happen?' Without Vic to support them what would become of Alice and her little one?

For months Alice had lived almost in secret

in her father's house, but now she had a baby she could no longer escape Ned. Little Ben knew nothing of his grandfather's feelings, all he knew was that he was hungry, uncomfortable or lonely. He cried.

At first Ned attempted to ignore him. The fact that Alice had given birth was a surprise to him but it hadn't been unexpected. He'd become used to living a separate life to his daughter under the same roof but he couldn't ignore the cries of a hungry infant. Or the local gossips. 'I call it spooky,' he overheard Clara Popplewell saying outside the fish shop, 'a baby born within the hour we 'ear its dadda's died.'

'That's if you believe Vic Piggott were the father,' said her companion.

'A babe's gotta 'ave a father,' said Clara.

'Oh, aye, and none more convenient than a dead one. She'll be sayin' next they got married on sly.'

In the factory and the pub the same topic of conversation came up and was hushed down as Ned walked past or joined a group of friends. The most hard-faced brought up the subject to his face.

''Ow's young 'un, then, Ned?' asked Jim Corbishley.

Ned ignored the question, drained his pint

and ordered another. The sure-fire way to shut up a landlord was to put more pennies in his till.

Fred Piggott had attempted to bring up the subject of their shared grandson but Ned had shifted the conversation before it had started.

Fred had cleared his throat. 'I 'ear your lass 'as 'ad it, then.'

Ned said nothing so Fred floundered on with, 'Shame my lad can't see it.'

'Aye, but lad's dead, in't 'e?' was all Ned could say, and the subject was changed at the suggestion of a game of darts.

Ned was wise enough to know he couldn't go on pretending that Alice and her baby didn't exist while they lived under his roof. Rather than admitting he might have been in the wrong and giving his child the support she longed for he decided there was only one solution to the problem. 'She'll 'ave to go,' he told Sarah, two weeks after the baby had been born.

'You what?' Sarah dropped her wooden spoon into the pan of soup.

'The girl. She'll 'ave to go.'

'What girl?'

Ned gestured upstairs.

'You mean our Alice? Your daughter?'

Ned grunted. 'Aye. 'er.'

'Why? Why will she 'ave to go? Where do you suggest she goes?'

Ned avoided his wife's eyes and concentrated on a crack in the wall opposite. 'She's brought disgrace to this 'ouse and I want 'er out,' he said gruffly.

'Don't be so stupid,' said Sarah.

It wasn't that Sarah was putting him down as much as the laugh that came after her words. She was laughing at him – in his own house. Ned sprang to his feet and lashed out fiercely with the back of his hand, catching Sarah across the side of her face. The blow took her by surprise and sent her spinning sideways into the range. The pan of hot soup was knocked over and spilt down Sarah's skirt on to her bare ankles. She cried out in pain and confusion. 'Don't you ever laugh at me again!' Ned shouted. 'This is my 'ouse! You 'ear? My 'ouse!'

Upstairs the baby started to cry, upset by the noise coming from the kitchen. Sarah stared at her husband in terror as he leant over the table and raised a finger to point at her threateningly. 'Get that girl and that baby out o' this 'ouse.'

'But, Ned...' began Sarah weakly, 'where's she to go?'

'I don't care. Just get 'er out!'

'She'll go. She will. Not yet, mind, 'er body's still weak. She needs rest...' The words came rambling out of Sarah's mouth like a waterfall rushing from a rocky crevice.

'She's got till the end o' the week.'

Sarah opened her mouth to remonstrate but Ned turned on his heel and stormed out of the house.

On the day Alice Buck left Coronation Street, clutching baby Ben defiantly to her bosom, the telegram boy made two visits to the Street. Sarah had arranged for her sister, who had a smallholding in Cheshire, to take in her errant daughter, but only after her sister had made it clear that Alice would be expected to work hard for her keep. Sarah assured Alice it wouldn't be for long, that her father would be talked round and that all would be well again soon.

Down the Street at the Rover's, the sight of the white envelope sent Nellie Corbishley into a panic but the contents of the telegram were not as cruel as they might have been.

'He's not dead?' said Jim, his tone almost disappointed.

'What's happened, then?' demanded Nellie, her mind racing through images of her beloved Charlie being gunned down by laughing Germans.

''E's bin injured and 'e's bin taken to Southampton. To an 'ospital.'

'He's in England!' cried Nellie in relief. 'When's he coming home?'

'It don't say,' said Jim. 'Just that he's injured.'

Nellie went to the Armoury to establish that Private Charles Corbishley had sustained bullet wounds to the chest, shoulder, head and arms, and was being nursed back to health in Southampton. The following weekend she set off for the railway station with her best hat on and carrying an overnight bag with two bottles of Charlie's favourite bitter nestling in her nightgown.

Unfortunately the telegram boy had not finished with Coronation Street that month. A week after Alice's departure he was knocking on the door of No. 9 to pass Sarah an envelope. With two sons fighting overseas she was convinced of the telegram's message and was puzzled when Gladys Arkwright read out the words to her: '"In London. Don't worry. I'll cope. Alice."'

'Whatever does it mean?' Sarah asked.

'I take it to mean she's not with her auntie,

185

Sarah love. She says she's gone to London.'

'London?' said Sarah in disbelief. 'We don't know anyone in London.'

Gladys folded the telegram and placed it in Sarah's shaking hand. She hoped it would be the last one she would have to read, but that same afternoon one was delivered to her own home. After reading the contents she sat in silence for over two hours until Ena called in on her way home from work.

Ena took one look at Gladys's drawn face, then saw the telegram lying where she had dropped it on the vestry floor. She bent, picked it up and slowly unfolded the piece of paper. She read each word carefully and hoped there'd been a mistake. A terrible mistake.

'He's dead,' said Gladys.

Tears blinded Ena's eyes.

'Our Phil's been taken...' Gladys started to sob and Ena rushed forward, falling upon her and weeping into her lap.

Phil Moss had been shot as he emerged from a trench to rush the German defences. The bullet that killed him had torn a hole through Ena's love letters, which he carried in his breast pocket, close to his heart.

CHAPTER SEVEN

October 1916

'I see Henshaw's gone bust,' Vi Todd said as she waited to be served in the shop.

Her mother, leaning against the back of the bacon slicer and taking the opportunity to forage for minute shreds of meat, nodded gravely. 'It's the price o' flour,' she said. 'You can't afford to buy bread when them as made it are charging ten pence.'

The other women in the shop muttered in agreement, each one trained at their mother's apron in the art of bread-making and each publicly condemning any woman who bought loaves from a baker.

Ena Schofield, normally wary of taking part in group conversations, felt at ease enough with the subject matter to offer an opinion. 'It's to do wi' not so much wheat comin' into country. Cos of war.'

The older women looked at her, considered her statement and then shook their heads.

'Nay, lass,' said Ivy, wrinkling her nose. 'That can't be right. Everyone knows we grow our own grain an' stuff. Always 'ave done. There's places which are just fields and fields of the stuff.'

'That's right,' agreed a tall woman, with a crooked nose. 'Yer got that wrong, lass.'

Ena smarted. She knew her facts were correct as she'd read them in a newspaper. Her cheeks flushed but she remained silent. She'd been brought up not to disagree with her elders and as the youngest person waiting in the queue to be served she was all too aware of her place in the pecking order. Vi Todd was nearest to her in age, just four years her senior, but the wedding-ring she wore gave her a worldly experience beyond mere years, and a married woman always took social precedence over an unmarried one. To be married was every girl's aim. To be a mother was every married woman's aim. Having given birth to a live baby and seeing it grow through childhood diseases into adolescence secured for a woman fourteen or fifteen years at the top of the female pecking order.

Once the child left home the mother's standing started to falter, unless – like Ivy Makepiece – she kept her offspring close by.

If this enviable feat was achieved, the mother, who had often become a grandmother by this stage, became the highest of the high: the matriarch, the female head of an ever-increasing family. With most men in the area dying before their fifty-fifth birthdays and women being blessed with a further ten years of life, the dowagers held court over large areas of the industrial north. Likewise, at the other end of the scale, older unmarried women spent their remaining days in bitter isolation, awaiting death.

Ena shuddered. It was every girl's fear and every mother's warning. Quite when one stopped being 'unmarried' and became a 'spinster' or 'old maid' Ena couldn't work out. Perhaps, she mused, when the girl became the last of her generation not to marry. It didn't really matter when the change took place, though, all that concerned the local girls was that such a fate shouldn't happen to them.

Ena glanced enviously at Vi Todd. There she was, twenty-two, and two years married. She'd never be a spinster. Even if swaggering Jack Todd never returned from the war she'd be a widow and there were plenty of older widowers on the look-out for young widows. Widows were preferred to spinsters because they had experienced male dominance and, as Ena had learnt from her mother's guarded remarks at the kitchen sink, men were only interested in one thing and it wasn't a girl's ability to make a decent Lancashire hot-pot. Ena's paternal grandfather had taken a young widow as his bride just three months after the death of his wife. She had overheard her father and Uncle Ralph drunkenly discussing the union and the 'old man's' wisdom in picking a 'widder' over a 'posy who still 'ad 'er ankles crossed'. At the time Ena had puzzled over the remark and had conscientiously spent months never crossing her ankles, not wanting to be thought a 'posy', whatever a posy might be.

Ena's train of thought had caused her to drift away from the shop conversation but she had been aware of it as a drone in the background. She gave a start when it ended as the shop bell jingled.

Emma Piggott shuffled in, a shawl over her shoulders, clutching a basket to her bony frame. The other women made room for her and smiled at her whilst exchanging glances with each other.

'Mornin', Emma,' said Ivy, who, as her

immediate neighbour, felt honour-bound to take the conversational lead. 'It's been a bit since I've seen you out. I was only saying the other day to my Vi, "I've not seen Emma Piggott for a good few weeks", didn't I, Vi? Didn't I say that?'

'Yes, Mam,' agreed Vi, eyeing Emma.

'You're lookin' well,' ventured a Mawdsley Street harridan.

'It'll do you good to get out,' went on Ivy. 'Get some colour into yer cheeks. Your Fred all right, is he?' She waited a beat for a reply but when none was offered she said, 'Good'. A satisfied customer collected her purchases together and left the shop. The remaining women shuffled up the counter, each reluctant to leave the spot they had warmed. Ena watched Emma as she kept her weary eyes focused on her feet, her shoulders humped forward, her thin fingers fiddling with strands of wool that frayed from her moth-eaten shawl. Her mother had only remarked the other day that she had been a classmate at Silk Street factory school with both Ivy Makepiece and Emma Piggott. Now, seeing both Ivy and Emma stood next to each other, Ena couldn't help but draw comparisons: both women were in their early forties, but while giving birth to at least seven children had aged Ivy, Emma appeared at least a decade older. Ena's heart went out to Emma: in many ways her fate and standing in society was even worse than that of the spinster – to have enjoyed her position in life as a mother then have it taken away, knowing she'd never be a mother again, never be a grandmother or a matriarch. It didn't bear thinking about. All Emma had in front of her were years as a childless wife and childless widow, for no man would consider marrying such an aged woman. The shell that had murdered Robert and Vic Piggott had turned their mother into a pariah. Ena couldn't help but wonder about Albert. She'd not had a letter for a while and this thought was nagging at the back of her mind.

Ena arrived at the head of the queue. She pushed thoughts of Emma to the back of her mind, glanced up at the shelves and requested a box of rice starch.

The day following her encounter with Emma Piggott found Ena sitting between a hard wooden pillar in the Mission Hall and her mother's twitching shoulder. Mary Schofield had woken to find one of her husband's whippets using her shawl as a bed and now, to her mounting fury, she discovered that the animal had left its little friends with her. Scratching in public was not uncommon in Weatherfield, where nearly all the street urchins played host to communities of lice, but Mary had always striven to keep her family clean. The realisation, half-way through the second chorus of 'I Know Not Why God's Wondrous Grace', that her best shawl had been infiltrated sent her into a foul mood.

While Mary scratched, Ena sat listening to the sermon. Sidney Arthur Hayes was an odd fellow. He lived at No. 5 Coronation Street, with his wife, Rose, and children, six-year-old Ada and little Frederick who had been born in the summer of 1915. Unlike his male neighbours Sid was not a manual worker: he earned his living sitting behind a desk, book- and ledger-keeping at the General Post Office. He was a thin-faced man with receding fine hair, who hid behind round spectacles. Ena had never seen him in a muffler or wearing the heavy boots favoured by her father and his friends. He was never spotted without a collar on his shirt and a tie around his neck. He alienated himself from the menfolk by his temperance and had never set foot over the Rover's threshold. Neither men nor women under-stood him but they deferred to him as a lay preacher and reader of books. The sure-fire way to win an argument in Coronation Street was to say that your source of information was Sid Hayes, for Sid Hayes knew everything, Sid Hayes was never wrong.

'...and I say it again, and will continue to say it until this wretched war is over,' Sid pounded the lectern in front of him and bellowed out at the congregation, 'the taking up of arms with the intent to maim or kill another human being goes against everything the Lord God taught us. "Thou shalt not kill"!'

It was a sermon Sid continued to preach and one that at first had made those listening uncomfortable and challenged them to consider their own thoughts on the subject. Now, two years into the conflict, the congregation had lost patience with the preacher. Many had stopped attending the services, others went along each Sunday but used the sermon time to nod off or day-dream. Others were hostile towards Sid.

Like Ena, Vi Todd sat next to her mother, Ivy Makepiece, and closed her eyes, willing Sid to stop his rantings. She sat content in the knowledge that in the two years her Jack had taken up arms against the Hun he hadn't killed a single person. As he assured her in his letters, war wasn't just about killing people, it was to do with maintaining principles and securing what you believed in. Jack had spent nearly eight months in the same series of trenches, situated in what had once been a field outside a small Belgian village. He hadn't seen any action and was carrying out his orders implicitly. He and his chums were to keep the trenches, not advance or retreat, just keep them. Vi was certain that if he had to Jack would kill someone – he had, after all, been trained to do just that – but it was comforting to know that he wasn't in a position to do so.

Ivy wasn't so disturbed by the thought of killing. She'd lost her two eldest sons to the war already and had been brought up with stories of war. Napoleonic, Boer, Crimean... Men went off to war, fought and either returned or died a hero's death. Women waited and wept. That was the nature of things and it was ridiculous to quote the Almighty as a prophet against war. Everyone knew that most wars were fought in His name. As Sid drew his sermon to a close, Ivy made no attempt to lower her voice as she turned to her daughter and said, 'Anythin' to dodge the call-up.'

Sid broke from his rehearsed summing up and spoke directly into the congregation: 'I beg your pardon, Mrs Makepiece?'

'Aye, and so you should,' retorted Ivy. 'I've sat through enough of yer drivel, Sid 'Ayes, to last a lifetime. It's bin more than a body could stand sittin' wi' you goin' on and on about how war's such a terrible thing.'

'It is a terrible thing. Surely, Mrs Makepiece, you of all people agree with me on that.'

Ivy rose to her feet and shouted over the heads of those in front of her, 'Why? Cos the Lord chose to take two o' my lads who were man enough to stand up and fight for what they believed in?'

Sid flinched at her tone but answered carefully, 'What did they believe in, Mrs Makepiece?'

The question threw Ivy. Heads turned to look at her, many silently urging her on. At last someone had stood against the tide that washed over them each Sabbath.

'Isn't it the case that they were not fighting for what they believed in,' pressed Sid, 'but rather that they were pressured into going off to fight in a war that had nothing to do with them, against human beings they had never met? They were pawns in political manoeuvrings that bore no relevance to their own short lives. What did their deaths achieve?'

Ivy gasped, as if she had been slapped across the face. 'They died fighting for freedom,' she said, her voice shaking.

'Whose freedom?' asked Sid quietly. 'Not their own.'

'I'm not listenin' to this.' Ivy pulled her shawl tightly around her and pushed down the row of chairs to leave the hall, with Vi scurrying along behind her.

Gladys Arkwright, on a stool at the harmonium, played the opening bars of the final hymn. Cut off from his sermon, with his conclusion undelivered, Sid nervously smoothed down his suit. Ena slid from her chair and crept towards the harmonium in case she was needed to turn the pages for Gladys.

Mary Schofield took the opportunity to give her shoulders and neck a good scratch.

Taking Sunday tea later that afternoon in Gladys's vestry the two friends discussed the wisdom of Sid's drum-beating to his own cause. Ena was surprised when Gladys admitted that she had written to the Mission superintendent, expressing her concern.

'Did you hear back?' Ena asked in awe.

'Yes. He said it wasn't my place to criticise or question the judgement of a member of the Mission committee.'

'But you weren't being spiteful.'

'I doubt he saw it that way,' said Gladys, forcing a smile and offering a plate of fruit cake.

Ena took a piece and munched in quiet contemplation.

'You have to learn, Ena, that if a man holds a position of authority, it does not automatically follow that everything that comes out of his mouth is correct. Men are human and humans err. I'm not saying that Mr Hayes hasn't the right to his own opinion but he should make more of an effort to understand the feelings of the local community. He certainly doesn't lack the courage to stand by his convictions.'

'Me dad calls Mr Hayes a conchie,' said Ena.

Gladys sighed. 'Men have always objected to war on account of conscience. I don't know, when women object to war people put it down to us being all emotional and having less education. When men object, often it's because they have too much education. Men like your father and Ivy Makepiece's husband – you won't remember him, he was as vocal as his wife – they do what they're told. 'Turn that handle', 'Mine that rockface', 'Go to war.' They don't understand men like Mr Hayes. Men who think for themselves. Mr Thwaite was just the same. Look what happened to him and his poor wife.'

The memory of the assault on the Thwaites' shop still visited Ena during the night and she shuddered at the thought of Lottie Thwaite's bloodied face. 'You don't think there'll be more trouble, do you?' she asked.

'I wouldn't be surprised,' answered Gladys sadly. 'Man has a habit of inflicting terrible unkindnesses on his neighbour. Perhaps that is why the Lord chose that particular commandment to be the most important.'

'"Love thy neighbour as thyself,"' whispered Ena.

'Amen.'

The sudden noise of glass shattering was followed, moments later, by hysterical screeching, and the residents of Coronation

Street appeared at doorways and windows. Across the cobbles the vestry door opened and Gladys and Ena tumbled out to join the people standing around the broken window-pane at No. 5.

Sid Hayes stood surveying the mess left by the brick that had smashed into his home as Ivy Makepiece wiped red dust from her hands on to her apron and spat on the pavement at Sid's feet. 'Write a sermon about that,' she hissed.

Her children stared at Sid, waiting to see how he would react.

'Is everyone all right?' asked Gladys, steering her way through the onlookers to reach Sid.

'A brick through the front parlour window,' he said matter-of-factly. 'Glass everywhere. Just missed Frederick asleep.'

'Is he hurt?' she asked anxiously.

'Just startled. Rose has him in the back room.' Sid's voice was dull but his gaze was locked on Ivy's defiant face.

'I'll go and check up on him,' said Gladys. She flapped her hands towards the neighbours. 'Go back to your homes, there's nothing to see out here.'

Disappointed that no hair was pulled out or clothes ripped, the residents dispersed.

Ivy gave Sid one last glare then slammed the front door of No. 11 behind her.

Ena waited for Gladys to enter the Hayes' family home before she retired to the vestry. She decided to put the kettle on. Drama always made her thirsty.

The wrought-iron gates that formed the main entrance to North Cross Cemetery were locked during the hours of darkness. Local children chose to believe that this was a precaution against marauding spirits but older denizens of Weatherfield recalled a spate of grave-robbing and body-snatching at the turn of the century. Interference with dead bodies was something to be abhorred but attempting to contact dead spirits was a different matter. Congregationalists, such as Sid Hayes and Gladys Arkwright, and those who attended the parish church of St Mary stood firmly against it but, with the death toll rising in France and Belgium, attempts to contact the dead were on the increase.

Sandwiched between Earnshaw's Mill and the boundary of the cemetery was a tall, thin building, whose brickwork was coated with soot. Intricate carvings and woodwork marked it out as different from the custom-built terraced homes in the area. Each window-sill was supported by tiny animal-like carvings, each one writhing in a position of torture. Five wide steps led to the black front door, framed by spiralling pillars. A glass panel bearing the name 'Endleigh' loomed high above it. Folk said it was the oldest house in Weatherfield, and that if you stood on its steps you could no longer hear the wind rustling, birds singing or trains clattering. Old biddies and young urchins alike referred to it as the House of the Dead and unnatural practices were said to take place in its basement.

Ena had grown up listening to such tales but while others, such as her gullible friend Martha Hartley, believed them without doubt, Ena took it upon herself to satisfy her curiosity about it. The curate of St Mary's told her that the house had been designed and built only forty years before and that its only connection with death was that its architect owner had keeled over with a heart-attack before completing the interior. He had been a nature lover whose artistic talents never matched his enthusiasm and vision. The tortured creatures were meant to represent squirrels and rabbits. Since the owner's death the house had remained empty.

Late in 1916, however, life – and death – caused light to brighten the house for the first time. A lease was acquired on the basement and a brass plaque secured to the railings, which led down into the belly of the house. 'Dr R. J. Sharples' read the plaque, 'Doctor of Divinity'.

'I don't know 'ow you talked me into this,' hissed Ena to her best friend, as they rushed down Victoria Street.

'Ye're comin' cos ye're me friend an' ye're as curious as I am,' said Martha. She was all too aware that if her mother found out about the night's outing she wouldn't be able to sit down for a week.

'Why should I be curious about such a place?' said Ena. 'It's nothin' but rot. The Bible's very plain on what 'appened to the Witch of Endor.'

'Oh, aye?' said Martha. 'Who were she?'

'Didn't you learn nothin' at Sunday School?' Ena was shocked.

'I liked the parable of the lost coin,' Martha smiled to herself, 'but you know I missed a lot of schoolin' on account of me epidemic.'

Ena decided to be lenient with her friend: eighteen months laid low with TB was as sound an excuse as any. 'Well, she was one of them that say they can see into the future an' she came to a sticky end.'

'Well, this fella don't see into the future, does he? He just reaches out to the other side.'

''Appen,' sniffed Ena.

'Oh, don't go bein' all huffy before we've even got inside door. There's a woman in our Street went last Saturday night an' she made contact wi' her lad who was killed in the same battle as your Phil.'

'If you believe such stuff,' said Ena scathingly.

'Well, it don't mek no odds if you believe or not. Facts is facts and she spoke to 'im for five minutes. He told 'er he loved 'er and she bawled 'er eyes out.' Martha gave Ena a sly look and added, 'Perhaps yer Phil'll try and contact you.'

Ena blushed. Much as she heaped scorn upon such nonsense she couldn't deny the flicker of hope that nestled in her heart that she might reach her dead fiancé.

Weatherfield did not boast many street-lamps, just one on the corner of each main road, so the walk from Victoria Street to the cemetery railings was in pitch blackness. The odd alehouse *en route* cast rays of light

204

on to the pavement but otherwise the streets were in darkness. Ena had once taken a tram ride into plush Oakhill and discovered that, in the bigger houses, people occupied their front parlours for daily use so light was thrown into the wide streets in front of them. In the terraces of Weatherfield parlours were used only for best or for laying out the dead in their coffins. Now the fronts of the houses looking out on to the cemetery remained dark, cut off from the life that went on at the rear of each home.

A lamp mounted on the side of the House of Death guided the two girls down the rickety service steps to the basement below. Ena knocked on the door and was surprised when a young face appeared as it was opened.

'We've come for the meeting,' said Martha, lowering her voice as if delivering a password.

The young man pulled the door wide and smiled at the arrivals. 'Do come in. Can I tek yer shawls?'

His accent wasn't local but Ena had trouble placing it. 'Where are you from?' she asked.

The young man looked startled. 'Bury. But I travel around some.'

'Oh,' Martha giggled, 'it must be lovely to travel.'

'Oh, aye, it is,' said the man. 'I've bin all over – Oldham, Preston, Blackpool, Rochdale, all over.'

'Fancy,' sighed Martha, eyeing the man appreciatively.

'Are we on time?' asked Ena, nudging Martha in the back to make her move further into the room.

'The doctor won't start until we 'ave a full circle,' said the man gravely.

'Suppose yer don't get one?' asked Martha, 'I can't stay long or me mother'll miss me.'

'We always get a full circle,' the man reassured her.

'Come on, Ena, let's get sat down,' said Martha, smiling sweetly at him.

'I 'ope you find what you're lookin' for,' he said.

The appearance of a medium or spiritualist would normally have sent Sid Hayes straight into the pulpit to warn his flock of the dangers in consorting with such a man. However, the coming of Dr Sharples coincided with another arrival at No. 5 Coronation Street – Sid's call-up papers.

The government had announced the need for conscription, starting in May 1916 as the number of men rallying to the flag had fallen. The mass slaughter on the Somme meant that married men and those previously deemed unfit for service were to go to war. Sid had been anticipating his telegram and had spent hours debating with like-minded associates as to his course of action. His decision to refuse to take up arms had surprised no one and he was sent to a military tribunal to state his case. Refusing to be daunted by the stern-faced panel who faced him, Sid attempted to deliver a sermon, repeatedly saying that to his mind it was morally wrong to fight and that to take a life was against the Christian ethic. He was disappointed when the authoritative men appeared bored with his speech, cut him off and offered him the chance to take up non-combatant duties.

'Such as?' he asked warily

'Burying the dead.'

'Carrying stretchers.'

'Digging holes.'

Sid was puzzled. He'd been anticipating arguments, brow-beating, threats of imprisonment and physical torture. These options sounded too easy and he would have liked time to ponder the choices but time was at a premium. Prompted by the panel, he cautiously agreed to join the Non-Combatant Corps.

Two days later he left his home and family, then went off down Rosamund Street with a uniformed policeman keeping step beside him – in case he decided to run.

The desire to run was building up inside Ena as she sat in the cold, musty basement of the House of Death. The room was filled with nervous-looking figures, mainly women in their forties and fifties, all sharing the same guilty, grief-stricken faces. 'We shouldn't be 'ere,' she whispered to Martha.

'I know. I keep thinkin' what's on the other side of that wall...' Martha gestured to it. 'The cemetery on the other side, 'an' you know what you find in cemeteries, don't you? Dead people.'

Ena shook her head in mock disbelief. 'Fancy that... Eee, I'd never 'ave worked that one out meself.' She sat further back in her chair, seeking comfort from its hard back pressing into her blouse. She wished she'd kept hold of her shawl, and peered into the gloom for a glimpse of the young man who had whisked it away. He was nowhere to be seen.

A door at the far side of the room opened and an imposing shadow crept across the flagged floor, like a gloved hand reaching out to grasp those in the room. Martha gave a yelp, but Ena ignored the phantom and watched the doorway as Dr Sharples made his appearance. The shadow had been a red herring, she decided, as the man who cast it appeared little more than five feet tall. He was middle-aged with wispy fair hair, which he wore brushed over a bald patch across the centre of his scalp. His voice, when he greeted his guests, was deep and echoed around the room. He invited the startled company to join him at his circular table and at once passed around a collection plate. Ena dropped in her three pennies reluctantly.

'We must all hold hands in an unbreakable circle,' instructed Dr Sharples. 'The one who causes the circle to break before time will live to regret it.'

Martha squeezed Ena's hand and the hand of the woman on her left. There was so much regret in Martha's life that she couldn't bear to risk any more.

Ena joined the circle and eyed the doctor cautiously.

'Are we all believers?' he asked.

The group voiced their assent.

'All?' he asked again, with a raised eyebrow.

'I 'ave an open mind,' muttered Ena.

Martha cast her friend an anxious look, hoping she wasn't going to cause bother and upset.

'Better open than closed,' said the doctor, with a smile.

'Quite,' retorted Ena, shifting in her chair. As she moved she caught sight of an angular figure sitting to his left and recognised Emma Piggott. No longer bothered whether the medium was true or false, Ena longed for the whole charade to be over so that she could escape. She prayed that Emma wouldn't notice her. If it should get back to Mrs Arkwright that she had visited such a place, sat holding hands and conversing with such a man ... Ena shuddered at the thought.

The lights dimmed and Emma faded into the blackness. All was quiet, apart from the pounding of Ena's heart. The doctor emitted a low moan.

'Is he all right?' whispered Ena.

''E's mekkin' contact,' replied the woman to her right. ''E's contactin' his guide.'

''Is what?'

'Guide. 'E 'as a guide on the other side.'

Ena fell quiet and stared hard at the doctor as he groaned, rocking back and forth in his chair. His face contorted and his eyes rolled from side to side. Ena screwed up her nose in distaste.

Watching every jerk, every flicker and twitch, Martha began unconsciously to mimic the doctor's movements. Ena nudged her friend and dug her fingernail into her palm. Martha opened her mouth to protest but was silenced by the scream that rose from within the doctor's body as he fell against the back of his chair, his body suddenly limp.

''E's dead!' said Martha in awe.

'Well, if 'e is, 'e certainly gave us a show for us three pennies,' said Ena.

'Why do you wake me?' The voice was light and feminine, and seemed to be coming from the lifeless body of the doctor.

'Eh up,' whispered Ena. 'Summat's 'appenin'.'

'I am Matilda Bracegirdle... What do you want from me, Ronald Sharples?'

The voice wavered and faded, to be replaced by the stronger voice of the doctor. His mouth made no movement as he answered, 'I have friends who seek loved ones, Matilda. Will you help them?'

'I will always help when I can,' came the reply. 'I feel you have friends who are in pain. Is that the case? Heartache is a terrible pain.' The doctor's normal voice returned, asking for those in emotional pain to identify themselves.

A couple of women cried out, longing to believe in a miracle.

'It is hard to be a mother and to lose a child,' said Matilda's voice.

A woman sobbed.

'To lose more than one is a terrible thing...' the voice continued.

A shift in the light from the gas mantle flickered across Emma Piggott's face and Ena saw tears rolling down her cheeks.

'I have somebody here... He wants to reach out through me...'

Matilda's voice faded and was replaced by a youthful, distorted male voice: 'Mother?'

Martha felt the hand of the woman to her right shake as she whispered, 'Jack?'

'Mother, it's me, Jack ... only they call me John here...'

The woman's body convulsed as she clung to Martha's hand and half rose from the table. Ena glanced from the slumped figure of the doctor to the looming shape of the woman, seeking the source of the voice.

'Oh, Jack ... oh my boy...'

'You needn't worry, Mother, all is well...'

'I miss you, Jack!' the woman screamed across the table, tears rolling down her ashen face.

'I miss you too, Mother, but we'll be together again soon ... come another time...'

'I'll come back next week, and I'll bring Aggie an' yer dad!'

'No,' cautioned the voice, 'not me dad... Tell him I'll see him in his dreams.'

'Oh, Jack, will yer? Oh, come to my dreams, too, won't you, lad?'

'I will, Mother. I have to go now...'

The woman lowered herself into her seat, her body jerking with sobs.

Martha watched her, her mouth opened in wonder.

Ena didn't know what to say so said nothing. Her eyes continued to dart around the circle. She wasn't sure what was going on but one thing was certain: she didn't want to be contacted by Phil Moss in such a place.

Matilda returned to say she had another friend but couldn't work out what his name was, only that it began with R.

'Reg?' cried a woman, biting her lip. 'Me

mother 'ad a lodger called Reg...'

'Not Reg,' said Matilda, almost teasingly. 'He keeps talking about his brother.'

Quietly Emma spoke one of the names of her dead sons. 'Victor ... his brother's name is Victor...'

Matilda sighed, and the lights went out. Martha let out a scream. Others followed her gaze as, out of the gloom, behind the doctor's chair, a youth appeared in uniform.

''Ello, Mam, fancy seein' you 'ere.' The voice was light, almost flirtatious.

Ena saw the smile break across Emma's face and her eyes shone. 'You look well, Robert,' she said, as if she regularly conversed with ghosts.

'Fit as a fiddle, Mam.' His tone changed as he went on, 'But you're looking like a bag o' bones, Mam. You've bin worryin', 'aven't you?'

Emma nodded.

'You mustn't ... I'm all right. Please take care o' yerself, Mam...' And with that the youth disappeared into the darkness.

Unlike the mother before her, Emma remained seated and breathed calmly. Tears continued to roll down her cheeks, though, and she made no attempt to wipe them away.

The company sat in silence, waiting for Matilda to return or for another apparition to appear. The doctor remained motionless and all was still until a male voice spoke out of nowhere: 'Ena, is that you?'

'She's broken the chain!' shouted a woman, as Ena leapt to her feet, her chair legs scraping across the paved floor. Her head spun as she knocked into more chairs and fought blindly for the door.

Behind her chaos ensued around the table. The doctor convulsed and groaned as if in death throes, women shrieked and the lights flared into life, causing everyone to blink. Martha stood looking after her friend forlornly, muttering, 'She broke the circle ... she broke the circle...'

When the letter arrived from Sid, Rose Hayes could think only of one person to turn to. Gladys Arkwright was amazed to discover that for all his preaching and campaigning for those less fortunate than himself Sid had never taught his wife to read and write. She took the letter from Rose, offered her a cup of strong tea and cast a quick eye over the letter's contents.

''Ave they shot 'im?' asked Rose.

Despite herself, Gladys laughed. 'Of

course they haven't,' she said. 'Why would they do that?'

'He reckoned on them shootin' 'im. 'E said as much the mornin' they carted 'im off.' Rose sounded resigned. Gladys wondered if she would have minded if her husband *had* been shot.

'Look, it's from Sid himself,' said Gladys, waving the letter at her. 'He says he's in a military prison and he wants you to write to him.'

'I can't write,' said Rose, her voice raised in panic.

'Well, you tell me what to write and I'll write it down for you,' said Gladys helpfully.

'I don't understand why he's in prison,' said Rose, her brow troubled.

'According to the letter, he's been sent there for six months. He says he was asked to unload a railway carriage but refused to touch the chests containing rifles and ammunition. He's been given hard labour but he says you're not to worry because he's still in Blighty and he's made lots of friends. One of them's a Seventh Day Adventist.'

'Oh,' said Rose, bewildered. 'Does he say what to do about the rent? Only I'm fallin' behind and the money's stopped comin'.'

'That'll be because he's been court-martialled,' said Gladys. She looked at the pathetic creature on her sofa and shook her head. 'I'll talk to the Mission superintendent, see if he can put some work your way. You don't mind a bit of polishing and cleaning, do you?'

'Don't sound as if I've got much choice in matter, does it?' said Rose sadly.

'Why did you run off like that?' asked Martha, at the earliest opportunity she had to quiz her friend. 'The doctor was really put out.'

Ena shrugged and looked down into the murky depths of the canal. The pair stood on the old packhorse bridge, enjoying the crisp bite of the morning frost. 'Whoever it was said my name in that place it wasn't Phil, that I'm sure of.'

'But it sounded like 'im,' said Martha.

'Martha Hartley, when did you ever met Phil Moss?' asked Ena.

'Well,' said Martha uncomfortably, 'just because I never met 'im it don't follow that I don't know what he sounds like. I've seen 'is picture and 'e sounded like I thought 'e'd sound.'

'He sounded like a thousand other chaps, and there was no way I was 'angin' around that place to be made a fool of.'

'Nay, Ena, nobody was out to mek a fool of yer.' Martha stroked her friend's arm. 'Dr Sharples only wants to help those in mournin' to reach through the abyss.'

'The what?'

'The abyss. That's what he called it after you'd tekken off. That woman whose son appeared, she's goin' to see Dr Sharples for a private session.'

'I bet she is,' murmured Ena sadly. 'I reckon it'll cost 'er a tidy sum an' all.'

'Well, you wouldn't expect the doctor to do it for nowt, would you? You saw for yerself what it took out of the poor fella.'

'I'm not sure what I saw,' said Ena wearily. 'Not sure at all.'

Ena hated lying to anyone, especially her mother. When Mary Schofield asked after her daughter's shawl Ena flushed and murmured that she'd mislaid it. Mary hadn't pressed her and Ena stayed up for weeks knitting herself a new one to see her through the harshest winter months. She never ventured near the House of Death again and was relieved to hear that Martha had no intention of doing so without her. However, word of Emma Piggott's involvement in spiritualism spread around the neighbourhood, and Ena feigned shock and surprise when, over their Sunday-afternoon tea, Gladys Arkwright told her about her neighbour's new pastime.

'She goes every week,' said Gladys, disapprovingly.

'And she hears from her sons?' asked Ena.

'Not every week. Sometimes she hears from one, sometimes the other, once from both at the same time. Sometimes there's no message for her.'

'What do you reckon to it?' asked Ena, helping herself to a biscuit.

'Well,' said Gladys awkwardly, 'I'm not saying I don't believe in it. The Almighty warned us against dealing in such matters but he never said it was a load of old rot.'

Ena fell silent and munched her biscuit. It being the third Sunday of the month it was an arrowroot biscuit. Gladys baked four different types each Saturday night of the month: first nut rocks, then almond fingers, arrowroot and ginger. She never experimented with different recipes, preferring the contents of her biscuit barrel to match everything else in her ordered life.

'Mr Hayes spends his day sewing mailbags,' said Gladys, after a pause. 'He stitches with hemp.'

Rose Hayes had received only one other letter from her husband as regulations restricted him to one each month. Gladys had pointed out that there were no such restrictions on Rose and she could write as often as she wished. So far Rose hadn't taken her up on her offer and Gladys believed sadly that she had no desire to make contact with her husband. Rose was a woman of simple beliefs who resented Sid's forceful manner and enjoyed life away from his dominating presence. But true to her word, Gladys had taken her plight to the Mission super-intendent and Rose had been employed to help clean the six Mission Halls in the neighbourhood. Her wages – the first she had ever earned – barely covered her food and rent but she savoured her independence, and she looked forward to the hours spent alone after work at No. 5 with little Ada bouncing around the house and the baby, Frederick, gurgling and chuckling.

It was a small group who buried Frederick Hayes on the first Sunday in November 1916. The child, not even eighteen months old, had become ill and died of diphtheria within a week. The sudden extinction of life had shocked the residents of Coronation Street and sent Rose into a screaming fit, so violent that Mrs Corbishley at the Rover's Return had to open a bottle of brandy to calm her. Gladys had written to Sid immediately, and the Mission superintendent had petitioned for compassionate leave. None had been granted and Sid remained behind bars as his son's coffin was lowered into the ground at North Cross Cemetery. Gladys and Ena supported Rose at the graveside. Apart from Sid's aged mother and Rose's neighbour Gertie Hewitt, from No. 3, there were no other mourners. Gladys had laid on a small spread of sandwiches and cakes in her vestry and led Rose homeward after the short ceremony.

Walking behind the group, Ena paused as she left the cemetery and glanced up at the House of Death. She hadn't been mistaken: someone was watching from the porch. She cleared her throat and wished she'd been able to finish knitting her new shawl before the funeral. It was bitterly cold, and in other circumstances she would have worn her bright orange cardigan but black was the only colour to wear at a funeral.

'Hello.' The man's voice cut into the crisp air.

'If I'd known folk were that interested in watching a bairn's funeral I'd 'ave got 'is mother to sell tickets. Lord knows, she needs the money.'

'I'm sorry. Was it a family member?'

'No. A friend's child,' said Ena. She shielded her eyes from the glare of the midday sun to get a better look at the young man.

'It's you, isn't it?' he said.

'By 'eck, lad, you're fast off the mark.'

'No,' he blushed, 'you're the girl who ran out a few weeks back ... Ena.'

The way he said her name sent a shiver down her spine. She knew she'd heard it said that way once before and turned her back on him, determined to catch up with the others.

'Don't go,' he pleaded, and stepped down the five deep steps. 'I'm sorry.'

'For what?' she challenged, daring him to confess, to tell her what she had already guessed.

'For ... I'm not sure. Would you like yer shawl back?'

Ena laughed. 'You've been caught off-guard, lad,' she said. 'You're not from Bury I know Salford when I 'ear it.'

The young man flushed. 'I kept yer shawl.

222

You can 'ave it back. It won't tek me a minute to fetch it.'

'Don't bother yerself. It were old anyway. I'm mekkin' another.'

'Ena...'

She turned and glared at him. 'I dunno who dragged you up,' she snapped, 'but I've always bin led to believe that manners maketh man. We 'aven't been introduced and I'd be grateful if you'd stop callin' me by me name.'

'I'm sorry,' he said, smiling at her disarmingly. 'My name's Alfred Sharples.'

'As in Dr Sharples?'

'He's my father.'

'Where's your mother?'

'Dead.'

'Not called Matilda by any chance, was she?' Ena saw from the pain that flickered across his face that she'd gone too far. 'You know I don't 'old wi' what you and yer father do in there, don't you?'

Alfred shrugged. ''E only gives them what they want – the chance to say one last goodbye. There's no 'arm.'

''Appen,' agreed Ena, 'I dunno what's right and what isn't any more. The whole world's gone mad around us.' She looked at the smiling man and clicked her teeth. 'You a conchie?' she asked. 'Yonder bairn's father's a conchie. He's locked up in some prison for it.'

'I'm no conchie,' said Alfred. 'I was one of first out there, fifteenth battalion, First Salfords. Took a bullet in me shoulder in Henencourt, last New Year. I'm just waitin' for the all-clear an' I'll be back wi' the lads.'

'Yer father'll miss yer,' she said ruefully. 'The ghostly soldier boy's a great touch.'

Alfred shuffled uncomfortably, cast his eyes to the ground and said, 'Aye, well...'

'Aye,' replied Ena. 'Goodbye, Alfred Sharples. I don't think I'll be seein' you again.' She turned and walked away from the house and the cemetery. Her mind was whirling with conflicting thoughts: she recalled the look of serenity on Emma Piggott's face when she believed she was talking to her dead son, and the thrill she had felt on believing she might have made contact with her own Phil. Who was she to condemn the Sharples for giving people like her the chance to say goodbye?

'Goodbye, Ena,' called the man.

She didn't answer, just hurried across the street, thinking of the letter she would write to Albert when she got home.

CHAPTER EIGHT

January 1917

Jim Corbishley lowered his newspaper with a groan. His wife, Nellie, glanced up from her mending and asked, 'What's to do?'

'Colonel Cody's dead.'

'Oh,' said Nellie, none the wiser. 'Was he in the Fusiliers? Does our Charlie know 'im?'

Jim shook his head in despair. 'Ye're daft, woman. Colonel Cody is Buffalo Bill. You must 'ave 'eard o' 'im.'

'I'll thank you not to talk to me in that manner,' barked Nellie. 'I'm not one of yer floozies sat on a bar stool in Manchester. I'm a decent, 'ard-workin' woman and a bit o' respect would go a long way.' She sniffed. 'It's not my fault I've not 'eard of this Cody chap. I see that many folk over that bar top. 'Ow am I to know all an' sundry that come in?'

''E's American,' said Jim. ''E's never set foot in Rover's.'

'Then 'ow in God's name am I meant to 'ave 'eard of 'im?' challenged Nellie, furiously darning a sock. 'Maybe if you took me out from time to time then I might 'ave met him or 'eard of 'im, but no, I couldn't expect that o' you, could I?' She glared at her husband with contempt. 'When were the last time you took me out?'

Jim opened his mouth to answer but Nellie continued, 'I'll tell you when it were. Sunday the eighth of August 1915. Over a year ago. A year!'

'Nay,' said Jim. 'I took you out last October. We 'ad a day out. It rained.'

Nellie flung down her sewing and glared at her husband. 'We 'ad a day out?' she shouted at him. 'A day out? That was my mother's funeral!'

A grin spread across Jim's craggy face. 'Aye, that's right.'

Nellie bit her tongue and marched out of the room. In the hallway she passed Sarah Bridges, the young resident barmaid, who neatly stepped aside to avoid her and slipped into the living room.

With Nellie gone Jim laid aside his newspaper and started to roll himself a cigarette. Sarah glanced at the paper as she passed and squinted down at it. 'Who's Colonel

Cody?' she asked softly.

'Just some old American,' said Jim dismissively. 'No one for you to worry yer pretty little 'ead about.'

Sarah lowered herself into an easy-chair and stretched provocatively, knowing full well that Jim's eyes would be fixed upon her rising bosom. She emitted a tiny squeal and shuddered. 'Mrs Corbishley seems out o' sorts,' she said.

'Tek no notice,' advised Jim. 'I don't. She's a law unto 'erself.'

'Maybe she's upset about Charlie.'

'I don't see why,' said Jim. 'She knows where 'e is. Tucked up safe an' sound in that there Southampton 'ospital, 'avin' nurses waitin' on 'im 'and and foot. She's got no cause to fret. It's not as if 'e's still out there gerrin' shot at.'

'Still,' said Sarah, with a smile, 'she's bound to think of 'er only son on 'is birthday.'

Jim's eyes shot to the date on his newspaper. The eleventh of January. He groaned. How was he supposed to remember birthdays? He had a business to run.

Minnie Carlton hurried down the sloping hill beside the viaduct. She was late, and

227

Ena hated to be kept waiting. The wooden soles of her shoes smashed against the cobbles but she wasn't a fast runner. Her mother said it was because she didn't have the build for it, but Minnie knew it was because she could never be bothered to lift her feet high enough. Not even the prospect of keeping Ena waiting could prompt her to speed her trot into a gallop.

The alleyway was dark so Minnie kept close to the viaduct wall, her eyes darting from left to right as she rushed along. Five years previously a woman had been found with her throat cut here, and even though the murderer had been caught Minnie was a great believer in lightning striking twice. She smiled with relief as she approached Gypsy Corner and saw the familiar shape of Ena Schofield beneath a gas-lamp.

'You're late,' was Ena's greeting.

'I know. I couldn't find me 'anky.'

'What do you want yer 'anky for?' asked Ena, irritated.

'In case it's sad. I always get weepy if it's sad.'

'Since when 'ave you seen owt sad at Band of 'ope?'

'Oh, Ena, sometimes they show you slides of the little children in Africa. That can be sad. They 'ave no clothes an' 'ardly any food.'

Ena sniffed. 'If you find that sad then don't go wanderin' down Gladstone Terrace way cos there's plenty down there wearin' bits o' rags scavengin' for food.' She sighed at Minnie's pained expression. She was, without doubt, the most emotional and generous of Ena's friends, but gullible too.

'I 'ope it's not about little African children,' said Minnie, her fingers toying with the frayed end of her blouse.

'Well, if we don't stop chunnerin' and go in we'll not find out. I've been stood 'ere twenty minutes an' I've seen 'em all go in. There's a fair few tonight and we'll be lucky to get seats.'

The two friends made their way towards the Gothic building across the street. Built as a Pentecostal chapel it had been taken over by the Band of Hope just before the war, and educational and instructive meetings were held every Saturday night. These meetings were presented in a Christian context with an evangelical message. The only way they differed from those of the other neighbourhood chapels was that each message was accompanied by a magic-lantern show.

The hand-coloured slides that the lantern brought to life were projected upon a huge screen. Images of mysterious animals, wonders of the world, exotic-looking peoples, Biblical landscapes and even members of the British Royal Family were shown for all present to marvel at.

Ena and Minnie crept into the crowded hall and found seats at the back. The place was busier than usual because posters had spread word of the meeting around town: 'Dr Charlesworth will show slides of his visit to the savages of Africa.' No one could resist tales of cannibals.

Dr Charlesworth, a short squat man with glasses perched at the end of his nose, was being introduced enthusiastically as Ena and Minnie sat down. Ena had to ask the man sitting next to her to move his coat, which was on her seat. As he apologised, Ena recognised his voice and her stomach tightened.

'We meet again, Miss Schofield,' he said.

'Aye, Mr Sharples, so we do.'

'Come to gawk at the savages?' he asked.

'I don't gawk,' replied Ena frostily. 'My friend and I come 'ere most Saturday nights. It's very educational.'

'Sssh,' whispered Minnie. ''E's startin'.'

An hour later, after the congregation had been transported to a far-off land of wooden huts, witch-doctors, tribal dances, hungry crocodiles but, disappointingly, no cannibals, a hearty round of applause marked the end of the meeting.

'Are you stayin' for tea?' asked Alfred.

'I normally do,' said Ena.

She looked around for Minnie but her friend had already darted away. Ena smiled weakly at Alfred and made her excuses in order to find Minnie. She ran her to ground in the queue to ask Dr Charlesworth questions.

'Whatever are you doin'?' asked Ena.

'I've a question,' said Minnie smugly.

'Oh, aye?' Ena viewed her friend with suspicion. She'd noticed Minnie fumbling for her handkerchief when the slide of the crying child had come up.

'I want to ask if he saw any lions or tigers. I like lions and tigers.'

''Ow do you know if you like 'em or not?' said Ena. 'When 'ave you ever seen one?'

'In picture books,' replied Minnie, shuffling forward in the queue.

The man standing directly in front of her turned and smiled at her.

'I like lions and tigers too,' he said. 'My

231

name's Armistead Caldwell,' he went on. 'It's a bit of a mouthful. My father was big on battlefields.'

Minnie smiled at the young man and replied, 'My father was big in the shuntin' yard.'

''E shovelled coal,' Ena added.

''E died eight year ago,' said Minnie. 'TB.'

'This is my cousin Harry,' said Armistead, nudging his neighbour, a tall lanky fellow with outsize limbs.

Harry grinned at the women, revealing a gap where his two front teeth should have been.

'We're on leave,' continued Armistead. 'Looks like the doctor's busy tonight. 'Ow about we buy you ladies some refreshments?'

Minnie looked gleefully at Ena, who glanced back to where Alfred Sharples sat, then nodded and followed the others to the tea counter.

Ivy Makepiece sat in the central position in the Snug bar of the Rover's. There were more comfortable seats beside the fireplace but Ivy preferred the stool on which she sat. It faced the bar and offered a decent view of the comings and goings in the Public. All that was going on was that Jim Corbishley was bent over the bar chatting to the new tenant of No. 1 Coronation Street.

Ivy beckoned Sarah Bridges over. 'Want toppin' up, Mrs Makepiece?' asked the girl.

'No, I'm after information,' said Ivy. 'What's the name of that fella?' She jerked her head in the direction of the Public.

'That's Mr Marsh,' said Sarah.

'I knew I knew his face. Ugly brute, ain't 'e?'

'Oh, I dunno,' said Sarah. 'I've seen worse.'

'Still,' sniffed Ivy, 'you're from Liverpool, aren't you?'

Sarah laughed and leant against the bar. She scratched the back of her neck and sighed. With all the young men away, Coronation Street was incredibly dull. Things had been different in the two years she'd lived over the pub before the war. Then Charlie Corbishley had been around. Knowing that his mother disapproved of dalliance with the staff, Charlie had taken to wooing Sarah in darkened corridors, fumbling with her clothing in the beer cellar and creeping into her bedroom at night. Sarah had been more than willing to succumb to his advances and matched his passion with her own.

When Charlie's eye had roamed, Sarah had merely made eyes at one of the strapping young blokes in the Public. Charlie had always returned for more and she fancied he would do so after the war. She didn't mind the frosty looks she received from the inhabitants of the Snug. Life was dull enough without sitting at home crocheting table mats and waiting for Mr Right to come a-calling. Besides, she was a barmaid, and she always had the excuse that she wasn't a native of Weatherfield, or Manchester. For the closed minds on Coronation Street, those from different counties or towns were never as moral as the home-bred.

Since Charlie had gone swaggering off to war the floorboard outside Sarah's bedroom had stopped creaking at night. She'd started a liaison with a bandsman but had run scared when he'd talked of marrying her and 'rescuing her' from her job. Sarah didn't want rescuing: she loved the back-street alehouse because in its grimness she shone out. She was shrewd enough to realise that without her stage her light would fade into the background.

Even if the young men were absent there were still plenty of older ones about, and from the encounters Sarah had experienced she felt there wasn't much difference between them in the dark. She felt eyes upon her and casually turned to face the Public bar. Both Jim Corbishley and Alfie Marsh were gazing admiringly at her. She pulled her lips into a smile then turned back slowly to Ivy in the Snug, swaying her hips as she did so.

'By 'eck, lass, you do that well,' commented Ivy, admiringly.

Sarah smiled broadly at her and said, 'I've 'ad a fair bit o' practice.'

'So,' said Ivy, leaning forward, 'if you 'ad to, which of them would you set yer cap at?'

Sarah considered: both men were old enough to *be* her father but as Ivy was old enough to be her mother she decided the question was a fair one. 'Mr Corbishley,' she said. 'I've always fancied runnin' a pub.'

Ivy cackled. 'Good choice but yer forgettin' summat.'

'Oh, yes?'

'There's a Mrs Corbishley, and she holds the purse strings.'

'That's true,' said Sarah, with a glint in her eye. 'Very true.'

Minnie Carlton surprised her best friend. Ena had always considered her the most slothful of women but the speed at which she pursued Armistead Caldwell took her breath away.

'I know the lad's only got a few days' leave,' said Ena, as the pair rushed to work on Monday morning, 'but you've not given 'im chance to draw breath.'

Since meeting Armistead on Saturday night, Minnie had spent the Sunday out walking near Bolton with him and had introduced him to her mother. It was beyond Ena what Minnie saw in Armistead, who, she thought, had a permanently startled look about him. 'He reminds me of a rabbit me uncle Len had. Every time anyone picked it up its little back legs would start jiggerin' and its eyes would flare up.'

'Armistead doesn't jiggle,' said Minnie defensively, 'and you've no right to say 'e looks like a rabbit. You leave yer comments for 'Arry.'

''Arry who?' demanded Ena.

'Armistead's cousin 'Arry.'

'I've nowt to say about Armistead's cousin 'Arry.'

'Well, 'e 'as plenty to say about you,' said Minnie kindly. 'Armistead says he thinks you're smashin'.'

Despite herself Ena felt her face colour.

She flapped her arms against her sides, which she often did when thrown. Minnie sucked her teeth and enjoyed her friend's discomfort.

'Well, all I can say is I've done nowt to encourage 'im,' said Ena finally. 'I 'ardly said owt to the lad.'

'Armistead says he wants to see you again.'

'Well, 'e can want, then. I'm not walkin' out wi' anyone.'

Minnie caught the tinge of sadness in Ena's voice and laid a hand on her arm. 'It's bin nearly a year since Phil passed on.'

'I don't need remindin' o' that,' said Ena sharply. 'An' 'e didn't "pass on". 'E were shot in the 'ead by a bullet.'

Pain shot through Pearl Crapper's left leg and she stumbled against the mangle, her hand thrust out to steady herself. She closed her eyes tight and held back the groan of despair that rose in her throat. She hadn't had the pain for three weeks and had hoped the cause of it had gone away. It had started nearly a year ago: at first she had experienced little more than twinges, but now the pains came without warning, sudden and ferocious, flooding her leg like burning sulphur.

She pressed down on the mangle roller, biting her lip and closing her eyes against tears that threatened to blind her. Hearing a noise from the next room she wiped them away and gritted her teeth. The last thing she wanted was the Corbishleys to think there was something wrong with their housekeeper. She knew Jim only tolerated her presence because she was a good cook, and Nellie was not the sentimental kind. Any hint that the old mare was going lame and Pearl could picture the gun barrel being pointed at her.

She managed to compose herself before the glass-panelled kitchen door opened and Nellie Corbishley walked in. Pearl sprang to life, pushed one of Jim's shirts through the mangle and watched the water dripping out of it.

'Have you not finished in here yet?' Nellie's tone was naturally critical and caused Pearl no alarm. It was only when she turned to face her employer that she noticed Nellie's worried expression. There was no need to ask what the matter was. In her hand was a telegram.

Pearl eyed it with concern. 'Should I fetch Mr Corbishley?' she asked.

Nellie shook her head. 'It'll be brewery

business,' she said unconvincingly. She took one last look at the telegram before sliding her finger under the flap of the envelope.

The message was short and to the point. 'Regret to inform Pvt. C. Corbishley died in hospital 11 January.'

Nellie hit the floor before Pearl had a chance to reach her.

Ena wasn't sure how she'd come to agree to making up a foursome with Minnie, Armistead and the ever-grinning Harry. She certainly had no wish to spend her Monday night sitting on a park bench throwing pieces of stale bread to a couple of mallards. On one side of her Minnie and Armistead sat holding hands and gazing into each other's eyes. On the other Harry shifted around as if ants were crawling inside his clothing. She stared at him silently, challenging him to make a move. He was nearly six foot tall but there was no bulk to him and she reckoned if he tried anything it wouldn't take much to knock him over.

'It's not that cold,' ventured Harry.

'No, it's not,' agreed Ena.

'But it's not that warm either,' he continued.

'Aye, I've known warmer,' she said.

'Still, at least it's not cold.'

Ena thought of Phil Moss: he'd never been one for words but when he did speak it had been to say something sensible.

'We go back on Wednesday,' said Harry.

'Where is it you're going back to?' asked Ena.

'Dunno,' said Harry. ''Appen France, 'appen Belgium.'

Ena sighed. It was a sad business when the lads didn't even know where they'd be fighting.

'Will you write to me?'

The question surprised Ena and she answered too quickly, without giving thought to the lad's feelings. 'No,' she said. 'I already write to a lad.'

She watched Harry deflate. His grin slipped from his face and he shuffled his feet on the grass. 'Oh, I see,' he said.

She wanted to say, 'No, you don't, I just write to this lad I met who was marching off to war,' but she held back. She knew that if she progressed any further with Harry he'd read far too much into it. They didn't have an understanding and they wouldn't.

Later, the four young people stood outside Minnie's home on Palmerston Street. Ena kept close to the open doorway waiting as her friend rushed inside to fetch a good-luck charm she wanted Armistead to have. Harry stood some distance away, kicking his heels, and Armistead leant carelessly against the brick wall next to the door. Inside the house Ena could hear the ticking of the clocks Minnie's father Bob had kept. Restoring them had been his hobby and the whole house was filled with clocks of different sizes and designs. To the uninformed eye there seemed no reason for the different times shown on each face. Those in the know, like Ena, understood that each was set to show the time in a different country. Bob Carlton had longed to travel but had never gone further afield than Rochdale. If Armistead heard the ticking he didn't mention it. Instead he smiled at Ena. An unsettling smile with eyes that bored intently into hers.

'She won't be long,' said Ena uneasily.

Armistead leant forward so his mouth was close to her ear. She flinched but stood her ground. He spoke softly but she heard every word. 'It's not Minnie I'm really interested in.'

She bristled.

'Could I see you before Wednesday? Alone?' he asked.

Ena glared at him. 'I don't think so.'

'Come on, Ena,' he said, brushing his hand gently over her shoulder. 'I really like you.'

Ena moved sharply away from the doorway. She wanted to run, to get away from the odious man and his disgusting overtures, but the knowledge that her friend would appear in a moment kept her rooted to the cobbles. She'd never seen Minnie so alive as she had been in the last few days, believing she had fallen in love with a decent, kind man. Yet how unlike Albert he was in all he did. How dare he say such things to her when Minnie was so besotted?

A black armband worn over his shirt sleeve was Jim Corbishley's only public acknowledgement of his son's death. He refused to close the pub and appeared his normal self to his regulars. Meanwhile, his distraught wife lay in bed with the curtains drawn. Pearl Crapper, who also burst into tears regularly, pressed soup and water vainly upon her employer. Any awkwardness the pub's customers felt in approaching the bar faded with Jim's jovial welcome and if anyone offered condolences he thanked them without adjusting his tone.

Sarah Bridges genuinely mourned her

one-time beau. All the characteristics about him that Jim had despised she loved – his cocky walk, confident grin and quick wit. While they had made Jim aware of his age they had made Sarah feel every inch a woman. Charlie had been master of an art form rarely found in the back-streets of Weatherfield: he had been a charmer, and now he was mourned by a woman who had experienced the depth of his attentions.

Sarah watched Jim carefully. She'd lived under his roof long enough to know that his nonchalance over Charlie's death was a ploy he had adopted to get over the pain. Having watched father and son rub each other up the wrong way in peacetime she realised that Jim regarded Charlie's death as a victory. The established order had been overthrown: death had taken the young buck and left the older man.

Sarah was a wise woman and knew when to consolidate her assets. Charlie would never return to Weatherfield and neither would many of his kind. That was, if the war ever ended and there was no sign of that yet. Sarah was a woman who needed men around her, to feel their eyes on her, to know that she was desired, and to be held in manly arms. She'd been too emotionally involved with Charlie, allowed herself to believe he was the perfect meal-ticket out of the back-street. He had been the sole heir to a public house, and his mother was the daughter of a prominent businessman in Salford. With him gone she saw the need to find herself another lover with prospects, and Weatherfield was a small pond with a limited supply of large fish in it.

Sarah was a lazy girl and, rather than trawl through available men further afield, she decided that Jim Corbishley was her best bet. He wasn't ideal as he had a wife, but she'd observed that there was no affection between Jim and Nellie. They even slept in separate bedrooms, which made life so much easier for a girl on the make. While Nellie Corbishley suffered nightmares involving her dead son, and Pearl Crapper snored out the night, Sarah Bridges slipped out of her nightgown to warm Jim's old bones.

On Wednesday 17 January, Minnie Carlton sneaked out of Hardcastle's weaving shed number five to bid her boyfriend goodbye. Her mournful face had irritated Ena, who had become impatient with her and snapped at the long-suffering Minnie.

Minnie had mistaken Ena's mood, thinking she missed Harry's company.

With Minnie out of the way, Ena concentrated on operating her looms as well as her own, which required her to keep a close eye on the darting bobbins of eight thundering looms. Although driven by machinery the intricate weaving of each loom demanded close inspection. It was an impossible task to watch more than six for any length of time. Minnie had struggled with two before the war and had only progressed to four as demand for domestic input had risen. Ena had always been one of the brightest and more competent weavers but as the minutes crept along with no sign of Minnie's return she struggled to keep on top of the looms.

Across the room Ena's friend Mary Makepiece caught her eye and mouthed to her over the din of the machines. Ena understood that her friend was telling her that a soldier was looking for her. Surprised, she frowned. Where?

Mary nodded out into the corridor and Ena turned to follow her gaze.

Armistead Caldwell was skulking in the gloomy half-light. Ena's shoulders sagged with her spirits. But desperate times called for desperate measures. One by one, to the amazement of the other women in the shed, she shut down the eight looms. Mary eyed her in alarm as Ena hurried out into the corridor.

'What do you want?' she demanded fiercely.

'I 'ad to see you. Where's Minnie?'

'Gone to wave you off, you daft 'aporth.'

'I couldn't go without seein' you, Ena,' said Armistead in a pitiful voice.

'I've nowt to say to you, Armistead Caldwell. I don't know 'ow you've the nerve to stand there. My best friend thinks she's in love wi' you.'

'I know.'

He sounded genuinely upset so she changed her tone, becoming less hostile.

'Go on, lad, go to war and forget any fancy notions you 'ave about me.'

'I do like Minnie but I like you better.'

'I don't want to 'ear it.'

'I think we could 'ave a laugh together.'

'I wouldn't be laughin' if Minnie were cryin' and, believe me, if you don't do right by 'er she will cry.'

'I can't 'elp it if she's keen on me,' said Armistead.

'By 'eck, you fancy yerself, don't you?'

246

Ena sniffed.

'Come on, Ena, say you'll be my girl.'

'No, Armistead. Now be told. I don't like you that way.' She took a step away from him. 'Go to wherever it is you should be. Kiss Minnie goodbye, and give 'er time to get over you.'

Armistead stared at Ena for a couple of moments before turning abruptly and walking away, towards the staircase. 'God speed, lad,' Ena muttered, before returning to the shed.

She approached the looms at the same time as Mr Fletcher, the foreman. He glared at her. 'Are these your looms?' he asked.

'Yes,' said Ena meekly, 'I'm sorry, but I 'ad to—'

'Fetch yer cards. You're sacked.'

Ivy Makepiece agreed to meet Sarah Bridges in private. Not that there was much privacy to be found at No. 11 Coronation Street, with one of Ivy's brood constantly hanging around the house on the look-out for food or attention. Sarah kept an eye on the kitchen door throughout her visit, ceasing her conversation whenever Susie or Will made a noisy entrance.

Ivy had established in her own mind why

Sarah wanted to talk before the girl broached the subject herself. Not many people came calling on Ivy and Sarah heard her fair share of gossip behind the Rover's bar. Ivy stared long and hard at the girl, seeing the tiny beads of sweat forming on her brow and top lip. The subject was going to be distasteful and that limited it to two possibilities. She eyed the girl's stomach but her belt appeared as tight as usual, her blouse tucked neatly into her waistband.

'Mrs Makepiece, you know I'm not one to listen to idle tittle-tattle,' said Sarah carefully.

Ivy nodded. In her experience Sarah never passed on the gossip she heard. She couldn't help overhearing things: it came with the job, along with strong biceps and a cheeky tongue.

'I 'ave 'eard, though,' continued Sarah, 'the talk concernin' yer mother's death.'

Ivy nodded again. Her face was set, not betraying her in any way. The gossips had had a field day over Hetty Harris's death in the summer of 1911. She knew they all suspected her of helping the old soul on her way out of the world, and if any other person had brought up her mother's death Ivy would have given them a mouthful and

248

thrown them out. However, her mind was already racing ahead of what Sarah was saying.

'I was wonderin',' said Sarah, 'if you might be able to 'elp me.'

Ivy judged it safe to join in the conversation. She poured herself a fresh cup of weak tea and put up a hand to stop Sarah talking. 'When me mother were alive I 'ad terrible trouble with mice. Terrible it were. All over the place. No use setting traps for 'em so I needed poison.'

Sarah paled at the word, her pupils grew larger and she opened her mouth slightly.

'Might you be 'avin' problems wi' mice at Rover's?' asked Ivy.

Sarah was silent for a couple of beats then nodded slowly. She didn't look at Ivy but said, 'Yes, that's it.'

'I thought so. Well, 'appen I can 'elp you.'

Sarah flushed and mumbled, 'I'd be very grateful, Mrs Makepiece.'

'It would be up to you 'ow you dealt wi' the mice. Once you 'ad the stuff.'

'Of course.'

Ivy inclined her head. 'I'll be in Snug tonight.'

'Thank you.'

'Terrible, isn't it? The price of brown ale,

these days?'

Sarah smiled. 'There'll be no need for you to pay owt so long as I'm behind the bar, Mrs Makepiece.'

Ivy raised an eyebrow. 'That's the sort of comment you expect a landlady to make, not just a barmaid.' Then she raised her cup to her chapped lips and slurped the tea. 'Here's to the future.'

Sarah raised her glass. 'The future.'

Pearl Crapper was concerned. No matter how grief-stricken, she'd anticipated Nellie would recover enough to attend Charlie's funeral in Southampton. However the morning of the funeral found Nellie vomiting into her chamber-pot. She'd not been able to keep anything down for forty-eight hours and painful retching dominated her day. Pearl had suggested calling in the doctor but Jim had diagnosed his wife as being sick with grief. 'It's just 'er sort of thing,' he had said, ''er way of remindin' us all that 'er reason for livin's died.'

Even Jim was surprised, though, when Nellie failed to rally for the funeral. He made a rare visit to her bedroom and, despite himself, was disturbed by her ashen appearance as she lay propped up in bed.

She looked drawn, her eyes sunken, her lips tinged with blue.

Jim had never intended to travel south for the funeral, thinking it a waste of time. While Charlie had languished in the Southampton military hospital he had never thought of visiting him and now that he was dead the trip seemed even more pointless. So while Jim served behind the bar and Nellie writhed in agony their son was buried by the hospital chaplain with two nurses in attendance, each unaware that the other had fallen for the dead patient.

Since she had tripped on a broken flagstone at the tender age of two, Ena Schofield had always taken her troubles to her mother Mary. The bond between the two women had always been strong, unlike that between Mary and her older daughter. Alice Schofield would never have dreamt of opening up to either of her parents. Mary knew that something was troubling Ena before she confided in her. Ena's natural optimism, outlook and positive nature were subdued and she appeared distracted. Mary knew it wasn't to do with being sacked from the mill. Ena had told her family that snippet of news as soon as it had happened. Indignant

Thomas had wanted to go round and sort the foreman out but Ena had calmly announced her intention to do her bit for the war effort.

The next afternoon she had returned home in a crisp new navy blue uniform and informed her impressed family that she was to be a conductress on the No. 14 tram, which ran from the depot on Rosamund Street into Salford and Manchester. Alice had made a cutting remark about Ena taking a man's job, but Thomas had soon silenced her.

With Thomas out playing dominoes at the Tripedressers with his mates, and Alice goodness knows where, Mary decided to tackle Ena as they ironed the family washing.

'What's to do, our Ena?' asked Mary, pausing to spit on the iron to test its warmth. There was no hiss so she placed it on top of the range and allowed herself a stretch.

'I don't know what you mean,' said Ena defensively.

'Yes, you do. You've 'ad a face on you that long it could be a pier.'

Ena sighed. She'd known she'd tell her mother at some point and now was as good a time as any. 'It's a lad.'

'Oh, aye?' said Mary casually. Inside her heart beat faster. Since Phil Moss's death she'd longed for Ena to find a new beau. It wasn't natural for a seventeen-year-old girl to live the life of an old maid because all the young men were either fighting or dead.

'You know that lad Minnie's fallen for?'

'The one with the daft name?'

'Aye, Armistead Caldwell.'

'Sounds like he should be 'awkin' patient medicines. "Armistead Caldwell's Cure-all Tonic".' Mary laughed at her joke and tested the iron again. This time a fiery hiss followed the spit. 'Is it a mate of 'is?' she asked.

'No, Mam, it's 'im,' said Ena sadly.

Mary stopped ironing and looked up in alarm. 'You've never fallen for same chap?'

'No,' said Ena. 'I think 'c's shifty and I'd trust 'im as far as I could chuck 'im.'

'I thought the same about yer father and I still married 'im, mind. They're easily trained are men. Easier than dogs.'

'I don't want to train Armistead Caldwell, I never want to see 'im again.'

Mary saw the anguish in her daughter's eyes and smiled sympathetically at her. 'I can guess what's 'appened,' she said.

'Can you?' Ena was surprised.

'Yer not the first lass to 'ave a friend's fella make a fool of 'imself over you. What 'appened? Did he make a grab for you when Minnie weren't lookin'?'

Ena nodded. ''E said I were the one 'e were interested in, not 'er.'

'And what did you say?'

'I said no.'

Mary nodded in approval. 'And now you think you ought to say summat to Minnie, eh?'

Ena looked at her mother in amazement. She always seemed able to read her mind.

Mary laughed at her awed expression. 'Yer me daughter, Ena. I know what goes on in yer 'ead. And before you ask, I think you know what I think.'

'I should tell 'er?'

'That's right.'

'But it'll break 'er 'eart.'

Mary carried on ironing, pointedly avoiding Ena's gaze. Ena sighed and carefully folded one of her father's shirts. 'I'll tell 'er tomorrow after work.'

Her mother was right. If it had been Ena in Minnie's place she'd want to know. And then she'd tell Armistead Caldwell exactly what she thought of him.

'I reckon we should fetch doctor,' said Pearl, her arms deep in the sink of dirty dishes.

Sarah, who stood by with a tea-towel ready to dry, stiffened. 'Yes, that's a good idea,' she said slowly.

Pearl sighed with relief. 'I'm glad you think so. 'Appen Mr Corbishley'll listen to you. 'E won't take a blind bit o' notice o' me.'

Sarah shrugged. ''E doesn't want to bother the doctor,' she said.

'Doesn't want to part wi' two shillin's more like,' replied Pearl. 'I think it's a cryin' shame the way 'e treats Mrs Corbishley. 'E's fair ignored 'er since she took to 'er bed.'

''E's a lot on wi' runnin' pub,' said Sarah.

'If 'e can find time to go watchin' two men knock seven bells out o' each other 'e's got time to climb a few stairs to see 'ow 'is sick wife is.'

Jim's outing to a local amateur boxing match the previous evening hadn't impressed Pearl. She would have had plenty more to say on the subject if she had known Sarah had accompanied him.

Sarah placed a clean plate in the crockery cupboard. 'A fella's got to 'ave an 'obby,' she said, masking the smirk that threatened to spread across her face. 'Besides, I thought Nellie were on the mend.'

Pearl had worked at the Rover's three years longer than Sarah and would never dream of referring to their employer in such a way. She looked at the barmaid with distaste and said, 'Mrs Corbishley is still very poorly.'

'If she's not gerrin' any worse I don't see the point o' callin' the doctor out.'

'But she's not gettin' any better,' said Pearl. 'I'm worried.'

'You're always worried,' said Sarah, not unkindly. She looked at the worn and weary woman beside her: grey hair scraped back over a pointed head in a bun, shoulders that sagged in a race with her breasts over which would hit the floor first.

'Will you 'ave a word wi' Mr Corbishley?' asked Pearl.

Sarah nodded. 'If you think it'll 'elp.'

Three minutes later Sarah put out a hand to stop Jim from walking upstairs in the Rover's hallway. 'Pearl thinks you should send for a doctor,' she said.

'What do you think?' he asked directly.

'I think you ought to kiss me,' she replied sweetly, before parting her lips to meet his.

'Fares please.'

Ena had been given a new lease on life since starting as a conductress. She'd swapped the noisy, constrictive mill for the travelling life, meeting different people rather than staring into the old familiar faces all the time. Already she was getting to know her regulars and her easy way with conversation made her a hit among those used to the severe male conductors who had worked the route before. The No. 14 wasn't an open-topped tram but Ena had her fill of fresh air as she stood on the tailboard as it travelled up and down the streets. Not that the air was ever fresh in Weatherfield, with its mill chimneys pumping out smoke, but it certainly beat wearing her fingers to the bone on the looms.

Now the tram was nearing its final destination, the depot on Rosamund Street. It had been a long day and Ena was looking forward to the potato pie her mother was preparing for dinner. It was dark and cold, and she had sighed in annoyance as a man jumped on board and ran up the stairs to sit on the top deck. Slowly she pulled herself up the stairwell and headed towards him. 'Fares, please.'

'Just to the depot,' he said, and his face broke into a smile. 'Miss Schofield.'

She handed him his ticket and took the money he offered. It was correct. 'Mr Sharples,' she said.

'I didn't know you worked the trams,' he said.

'I bet you don't know a lot of things.'

As Ena made no attempt to move away, Alfred was encouraged to carry on the conversation. 'I've been into town,' he said. ''Ad me final medical. I'm back off overseas next week.'

The news disturbed Ena. As he spoke she realised that she enjoyed bumping into Alfred. He always seemed so pleased to see her. 'Yer father'll miss you. 'E'll 'ave no one to 'elp 'im pull wool over eyes of the gullible,' she teased.

Alfred laughed. 'I stopped 'elpin' 'im wi' all that weeks ago,' he said.

'Really? Why?'

He shrugged.

''Appen someone made me realise the folly of me ways.' He grinned mischievously at her, and she found herself laughing. She didn't believe him for one minute but it was good to share a joke. 'Look,' he said, ''ave you got much longer to work?'

'I finish when we 'it the depot.'

'Really?' His face lit up. 'I don't suppose you'd let me walk you 'ome?'

Ena didn't have to consider the question. 'That would be nice,' she said.

After she'd handed in her ticket machine and pulled on the outsize overcoat that was part of her uniform, Ena caught up with Alfred at the depot doors and they started off down the street. 'Where do you live?' he asked.

'Inkerman Street, but I'm not goin' straight 'ome. I've to pay a call on my friend in Palmerston Street.'

'That's the other side of the viaduct, isn't it?'

'Aye.'

They walked in silence but it was comfortable. When she thought he wasn't looking Ena snatched glimpses of her companion as they walked under the gas-lamps. He wasn't the best-looking lad in the world, his nose was long and his eyes were close together, but she recognised a gentle spirit when she saw one.

He offered her a Woodbine but she refused. He agreed that it was disgusting when women smoked. She then blurted out

259

that she didn't drink either, and noted that he didn't condemn female drinkers so quickly. 'I've signed the Pledge,' she said.

'You religious, then?' he asked.

'I'm a Christian,' she replied, 'if that's what you mean.'

'I've never given the matter much thought.'

'Well, you ought. We're not on this earth for long and there's all of eternity to think about.'

He laughed and she turned on him sharply. 'What's so funny?'

'You're a rum 'un, Ena Schofield,' he said, his cigarette sticking out of the corner of his mouth.

'I'm not. I'm a decent, God-fearing lass. I see nowt wrong in 'onourin' 'Im who put us 'ere in first place, and if you don't stop laughin' I'll be walkin' rest o' way on me tod.'

Alfred straightened his face. 'Sorry,' he said. 'I didn't mean to upset you.'

'It takes more than that to upset me,' she said. 'I take it you enjoy yer drink.'

'Oh, aye,' he said shamelessly. 'When ye're in a trench stood ankle-deep in mud wi Gerry shootin' at yer 'ead, a drop o' rum's the only thing that keeps you going. I've seen new fellas startin' off shakin' their 'eads when they see the bottle mekkin' the rounds but 'alf a day later they're reachin' for it as it passes like the rest o' us. It warms yer and meks yer forget, just for a bit.'

Ena felt ashamed of her piety. 'I can't begin to imagine what it's like out there.'

'No,' he said simply, 'you can't.'

'And ye're goin' back to all that?'

'It's not like I've got much choice in matter,' he said. 'Doctor sez I'm better so back I go.'

She stopped walking and clutched his arm in alarm. 'You'll tek care o' yerself, won't you?'

Alfred glanced down at her hand and smiled ruefully. 'I'm not dyin' over there, Ena. If I was, that bullet would've gone through me 'eart, not me shoulder. There's only one bullet wi' my name on it and it were pulled out of me shoulder months back.'

'Good.'

'Would you write to me?'

It was the second time she'd been asked that question in a week, only this time she didn't need to think twice. 'Of course I will. Not that I'm one for much writin'.'

'No matter,' he said. 'Just a note now an' then.'

'Aye.'

'Aye.'

The couple stood outside the fish-monger's. The air was thick with the smell of fish and Ena kicked out at a fish head that lay abandoned in the doorway She couldn't think of anything to say.

A woman drew close to them and stopped. Ena was disturbed by the way she was looking at them. 'Hello, Alfred,' she said. 'I thought it were you.'

Alfred turned in alarm and gasped at the sight of her. 'Muriel...'

'You take some tracking down,' she said coldly.

Ena felt sick and she didn't understand why. Alfred looked stunned, as if he'd seen a ghost and, judging from the woman's tones, it wasn't a friendly one. 'Alfred...' she said quietly.

The woman sneered. 'Who's this, then, Alfred? Aren't you going to introduce us?'

'Ena, this is Muriel.' His voice was dead, his head bowed.

Ena looked at the woman. She was older than herself and Alfred, well dressed with a fur collar on her coat. Her face was hard, and as cold as stone.

'I'm his wife, dear,' the woman said.

Ena recoiled as if she had been slapped across the face. She stared at Alfred, who had the grace to look away. 'You're married?' she asked, her voice choking.

'I can explain–'

'I doubt it,' Ena interrupted, and before he could say anything else she ran down the street, her heart pounding, tears in her eyes. She felt humiliated and very hurt.

Mary Schofield looked up from her sewing, surprised to see Ena back home so early. 'I thought you were callin' on Minnie,' she said. 'Weren't she in?'

'I changed me mind,' said Ena sharply. ''Appen she's better off not knowin' the truth.'

Mary frowned as her daughter ran up the stairs and slammed into her bedroom overhead. Whatever was the matter now?

CHAPTER NINE

May 1917

Gladys Arkwright pulled on her white gloves and picked up her copy of the King James Bible. The book was well thumbed, with leather bookmarks and pieces of paper sticking out of it, marking particular passages. She moved over to where an ornate mirror hung between a painting of a stag and a framed picture of Jesus calming the storm. She gazed at her reflection and tilted her hat slightly to the right. For a moment she practised looking stern, then smiled brightly at herself. 'I think I'm just about ready,' she said.

Behind her, sitting on a horsehair *chaise longue*, Ena Schofield sighed. Gladys caught sight of her expression in the mirror. 'Are you going to have that look on your face all day?' she demanded. 'You look downright miserable.'

'I *am* downright miserable,' said Ena, fidgeting with her own Bible, a small, well-worn copy that had been given to her mother on her confirmation back in 1881.

'Could you try not to be? Just for today?'

'I'll do me best,' said Ena.

'I suppose that'll have to do,' said Gladys, looking round the vestry for her hatpin. There was no wind but Gladys always prided herself on being prepared for all eventualities. Her handbag contained a hand-stitched handkerchief and a bottle of smelling salts. Just in case. 'It's come round quick,' she said, as she rooted around the top of her Welsh dresser. 'Strikes me, we have Easter and then before we know it it's Whit. Third Sunday in May today. There was a time I used to bounce out of bed looking forward to it. Those were the days when I still had faith in human nature.'

'Don't you no more?' asked Ena.

'Put it this way, love, there's not much of it dwelling in Coronation Street.'

'Don't put me off,' said Ena. 'It's only my first time at it.'

Gladys shrugged. 'You'd rather I were honest, wouldn't you?' she asked.

'I suppose.'

Gladys waved her hatpin triumphantly and speared her hat with it. She looked at Ena's long face. 'Oh, Ena, for goodness sake get a grip on yourself. You're not the first lass to make a fool of herself over a married man and you're not going to be the last. That wife of his did you a favour. Stopped you getting involved more than you had. Has he come calling since?'

Ena snorted. 'As if he would. I wouldn't give him the time of day. I made my feelings very clear on the subject.'

'Good. So let's just forget Alfred Sharples even exists, shall we?'

'Aye, you're right.'

'Come on, lass,' said Gladys, in a kinder tone. 'There's souls to be saved, so let's be having you.'

Ena heaved herself up from the sofa and straightened her long, black skirt. She'd ironed a blouse especially for the occasion and wore her Sunday best hat – black straw with tiny cherries tied on to the band.

Gladys eyed her up and down appreciatively. 'Onwards, Ena, and remember, don't be discouraged.'

Ten minutes later, Ena and Gladys took up their positions outside the entrance to the Rover's Return Inn. Gladys opened her carpet bag and produced a tambourine which looked as if it had seen better days.

She gave it a rattle and tapped the pigskin to test it, then nodded to Ena, who cast an eye up and down the Street. At eight o'clock on a Sunday morning it was deserted. Wishing she'd never volunteered for the day ahead she smiled nervously at Gladys and then started singing.

'What a friend we have in Jesus,
All our sins and grief to bear!
What a privilege to carry
Everything to God in prayer!'

Ena's voice grew confident as she sang, with Gladys keeping time on the tambourine and tapping the toe of her boot on the pavement, but before she reached the second verse she was disturbed by the scraping noise of a sash window being pulled up sharply.

'Oy!'

Ena carried on singing while Gladys stepped out on to the cobbles to discover who had shouted. She didn't have to look far. Leaning out of the top window at No.1 Coronation Street was the bare torso of Alfie Marsh.

'What the bleedin' 'ell do you think ye're doin'?' he demanded.

'Singing praises to the Lord, sir. Would you care to join us?'

'No, I bleedin' well wouldn't. Shut up, will yer? I'm still in bed!' Alfie glared down at her, his moustache twitching angrily.

'The sun's been up for nearly four hours. It's a beautiful morning, sir. Are you certain you won't join us in a song of praise?'

Alfie looked at Gladys as if she were mad. 'If I come down there it'll be to put me fist in yer mouth. That'll stop yer noise,' he warned.

'Jesus loves you too, sir,' said Gladys, with a smile, and rattled her tambourine.

Another window opened, this time directly above the women's heads. Pearl Crapper looked down. 'I say, Mrs Arkwright...'

Gladys looked up and greeted her with a wave. 'Isn't it a lovely morning, Mrs Crapper?'

Pearl chose to ignore the question and shouted down, 'I've a sick woman up here in need of her sleep.'

'Don't worry,' said Gladys, 'nothing heals the sick faster than having the wonder of Jesus sung to them. Leave the window open and she'll be able to hear us all day.'

'All day!' Pearl stared down at the women, then remembered. 'Oh, it's not today, is it?'

'It certainly is,' beamed Gladys.

Pearl sighed. 'I'd best tell Mr Corbishley,' she said, and disappeared back into the bedroom.

The news Pearl bore to her employer made him groan across the breakfast table. He sagged his shoulders and ran a hand through his receding hair. 'It can't be a year since the last one,' he said in despair.

'It is,' said Pearl sadly.

'I don't see what the fuss is all about,' said Sarah Bridges, spreading a generous helping of quince jelly on a slice of bread. Pearl regarded her with disgust.

'I'll tell you what the fuss is about,' said Jim, spitting crumbs across the table. 'I've got a bunch of 'Oly Joes stood outside mi front door all day stoppin' all me regulars and tellin' 'em to sign the bleedin' Pledge.'

'How many sign?' asked Sarah.

Jim shrugged. 'I dunno. One or two.'

'Well, then, what's one or two? Let 'em sing. I like a nice hymn or two.'

'You won't be saying that this afternoon,' said Pearl sourly. 'After listening to "Tell Me The Old Old Story" for the ninth time. Fair drives the customers out of the place.'

'Aye,' agreed Jim. 'Worse than a fart in a

hat box. Religion and pubs don't mix.'

Sarah screwed up her nose at the analogy. Jim's coarseness was getting on her nerves. What had once seemed vaguely amusing was now offensive. The night before last he'd belched in bed before grunting and rolling off her. She now understood why Nellie had opted years ago for her own bedroom.

Pearl poured a cup of tea and made to carry it out of the room. 'If ye're interested I'll let you know if she drinks this,' she said drily, to Jim.

'You do that,' he replied, scanning the newspaper headlines.

'Shall I say you were askin' after 'er?'

'If you like.'

Pearl sniffed and left the room. Over the past few months she'd exerted all her energy in nursing Nellie. Some days she seemed almost back to her old self but then she'd have a bad night, bringing up the contents of her stomach and turning as pale as chalk. Jim's nonchalance annoyed Pearl. He had agreed to bring in a doctor, after Sarah had nagged him, but Nellie's health had picked up in the few days before his visit and he'd put her ailments down to the grief of Charlie's death. Jim had been quick to point out that this had been his own diagnosis, and since then Pearl had soldiered on in silence.

Martha Hartley peered round the corner of the Rover's Return into Coronation Street. Ena was still there, standing outside the pub doors singing bleakly to an empty street. Martha shook her head in despair. Surely there were better things to do on a Sunday lunchtime than sing in solitude?

She felt a tugging on her blouse and turned in irritation. 'Give over.'

'Is she still there?' asked Minnie Carlton anxiously.

'Yes, she is. You'd think by now she'd be in need of a break. I know I would, wi' my bladder.'

'We'll 'ave to go the long way round,' Minnie said mournfully.

'I don't see why,' said Martha. 'It's comin' to summat when you can't walk down a street for fear o' someone who calls 'erself yer friend jumpin' you and gerrin' you to sing hymns.'

'Yes, and I don't fancy it,' said Minnie. 'It's best if we just cut through Crimea Street then go down by the cemetery till we reach Tile Street and work our way back.'

'That's no good cos we'd 'ave to cross Victoria Street and she's bound to see us. We'll 'ave to go right down to the docks and work our way up.'

'I can't walk all that way. I've gorra bunion,' Minnie whined.

Martha gave her friend a hard stare. 'It were your idea in't first place. It's you that wants to go to the fair, not me. And why do you want to go? To 'ave yer 'and read. And why do you want yer 'and read? To see if you and that fella you don't stop goin' on about are gonna get wed.'

Minnie looked uncomfortable. Everything Martha had said was true but the way she'd said it, all critical and nasty, made it sound silly. 'I can't 'elp thinkin',' she said defensively.

Martha shook her head in despair. 'You'd do best to leave all the thinkin' to me and Ena. Face it, love, you weren't first in the queue when they were 'andin' out brains.'

Minnie flushed and would have retorted, if Ena hadn't interrupted her. 'I thought I 'eard yer voice, Martha. It's very kind of you to come lendin' yer support.'

Martha smiled nervously at her friend. 'Oh, is it today you do yer singin'?' she asked.

'Aye, it is, and yer just in time for the lunchtime rush.'

'Oh, Ena, I'm sorry, but I've just nipped out on an errand for me mother,' lied Martha.

Ena eyed her up and down and pointed to her feet. 'See you've got yer best Sunday shoes on. Them with the buckle.'

Martha flushed.

'Come on, it won't tek you long. Just a couple o' hymns to swell the ranks.'

As Ena walked back into Coronation Street Martha turned on Minnie. 'That's your fault,' she hissed. 'If you 'adn't kept on talkin' we could 'ave sneaked off and she'd 'ave never known.'

The presence of the temperance parade outside the pub did nothing to deter the staunch regulars of the Rover's. If anything they appeared to have rallied extra troops in an act of defiance. Jim Corbishley had a happy smile spread across his face as he threw coins into the till drawer and watched Sarah Bridges pulling pints.

'You're lookin' pleased wi' yerself,' remarked Ivy Makepiece, from her chair in the Snug.

'Am I?' Jim said, wiping spilt beer from off

the bar counter.

'That Arkwright woman tried to stop me as I came in. I just shoved 'er out o' way. She's bin after me to sign that bit o' paper for years. You'd think by now she'd 'ave given up.'

'She's a stubborn one,' agreed Jim.

'She's wastin' 'er time. None o' this lot are gonna give up the only bit o' pleasure they 'ave in their miserable lives.' Without drawing breath, Ivy changed the subject. 'Talking about miserable lives, 'ave you 'eard about that Gertie 'Ewitt from No.3 lettin' her own mother be buried on the parish?'

Although Ivy's role in her own mother's death was common knowledge it didn't stop her taking the moral high ground over her neighbour. The Makepieces and Hewitts had been sworn enemies for years, since a dispute over a job, and Ivy took delight in criticising Gertie or any of her clan, especially now, when her Ralph had been killed while Thomas Hewitt was still unscathed.

'Really?' Jim hated listening to the local gossips but knew to sound interested in order to encourage Ivy to spend more over the bar.

''Er own mother, shut away in that awful workhouse, dyin' all alone on an infested mattress. It's not 'ow I'd want to go. And what does that Gertie 'Ewitt do? I'll tell you what she doesn't do. She don't claim 'er mother like a decent Christian should. Oh, no. She lets the parish bury 'er in a pauper's grave.'

Ivy's tirade ended abruptly when Sarah called across from the beer pumps, 'Jim, bitter's off.' Sarah shrugged apologetically to the waiting customers, and offered mild or bottles as an alternative. The customers grimaced.

Jim set off to change the barrel in the cellar, leaving Sarah kicking her heels. She nodded to Ivy and wandered over to her. 'Funny creatures, fellas,' she said. 'I can't stand the taste o' bitter but this lot won't touch owt else.'

'Men *are* funny. My Alf were the same. Fine if I 'ad 'is tea on table the moment 'e stepped foot in the 'ouse but if I didn't...' she pulled a face. 'Blue murder.'

'Did 'e 'it you?' asked Sarah.

'Oh, I've been black and blue. When 'e were taken I may 'ave bin left wi' seven bairns but at least me ears stopped ringin'.'

'I couldn't do wi' a fella 'ittin' me,' said Sarah in disgust. 'There's no call for that.'

Ivy sat back in her chair and motioned for

Sarah to lean across the bar. She glanced around to ensure no one was listening then hissed, 'Talkin' about fellas, how are things between you and...?'

'Jim? Oh ... you know.'

Ivy looked upwards and grinned. 'You know, I'd 'ave laid money on 'er droppin' off 'er perch be now.'

Sarah shifted awkwardly. 'She should 'ave done but she's very well cared for. That Pearl Crapper's a cross 'tween a nursemaid and a guard dog. She's taken to sniffin' 'er food now.'

Ivy pulled a face. 'What you doin' about that?' she asked.

Sarah sighed. 'To be honest, I'm not that bothered no more. If she wants to 'ang on to life that much then I reckon I'll just let 'er be. Not that you can call it much of a life. Bein' wed to Jim Corbishley.'

'Is it no good ... you know ... bed?'

Sarah blushed. 'There's a lot o' talk but very little action.'

'My Alf were just the same. The pencil were always sharp but the lead kept runnin' out.'

'Well, Jim's lead's broken, or it might as well be for what good I get out of it.' Sarah played with a curl and cast an eye in the

277

direction of the Public bar. She winked at Ivy and sniggered. 'Anyway, 'e's not the only one in me life just now.'

Ivy's eyes widened and she craned her neck sideways to see into the main bar. The usual crowd stood around drinking, or waiting for the bitter to come back on. Harry Popplewell from No. 7, overweight Fred Piggott, sour-faced Ned Buck, Alfie Marsh from next door and Tommy Foyle, the wounded shopkeeper. Ivy ruled out Ned and Alfie considering them too old for herself, let alone a youngster like Sarah, and Harry and Fred didn't seem the roving sort so that left only one. ''Im from shop?' she asked.

'I did consider 'im but I 'eard tell the bullet hit more than 'is leg, if you know what I mean.'

Ivy nodded sagely. 'Which one?' she asked.

'Alfie Marsh,' said Sarah slyly. 'He's what I'd call a real man.'

'Really?' Ivy's mind raced.

The conversation was cut short by the arrival of Jim from the cellar. 'Bitter's back on,' he announced to cheers.

Sarah disengaged herself and went back to the pumps. 'Right, Mr Marsh,' she said, with a cheeky grin, 'you're next.'

Inside No. 3 Coronation Street, Gertie Hewitt was almost in tears. All day she'd listened to Ena singing and Gladys preaching – the sound seemed to echo around her terraced house. Although the spring sunlight was a welcome change from the long shadows of winter, the house still felt cold and bare, the joy gone since Thomas had been seduced into joining up that fateful night at the Bijou. He'd been home only once on leave, and had been a changed man, with dull eyes and a battle-scarred mind. Flo, now eighteen, continued to work at Baker's factory, alongside Martha Hartley, whilst Molly, the baby, was growing up without a father. Gertie's eyesight was going and she had been sacked from the mill after failing to spot mistakes on her loom work. The family were supported by Flo's wages now and what bits of food Gertie could pilfer from the local shops and markets.

The first time she had stolen an apple from the Corner Shop Gertie had been filled with remorse, but the sight of hungry Molly devouring it had urged her on to repeat the offence again and again. She'd become skilful in stealing from under shopkeeper's noses, with her outsized shawl, now hanging off her bony shoulders, providing plenty of room for packets and tins.

Gertie had been ashamed to let her mother spend her final days in the old Weatherfield workhouse. At the turn of the century the sinister building had housed hundreds of the poorest of society, who, on entering the large wooden gates on Arkwright Street, knew that their fate was sealed. Hardly anyone left the workhouse other than feet first in a cardboard coffin, to be buried in a pauper's grave. No service, no hymns sung over the dead, just a hole in the ground and a few gabbled words. Much of the workhouse had fallen into disrepair and Bets Pegg had died after only three weeks in the draughty, miserable place. The warden had told Gertie that she'd simply lost the will to live. Gertie had attended her mother's funeral in St Mary's graveyard and had prayed no one had recognised her. Her prayer hadn't been answered, though: from the sly looks she had received in the Street and the shop she was aware that people *knew*.

Flo had spent her Sunday afternoon visiting a friend, eager to escape the hymn-singing, but as Molly was in bed with a fever Gertie had been imprisoned, forced to listen to Ena singing verse after verse, chorus after chorus. When Molly had eventually fallen asleep Gertie felt able to nip out and borrow a cup of sugar from Mrs Marsh next door. As she entered the hallway she realised something was amiss and paused against the banisters before she worked out what it was: the singing had stopped.

Outside the Rover's Return, Gladys packed away her tambourine and smiled at the weary Ena, who tried, but failed to muster a smile in return. 'We've done very well today,' said Gladys heartily.

'But no one signed the Pledge,' croaked Ena.

Gladys waved a hand dismissively in the air. 'We did the ground work, the Lord will do the rest.'

The Rover's door opened and Jim saw out his lunchtime customers. As usual, it was Ivy Makepiece who tottered out last. She blinked in the sunlight, then cleared her throat and spat into the gutter.

'Off you go, then, Ivy,' said Jim, moving back into the empty pub and bolting the doors after his customers.

Ivy stood for a moment, and rotated her hunched shoulders. She was hungry and hoped her daughters had left her something tasty from the lunch they had made for the children. Ivy had long since given up cooking and cleaning. What was the point in having three capable girls in the house and waiting on them hand and foot? She'd done her bit, and now it was their turn to look after her.

Ivy regarded Ena and Gladys disdainfully as they walked back to the Mission vestry. She set off in the same direction but as she passed No. 3 the front door opened and she came face to face with Gertie Hewitt. Gertie attempted to ignore her and stepped back into her house, making as if to close the door behind her.

However, drink had spurred Ivy and she was in a feisty mood. Surprisingly quickly, she stuck out her arm and caught the door, forcing it open. Gertie glared at her and tried to wrench her hand free but Ivy stood firm. 'You're good at slammin' doors in folk's faces,' said Ivy, with a sneer. 'Wonder 'ow yer mother felt 'avin' it slammed in 'ers?'

Gertie did not flinch.

'Talk about a daughter's gratitude,' continued Ivy, 'you go through hours of painful childbirth and what do they do in return?

Let the parish bury you on the cheap. Not even a wooden cross to mark the spot.'

Gertie gave up trying to close the door and folded her bony arms defiantly.

'Ye're one to talk about daughterly gratitude,' she said, 'you who murdered yer own mother.'

Ivy glared at her. ''Ow dare you say such a lie?' she screeched. Ena and Gladys turned to look at her as she pulled herself up to her full five feet two inches. 'My mother, God rest 'er soul, died of a 'eart attack. It said so on the death certificate. Course we can't ask you what it said on your mother's death certificate, can we? On account of you never settin' eyes on it.' Ivy stared at Gertie then spat on her doorstep. 'You're an evil-minded slut and Coronation Street would be a better place without you and yours in it!'

The door to No. 9 opened and Ned Buck stepped out on to the pavement. 'What's the racket?' he shouted. 'Can't a fella get 'is 'ead down no more on a Sunday? If it's not bleedin' hymns it's women shoutin' at each other!'

'It's 'er you want to be 'avin' a go at,' yelled Ivy, pointing at Gertie. ''Er who let 'er own mother die in workhouse.'

'Is that right?' Ned sucked his clay pipe.

'That ain't no way to be carryin' on.'

'That's just what I were sayin', Mr Buck,' said Ivy piously.

Now Gertie slammed the door shut in Ivy's face. She leant against the back of it, tears of fury welling in her eyes. Hunger was something she could just about cope with, but Ivy Makepiece's public goading was a different matter.

The evening stillness of Coronation Street was shattered just after nine fifteen by the sound of breaking glass. Ena, who had been asleep on Gladys's bed, woke with a start and struggled to work out where she was. By the time she got her bearings Gladys was already at the vestry door, peering outside.

'What was that?' asked Ena.

'From what I can gather, someone's thrown a brick through the window of the Hewitts' house.'

'Who'd do a thing like that?'

'Well, judging from the speed Ned Buck bolted into his house, I'd say he did.'

Gladys watched a couple of doors opening on the other side of the street. Ivy Makepiece appeared at the doorway of No. 11 and peered down towards the broken window. She was joined by Alfie Marsh, who shouted to his wife to stay indoors.

'You know,' said Gladys, 'I've never seen Mrs Marsh... He keeps her in there all the time. What a life the poor woman must have.'

Gertie's door opened and she stepped out tentatively on to the pavement. She cast a wary eye around the street, anticipating another attack. Close on her heels came Flo.

'Who's out there?' asked Flo.

Gertie didn't answer. Instead she glanced at Ivy then darted back into the house. Flo stepped out and took in the smashed window. Breaking windows was a spiteful thing to do, she thought, especially if you knew the owner couldn't afford to replace them.

'It'll be kids,' said Alfie gruffly.

'Why us, though?' asked Flo.

Alfie shrugged. 'Kids don't need reasons.'

Flo was propelled out of the way by Gertie as she descended the stairs and stormed out of the house carrying the chamber-pot that had sat, unemptied, beneath her bedstead all day. She moved with surprising agility down the street, crunching broken glass under her clogs.

'Bitch,' she screamed at Ivy, then threw the contents of the pot into her face. The impact shocked Ivy and froze her sneer. She stared at her enemy, then screeched in fury and flung herself upon Gertie.

Flo was rooted to the spot but Alfie Marsh roared with delight as Gertie and Ivy fell on to the cobbles, clawing at flesh, clothing and hair.

When Gertie cried out in pain Flo sprang into action: she jumped on top of Ivy and tried to wrench her off Gertie. The commotion attracted attention from other households and, seeing their mother being assaulted by Hewitts, Mary and Lil Makepiece hurried to help her. For a slight young woman Flo put up considerable opposition to the Makepiece girls and the mass of kicking legs and pounding hands rolled around the street over the cobbles.

Alfie Marsh cheered on the fight, unconcerned that Gertie had lost two teeth, that Ivy's nose and ear were bleeding, and that Flo had pulled a clump of hair from Mary's head.

From the Mission doorway Gladys attempted to block Ena's view, saying that it was no sight for good Christian women. When Ena suggested that they try to help, she said, 'You don't try and stop women in a fight. There's only one sure way to

286

separate them,' and nodded towards the Rovers' door where Jim Corbishley stood with a large pail of water. He stepped forward and tipped it over the heap of women. As one they gasped and relaxed their hold on each other, giving Jim and Alfie the chance to wade in and pull them apart.

'Now then,' shouted Jim, 'that's enough.'

Ivy shook herself free of the landlord's hands and glared defiantly at him. 'Don't you dare to tell me that's enough, Jim Corbishley. I never started this fight but I'm damned certain I'm goin' to finish it!'

As Gertie struggled to regain her composure and smeared blood from her cut lip over her cheek with the back of her trembling hand, Ivy ran back into her house only to reappear almost immediately. In her hand she carried her rent book. She made certain her neighbours were watching before she opened it and lifting it high in the air, thrusting it towards Gertie.

Gertie drew breath sharply. She knew Ivy was offering the ultimate challenge: her rent was paid up to date. Gertie hung her head in shame: she couldn't run into the house and brandish her own rent book. She was defeated and Ivy's victorious face showed that she knew it. Flo put out a hand for Gertie's and led her indoors.

Three days after Gertie and Ivy's public fight, Sarah Bridges decided she couldn't carry on. What had started out as a dalliance with her employer had turned into an oppressive situation in which she felt trapped and used. She was an ambitious young woman and knew she was wasting her life serving behind the Rover's bar. It was no longer enough that she was the pub's main attraction. Appreciative looks over the counter didn't keep a girl in jewellery or perfume and she'd been mistaken in thinking that Jim would be a generous lover. His gifts and little attentions had been quick to wane and now she felt more married to him than poor Nellie, who continued to languish in her bed. At least Nellie didn't have to put up with his drunken fumblings.

Sarah felt guilty about Nellie. True, at first she had hoped the potion with which Ivy provided for her, the result of soaking arsenic-covered flypapers in water, would send Nellie forward into an early death. She'd convinced herself that, with her beloved Charlie dead, Nellie had nothing to live for, and that Nellie knew what was going on and readily drank whatever was offered, in the hope of a speedy encounter with St Peter. Now, if she had Jim Corbishley as a husband, Sarah felt certain that she'd embrace death enthusiastically too. Her heart hadn't been in the poisoning, though, and she had abandoned the fly papers. Nellie continued to languish, though, her digestive system wrecked and her will to live minimal.

Sarah had no axe to grind with Nellie, who had always been a fair, if firm, landlady. Nellie had taken her in when she'd first arrived in Manchester from Liverpool with her battered case and worn-out shoes. She'd clothed her, sheltered and fed her, and Sarah had attempted to kill her.

Sarah stood in the open doorway of Nellie's bedroom. The curtains were drawn, blocking out the spring light and Nellie lay in bed, her slight body covered with sheets, blankets and an eiderdown, her head supported by a single pillow. A jug containing washing water stood on the wash stand next to the bed, a cracked bowl bearing the same floral print next to it. It was empty, as Pearl Crapper was too conscientious to leave it full of used water. On a small table beside the brass bedstead lay a book, *Jane Eyre*, and a glass of water, in which floated an upper set of false teeth. Sarah felt sadness as she stepped back on to the landing.

As she did so a floorboard creaked and Nellie turned her head. Her eyes were dead but they met Sarah's own. Slowly Nellie beckoned her to step into the room, to come closer and attend to her. Keeping her gaze on Nellie's sunken eyes and pale face, Sarah slowly walked over the faded rug towards her.

Nellie attempted to raise her head from the pillow. Her mouth moved silently so Sarah leant forward, placing her ear close to Nellie's cracked lips. Her own glossy hair brushed against the invalid's cheek.

'Finish it...' Nellie croaked, '...please...'

'I don't understand,' whispered Sarah, terrified.

'Don't leave me with him,' gasped Nellie, *'please.'*

Sarah drew back and gazed down at her. Her eyes moistened as Nellie stared up at her and repeated, 'Please...'

'I'm so sorry, I never meant...'

Nellie lifted a finger and shook it. 'I want to die,' she said.

Sarah and Ivy met in secret. The older woman's face carried the marks of her battle with Gertie: one eye was half closed with vicious bruising and the skin of her left cheek was grazed. The knowledge that she had won the encounter did little to ease the aches and pains inflicted by the rough cobbles, and she carried a deep resentment towards Jim who had drenched and humiliated her. The prospect of helping his sick wife escape him once and for all appealed to her.

Whilst Ivy locked herself away in her scullery, standing on a chair to root out a small earthenware jar long since hidden away, Sarah made her own plans. If all went according to plan Nellie would be dead within the week and Sarah had no intention of hanging around when questions were asked. She had always travelled light. The only addition to her belongings since joining the staff at the pub were trinkets Jim had bought her in the first flush of infatuation. They held no sentimental value for her and would convert to cash over the pawnbroker's counter.

One thought troubled Sarah. She'd been careful not to administer the arsenic to Nellie herself, always placing it in the food and drink Pearl prepared in the kitchen for the invalid's tray. Now, though, Sarah felt it would be relatively easy to administer the lethal dose in a drink directly to Nellie – after all, she did want to die. However, the thought of actually murdering someone, of lifting that frail head and pouring poison down the throat, didn't appeal to her at all. And she didn't see why Jim shouldn't be involved...

'One dose won't do it. Two should. Maybe three,' Ivy muttered.

'What is it?' asked Sarah, peering into the jar Ivy handed her, which contained a small quantity of grey powder.

'You don't want to know,' said Ivy mysteriously. 'All you need to do is make sure she takes it all. It tastes bitter but there's no smell, so put it in warm milk.'

Sarah's hand shook as she took the jar.

'You sure about this?' asked Ivy.

Sarah nodded. 'It's what she wants.'

Ivy could understand why Nellie wanted to die: married to Jim, with her only son and comfort dead, the future must look bleak. She sighed. Her own future didn't look too bright either but she was a fighter. Ivy Makepiece would never give up. As long as she had a breath in her body she'd battle on.

Jim took the cup of warm milk up the stairs and cautiously entered his wife's bedroom. He hadn't been keen on making this rare visit to her room but Sarah had nagged him, urging him to show some husbandly concern.

'It's only a cup of milk,' she'd said. 'You won't 'ave to sit and chat to 'er.'

The creaking floorboard in the doorway warned Nellie of her husband's arrival. She instinctively knew that Sarah had prepared the milk and that she had done so for her benefit. She gazed at her husband and felt nothing: no love, no hatred, nothing. Only indifference. If he was to be her administering angel then so be it. He looked awkward, standing over her, cup in hand, unsure what to do.

She decided to help him and craned her neck, which made him place a hand roughly under her head, to support her as she drank. When her lips touched the warm liquid, she didn't hesitate. She drank.

Jim stood awkwardly, one hand under Nellie's head, the other supporting the cup at her mouth, his back bent over the bed. Passing on the landing, Pearl Crapper took in the sight and gasped. To see Jim in her mistress's bedroom was one thing, to see him helping her to drink was another. What was she drinking? It was nothing that Pearl had prepared. Alarmed, she rested her foot on the creaking board and rocked forward. The wood groaned beneath her weight.

Jim's head whipped round and, sensing trouble, Nellie tried to gulp down the last of the milk.

'You should let me do that, Mr Corbishley,' said Pearl coldly. She stepped into the room and held out her hand. Jim shrugged and handed over the cup, which still contained a third of its original contents. If Pearl wanted to nurse Nellie that was fine by him. He had the racing results to check.

As Jim left the room Nellie closed her eyes and gulped down the last of the milk.

Next to the bed, Pearl raised the cup to her own mouth and cautiously licked it. She noticed the bitterness immediately and shuddered, her suspicions confirmed.

Under cover of night Pearl sneaked out of the pub with the cup. Dr Hawkins lived in a large house on the Oakhill Road – Pearl had visited it before as her friend cleaned for the doctor and his wife. She had never called on him as a patient, though, unable to afford his fees, but she figured that poison was poison and no doctor would turn her away.

Her departure from the pub did not go unnoticed. As she watched Pearl's bulky frame hurry into the night, Sarah hastily reworked her plans. By the time Pearl returned to the Rover's with the doctor and a bobby in tow, Sarah had fled Coronation Street. But she was not alone.

The news of Jim Corbishley's arrest spread rapidly through the Street and the neighbourhood. There hadn't been many attempted murders in Weatherfield and the residents lapped it up.

'It's just like Crippen,' said Martha Hartley to Minnie Carlton. 'It's always the quiet ones you 'ave to watch.'

'But, Martha,' said Minnie, 'Mr Corbishley wasn't a quiet one. My mother says 'e was a very noisy one.'

'What does your mother know?' sniffed Martha. 'She wasn't there, was she? When it 'appened.'

'Neither were you,' said Ena, 'but it don't stop you goin' on as if you know about it.'

'I'm only repeating what's common knowledge. That 'ousekeeper caught 'im red 'anded and there was poison in that cup.'

'I'm not bein' drawn,' said Ena, tight-lipped.

Martha shook her head. 'You know your trouble, Ena Schofield? You always think best o' folk.'

'And your trouble is you're always ready to think worst,' retorted Ena sharply. It pained her to think of a man plotting the death of his wife. She thought of her own parents and how close they seemed. The thought that after wedlock a couple could grow so far apart disturbed her. It reminded her of Alfred Sharples and his wife, and she was trying so hard to forget about him.

'I 'ear Coronation Street is swarmin' wi' bobbies,' said Martha, refusing to be deterred by Ena's critical tone.

'They've moved Mrs Corbishley to the 'ospital,' said Minnie knowledgeably.

'That poor woman,' murmured Ena.

''As that Gladys friend o' yours been to visit 'er?' asked Martha.

'She may have,' Ena replied. 'They are neighbours.'

''Asn't she said?'

'We don't tittle-tattle,' said Ena.

Martha pulled a face. She couldn't see anything wrong in peddling gossip. It was easier than reading the news in a newspaper. 'The murderer's locked up,' she said with satisfaction.

Ena laughed. 'As far as we know, no one's dead, so 'ow can there be a murderer?'

'You know who I mean,' said Martha in disgust, 'and his fancy piece 'as flown as well.'

Ena didn't say anything. From what Gladys had told her no one had seen anything of Sarah Bridges in days. Her case had been packed and she hadn't been seen since Mrs Crapper went to the police. However, she wasn't the only missing person: no one had seen Alfie Marsh from No. 1 since that night either. Gladys had tried calling on Mrs Marsh but the woman had never opened the front door, and Ena had heard from Martha that the local gossips were suggesting she had never existed. It did seem odd that no one had ever seen her.

Ivy Makepiece was very forthright: 'She never goes into the shop, she never 'angs out 'er washing, she never sees neighbours... There's summat queer goin' on in that 'ouse.'

The residents agreed with her. In fact there was something very strange about the whole situation on Coronation Street. As soon as she had regained enough strength,

Nellie Corbishley told the police that she had instructed her husband to give her the powder in the belief that it would cure her ailments. In a desperate attempt to keep his neck out of a noose, Jim had backed up his wife's story, and with no charges to level against him, the police had reluctantly allowed him to walk free. Jim looked upon Sarah's departure as evidence of her guilt in the matter and wanted the police to bring her in but Nellie threatened to retract her statement if he did so and would instead admit that she had feared Jim had been poisoning her for months.

Jim smarted over his lover's disappearance. It wasn't so much that she had deserted him as that it appeared she had left with Alfie Marsh. *Alfie Marsh*. Jim had never been naïve enough to think Sarah would always be his but to lose her to Alfie Marsh, an aging lout, was a real slap in the face.

For a short period, after the departure of Sarah Bridges, life in Coronation Street reverted to normal, or as near normal as possible. Nellie Corbishley slowly recovered her health in the infirmary, where Pearl Crapper kept a bedside vigil. Jim carried on in the pub and started to enjoy a certain notoriety as a man once suspected of murder. After noting the rise in trade from curious drinkers, Jim rose to the occasion, winking at the men and offering them 'something special' to take home to the missus.

Even the mystery surrounding Mrs Marsh was cleared up: the timid, browbeaten woman eventually emerged from No. 1 in search of supplies at the shop. Gladys Arkwright sought her out and won her friendship, reporting back to Ena that Mo Marsh's greatest misfortune had been in marrying Alfie in the first place. 'Reading between the lines,' she said, in hushed tones over tea and biscuits, 'he thought she had money.'

'And she hadn't?' guessed Ena.

Gladys shook her head sadly. 'After they moved in he made her life such a misery that she kept going to stay with her sister in Blackpool. He told her the sea air would do her good, and whenever she was out of the way he was free to ... *entertain.*'

Ena raised her eyebrows. It was disgusting. Men were disgusting.

'The poor woman's got nothing to her name,' said Gladys. 'I fear she'll be off to the workhouse soon.'

Ena was troubled by Mrs Marsh's suffering, but she knew there was nothing to be done. Without a man or son to support them, women like her faded into nothing. No job, no hope, no future. Fifty years old and waiting for death to take her.

The rent man had heard the story often before and was hardened to it. It was no use Mo throwing herself upon his mercy: he took in the furniture inside the house and knew it was only good for firewood. She had nothing to sell. If she'd been younger he might have seen his way to giving her a few weeks' grace in return for bouncing the bedsprings but the pathetic old wretch had nothing he was interested in. Mo was given two days' notice to gather her belongings into a bundle and instructed to make her way to the workhouse.

Her departure was observed by Gertie Hewitt from No. 3. She stood as still as a statue in her front parlour and peered out of the good window, next to the boarded up one, to watch her neighbour slam her door for the last time. Her head was filled with the image of her own mother closing her front door before she made the same journey. Tears filled her eyes and self-disgust

300

rose inside her. Mo Marsh had no daughter to save her, but Bets Pegg had had one.

Mo Marsh never reached the workhouse. She never suffered the indignity of being stripped and checked for lice by hard-handed wardens. She never sat on a hard bunk in a room occupied by thirteen others. Never woke in the night to hear the screams of the hysterical wretches who were nearing the end of their days, never had to fight for scraps of food, or look out of the barred, draughty windows to weep for the past. When the workhouse was built many had commented on the forbidding path that the inmates had to take along the canal to reach its imposing gates. Mo wasn't the first to embrace the dirty, consuming waters and she wouldn't be the last.

On the day that Gladys, Ena, and Gertie Hewitt attended Mo's burial at St Mary's, a postcard arrived at No. 11 Coronation Street. Ivy Makepiece had never learnt to read so its sender's name remained a mystery until her daughter Mary came home from work. The card was from a place no Makepiece had ever heard of: Margate. Its greeting was short and sweet: 'On honeymoon with Alfie, life's a giggle, love Sarah'.

Ivy wrinkled her nose. She'd always thought Sarah Bridges a rum girl. She tore up the card and threw it on the fire.

CHAPTER TEN

November 1917

Mary Schofield wasn't her normal calm and collected self. Neighbours used to her solid common sense and unflappable nature noted the difference in her as she stared, transfixed, in her local shop, casting her eyes along the rows of packages and tins as if she'd stumbled into a grocery in France or Belgium. Shopkeeper Agnes Nettles coughed politely in an attempt to prompt her customer but Mary didn't notice.

Martha Hartley took a more direct approach. 'Excuse me, Mrs Schofield, but could you 'urry it up cos me mam needs eggs for bakin'?'

'Sorry,' Mary settled hurriedly on corned beef.

Martha raised an eyebrow. 'Corned beef on a Friday?'

'We've got a visitor,' explained Mary.

Martha's curiosity, at best barely dormant, leapt, and she smiled winningly. 'Oh, yes?'

she said. 'Who's that, then?'

Two older women, in the queue behind Martha, exchanged disapproving glances. They knew the importance of subtlety in these matters but, as both were interested in Mary's answer, neither rebuked her.

'A friend of Ena's,' said Mary, wishing she could be allowed to get on with the shopping in peace. She wasn't used to buying food for young men and had no idea what they ate.

'Of Ena's?' said Martha with a frown. 'All Ena's friends live round 'ere. Why would they want to come visitin'? It's not Minnie Carlton, is it? She's not fallen out with 'er mother again, 'as she?'

'It's not Minnie. It's a young man she's been writing to, Albert Tatlock.'

Martha's mouth dropped open with indignation. Ena was supposed to be her best friend yet she had to hear from Ena's mother, in a shop, that she was going to be entertaining a man. Not just any man. Since the beginning of the war they'd all heard about the absent Albert and his exploits in the trenches. All the girls at Hardcastles and Earnshaws had posed the same question: how deep was the friendship between Ena and Albert? Martha sucked in her breath. To think that Ena had sworn blind Albert was just a pal. A lad she'd felt sorry for.

As soon as she got home Martha briefed her mother. Both agreed that you didn't invite lads you felt sorry for to stay at your home. There had to be more to it than that. Martha nodded sagely. 'You'll see, there'll be banns read soon enough.'

'Oh, I agree,' said Molly Hartley wisely.

'She's been desperate to get married since Kitchener made 'is first appeal,' continued Martha.

'Oh, I agree,' said her mother, tucking her hands under her flabby arms and nodding furiously.

'First there was that lad from the Mission. If it 'adn't been for that bullet she'd be callin' 'erself Mrs Moss now.'

'God rest 'is soul,' muttered Molly, crossing herself. She wasn't Catholic but it felt the right thing to do.

'Then that conman from the spook 'ouse. I never liked the look of 'im. Shifty eyes.'

Molly nodded. She seldom disagreed with her daughter. Martha had an opinion about everything and was always right. Always.

Having run out of Ena's beaus, Martha fell silent. Molly took the opportunity to add her own observation. 'I agree, Martha,

305

she should take a lead from you. You've never 'ad a fella come callin', 'ave you.'

The smile faded from Martha's face as her mother asked, 'Fancy a brew?'

Albert Tatlock arrived at No. 14 Inkerman Street late that Friday night. The family had been expecting him since tea time, but, as Thomas had pointed out to his womenfolk, time didn't amount to much in wartime. 'It'll be the trains,' he'd said. 'I 'ear they don't run to time, these days.'

Mary and her daughters took his word as gospel. None of them had ever travelled by rail, only by tram and charabanc.

When Albert finally arrived he was greeted with awkward handshakes and a plateful of dried-up corned beef hash. Mary had muttered apologetically about not knowing what time to expect him, but Albert didn't seemed to mind and tucked in to his food heartily. As he ate Ena and Alice watched him carefully. Like Martha, Alice was confused by her sister's friendship with the young soldier. She wasn't sure if she should view him as a future in-law or if he was, in fact, available. Alice Schofield had never sat at the tea table with an unattached young man before, and she experienced a sudden flutter in the pit of her stomach.

Ena regarded Albert with an interested eye. He was more thick-set than she remembered, and he seemed shyer than he did in his letters – she put *that* down to his being in the company of strangers. She understood shyness: once upon a time she'd been shy herself. Now she felt uneasy: it had seemed a natural thing to do, to invite Albert to stay during his leave. His family had all moved away and she didn't want to see the lad dossing down on a pal's floor. Mary had aired the bunk in the back bedroom and Ena had written enthusiastically to Albert saying she'd be insulted if he didn't rest his head in Inkerman Street. After all, she'd said, they'd been writing to each other for over three years now.

Ena had gone to great pains to impress upon her parents that Albert was only a friend, but Thomas couldn't have cared less what he was. For him, it made a comfortable change to have another man in the house. Mary, meanwhile, had taken Ena on her word and told her that any friend of hers was a friend of the family's. Ena hadn't felt Alice was owed any explanation, and let her formulate her own opinion. Thomas had high hopes of a manly outing to the Tripe

Dresser's Arms with his new comrade, but Albert said his journey had left him weary. Mary had encouraged Thomas to go anyway, and had dragged Alice into the scullery to help wash the pots. Ena and Albert were left alone.

Ena smiled at him encouragingly. 'It must be odd, bein' back in an 'ouse after all the months in mud.'

'Aye,' he said. 'Makes a change not to 'ave rats runnin' over me boots.'

Ena grimaced. 'If you're missin' them you should get down to the canal. We've got big ones down there.'

Albert grinned. 'You know what I miss most of all?' he asked.

'What?'

'The noise.' He was used to thundering guns, shells exploding, chaps singing along or chattering in groups, horses whinnying, the chaplain at prayer, officers barking orders, the solitary mouth-organ.

Ena regarded him with a soft light in her eyes. 'I've no idea what it's like out there,' she said quietly.

He didn't say anything. He didn't need to.

'Your letters paint a picture,' she continued, 'but I've no real idea.'

'It's hell,' he said.

'Aye.'

Ena's eyes were damp and she stared into the flames in the grate. Albert sneaked a quick look in her direction and noticed how sad she looked. 'Forgive me,' he said, 'but are you thinkin' about yer fiancé? Phil, wasn't it?'

Ena looked up sharply. 'Yes. I was,' she said.

'I was sorry to 'ear about 'im. We lost so many chaps those three days. Terrible waste.'

Ena spoke without thinking. 'But you survived.'

It wasn't meant as a rebuke but Albert felt it as a slap across the face. He dropped his head. 'Aye, I did.'

'I'm sorry,' said Ena, 'I shouldn't 'ave said that.'

Albert shrugged. 'If you want to know truth, there's times I wished I 'ad snuffed it. Wished a bullet 'ad got me and not some other chap.'

'You're talkin' daft,' said Ena.

'I'm not. There's your Phil. I 'ad no one at 'ome waitin' for me but 'e did... You. There were married men, men wi' kiddies. Wives and children left wi' no man. Aye, there's bin times... Course, that would 'ave been selfish.'

Ena frowned. 'Selfish? To wish yerself dead?'

'Aye. Sometimes when you're out there in the middle of nowhere with bullets comin' at you and screams, that's when you wish you were dead.'

Under other circumstances, Ena would have talked about God, about the sanctity of life, but looking at weary Albert and seeing her Phil sitting in his place, all Ena could do was nod slowly. 'If it matters, lad,' she said, 'I'm glad you're alive.'

He smiled thinly and rubbed his eyes. He couldn't put into words what it felt like to be back in a proper house: to sit beside a range identical to the one his mother had faithfully blackleaded each Tuesday; to eat off china rather than tin, taste food properly cooked through, and know that he'd be sleeping between sheets. He longed to get up the stairs and into bed.

As if she had read his thoughts Ena eased herself up from her chair. 'I'll show you your room.'

It was not going to be a leisurely leave for Albert and at seven thirty the next morning he was up and putting on his army boots. He cast a longing look at the bed, where the shape of his body was still imprinted in the sheet. He'd slept soundly. No nightmares.

Thomas had already left for work when Albert came down the stairs for breakfast. Mary had been surprised to see him up so early and had allowed herself a brief sit-down while he enthusiastically tackled her generous portions of porridge, then bread and dripping.

As he ate, Albert talked about his friend Dinky Low, whose wedding he was to attend that afternoon. He told her how they'd volunteered together, arrived in Belgium together, fought side by side and been like brothers. He didn't tell her of how they'd wept together over friends riddled with machine-gun bullets, or of how Archie Reynold's brains landed on Dinky's lap as they'd sheltered from the storm of bullets. Those things were best left unsaid.

'Must be an honour,' said Mary, smiling at Albert's healthy appetite, 'to be asked to be best man.'

'Aye, it is,' said Albert, 'and Dinky's always bin popular – 'e could 'ave asked plenty of others.'

'But 'e chose you. You must be a good friend to 'im.'

''appen I am,' Albert said.

By the time Ena had arrived downstairs, Albert had finished eating and, for want of something to do, had volunteered to polish the family's boots. Mary had been understanding enough not to put up resistance to the idea. She remembered her father recalling his experiences in the Boer War. 'I must 'ave polished enough boots to shoe all the Army 'orses, let alone the men,' he'd said. If the lad wanted to polish boots, who was Mary Schofield to stand in his way?

When she saw Albert at work Ena raised an eyebrow, but Mary shook her head, warning her not to comment. However, Ena leant over to inspect his work and said, 'I 'ope you've done mine. I want to look me best for this weddin'.'

Albert held up one of her boots.

'They'll do,' she said with a smile.

Ena had been invited to the wedding as Albert's guest. Dinky, an orphan like Albert, was being put up by his parents-in-law-to-be in their crowded tenement in Arkwright Street, a terrace huddled close to the back of the glue factory. Dinky had no recollection of ever having met Ena but she had a vivid memory of the tall, good-looking young man with the earnest eyes and the long, slender nose. She shuddered to think of herself back in the autumn of 1914, awkward, bashful and unsure of herself. The war might have claimed the lives of many but it had been the blossoming of her own.

As she sat at the table and attended to her own breakfast Ena felt redundant. A sampler stitched by her grandmother, which covered a damp patch on the front parlour wall, warned that 'The Devil maketh work for idle hands'. It had always been a proverb close to Ena's heart and she wished she could help with the wedding preparations. She had never even met the bride. 'Where's the weddin' taking place?' she asked.

'Some old mission hall,' said Albert.

'That'll be the Congregational Chapel on Bostock Street,' said Ena, with a grimace. 'They're a bit highbrow for me. They do the Stations of the Cross.'

'No, it's a little place near to where me auntie used to live. Back of Coronation Street.'

'Mission of Glad Tidings?' Ena perked up.

'Aye, that's the place. Madge chose it.'

Ena smiled to herself as Albert finished his polishing. She'd have plenty to occupy her hands with, after all.

Gladys Arkwright prided herself in the

pristine state in which she kept the Mission Hall. The interior of the building acted as a magnet for the dust and grime that issued from the neighbouring mills and factory chimneys, and Gladys waged a constant battle to keep it in check. She was grateful that the hall hadn't been built with pews permanently in place, like those in the parish church of St Mary's. Instead, the congregation sat on wooden chairs which Gladys put in place before each service. When they were not out in the hall, the chairs were stored beneath the stage and the likes of Ivy Makepiece thought Gladys made work for herself heaving them in and out of storage. However, Gladys preferred the heavy work to dusting row upon row of seats. It also meant that for small gatherings, such as Dinky's wedding, just a few chairs needed to be set out, creating an intimate ring around the platform. Gladys had noted that, as the war progressed, weddings had become smaller and smaller affairs, due to financial restrictions and the depletion of guests. Now, most young couples arrived with just a handful of family and friends and the brides were never late: the grooms were on military leave and time always seemed to be at a premium.

Ena regarded the arch of chairs with approval. 'They look champion, Mrs Arkwright.'

'I see you're in your best,' Gladys remarked. 'What side are you? Bride or groom?'

'I'm not either, really. 'Appen you should put us a chair by the best man.'

'Something I don't know about?' asked Gladys.

'No,' Ena replied, 'nothing at all.'

The walk from Arkwright Street, down the uneven surface of Viaduct Street to the Mission of Glad Tidings, brought home to Albert Tatlock something that the trenches of France had helped him forget: he was a short man. Knee-deep in mud this didn't seem to matter, but as he walked alongside six-foot-one Dinky his stature troubled him. Anxious over his impending nuptials, Dinky strode down the back-street with little regard for his best friend's comfort and Albert rushed along beside him, his hand fiddling in his pocket, ensuring the safety of the small brass ring.

His wedding day had placed Dinky in good spirits and he couldn't help but tease Albert over his lodgings.

'So is this Ena as wonderful as you remember her?'

Albert flushed. 'I never said she were wonderful.'

'I seen yer face every time you get one of 'er letters. Scurryin' off to read 'em in secret.'

'Gerroff,' said Albert, puffing. 'We're friends, that's all.'

Dinky laughed. 'So you keep sayin', although I reckon there's more to it than that, Albert Tatlock. I know you, you beggar.'

Albert flushed and stumbled, and Dinky slowed and glanced at his friend. 'I reckon you'd like to be more than Ena Schofield's friend,' he said, with a smirk. 'I reckon you're smitten.'

The colour in Albert's cheeks deepened. 'Give over,' he said. 'Ena's nowt but a friend. A good 'un at that.'

'Aye,' said Dinky shrewdly, 'but you'd like 'er to be more than a friend, wouldn't you?'

It took Dinky a few steps to realize that Albert was no longer beside him. He stopped and looked back to where the other man stood, frowning. He'd gone too far in the teasing. Dinky grinned apologetically. 'I'm sorry, I shouldn't 'ave said that.'

'No,' said Albert gruffly, 'you shouldn't.'

'I'll keep me mouth shut,' offered Dinky.

The pair continued in silence down Viaduct Street. Albert slipped his finger into the brass ring and felt its smooth roundness. For a second his thoughts flew to the idea of slipping such a ring on a female finger. Ena's finger– No. Ena was his friend. That was all.

Alice Schofield was put out by the way her family home had been taken over by the arrival of Albert and the wedding of a couple she hadn't even met. Returning from her Saturday-morning shift at the mill, she found her mother rolling pastry on the kitchen table. An enamel pie tin stood awaiting its pastry lid to cover the chunks of vegetables and scrapings of mutton inside it. Alice glanced at it and sniffed, pies were unheard of on Saturdays.

Mary didn't have to look up from her rolling to sense her daughter's disapproval. She was disappointed by Alice's attitude towards life. While Ena embraced it and did what she could to make her journey through it enjoyable, Alice clung to bleak shadows and seemed frustrated by all she was offered. There was no pleasure in Alice's soul and Mary was at a loss to know why she was so different from the rest of the family. She had always striven to show no favouritism to either of her daughters, but from an early age Alice had been secretive, sullen and always seemed on the edge of family life, regarding the others as if through frosted glass.

'Where's our Ena?' she snapped now.

'At the weddin',' said Mary, knowing Alice hadn't needed to ask her.

'Fancy.' Alice stared at the pie tin, her face set in an unattractive mould.

'And there's no need for you to stand there like that, Alice Schofield,' said Mary. 'I'm just showin' some decent 'uman 'ospitality to a lad who's got no mam of 'is own.'

'I'm sure I don't know what you're talkin' about,' said Alice, put out.

'Oh, yes, you do. And I'd do the same for one of your friends.' Mary stopped herself adding, 'If you had any.'

'It just seems to me that we always seem to be jumping through 'oops for our Ena yet no one puts themselves out for me. No one.'

As she threw rice over the heads of Dinky Low and his new wife, Madge, Ena thought

Madge looked sensational in her white cap and veil. Her wedding dress had been her mother's and had been altered only slightly at the waist. Madge spent the entire service staring lovingly into the face of her husband, watching the sincerity in his eyes as he made vows to honour and keep her until the day he died. Ena had attended plenty of weddings – had helped oversee many at the Mission – but never had one touched her heart as this had. If she had to sum it up she'd have to say that it was the sincerity of love shared between the man and woman that radiated around the hall. Dinky and Madge were obviously meant for each other and Ena felt privileged to witness their union.

Even Gladys, watching the couple leave to the shouts of well-wishers, noted the atmosphere. 'What a lovely couple,' she murmured to Ena.

As the bridal party set off for the spread Madge's mother had prepared at her home, Ena found herself falling into step with Albert. They wandered together, among the other guests, down Viaduct Street, taking the path trodden by Albert and Dinky only an hour before.

His previous conversation weighed heavily

319

on Albert's mind as he retraced his steps in the company of Ena Schofield. 'She's a beautiful bride,' said Ena, wistfully.

'Aye,' agreed Albert. 'He's a lucky lad.'

Ena smiled in agreement, and the pair walked on in comfortable silence. Albert's mind was racing ahead over the remaining few hours of his leave. After the reception he was to help Dinky move Madge into their new home. Ironically, the newly-weds were to move into a house once rented by Albert's aunt, Mary Osbourne.

No.1 Coronation Street had stood empty since Alfie Marsh had run off with the local barmaid and his wife had drowned herself on her way to the workhouse. A couple of interested parties had turned down the tenancy, claiming the house was unlucky, but Dinky wasn't superstitious and gladly took it on. Albert would help pull the barrow Dinky had borrowed from the vegetable market; today it would contain his and Madge's bits of furniture and their clothes. Then Albert would return to Inkerman Street for dinner with the Schofields, before meeting Dinky in time to catch the train back to barracks and eventually to France.

Ena noted Albert's solemn expression and

thought how horrible it must be for him to know he'd be back in the mud of the trenches so soon. She wished there was something she could do, something to bring some cheer or respite into his life. She toyed with the idea of removing the rosebud decoration from her dress and presenting it to him as a memento, a keepsake. But that was the sort of thing sweethearts did, not friends.

Then a voice startled her. Martha Hartley stood just feet away, waving and calling her name. She realised immediately that her friend had been waiting at the entrance of the back alley between Coronation and Mawdsley Streets, just to catch a glimpse of her with Albert. Ena also knew that Martha wouldn't be fobbed off with anything less than an introduction.

'Fancy seeing you,' said Martha, rushing over and falling into step with her friend. She stared meaningfully at Albert.

'Albert, this is my friend Martha. Martha, this is Albert.' Ena was annoyed at the interruption.

''Ello Albert,' purred Martha.

''Ow do,' muttered Albert. He always felt bashful in the company of strange women, and one look at Martha had convinced him that she was certainly strange.

Her beak-like nose darted out of her face, on which black-rimmed spectacles were perched, and was staring at him. In her turn, Martha decided he was nothing to write home about. She liked men to look like the King, tall and powerful, not short and stocky like Albert.

Feeling Albert's discomfort and the weight of Martha's scrutiny, Ena hoped that if she was ignored Martha would soon leave. She was mistaken.

Martha linked her arm with Ena's and began to chatter. 'I love a weddin', don't you, Ena? I love seein' the bride in 'er gown, lookin' like a princess from a fairy-tale and, you know, even the most ugly men look 'andsome on their weddin' days. It's as if God's said, 'E may not look much but today will be 'is day.' 'Ow do you know the groom, then, Albert? 'E's a very good lookin' fella, isn't 'e?'

''E's Albert's friend,' said Ena, before Albert could open his mouth.

'Where's the reception?' asked Martha, optimistically.

''Er mother's,' said Ena, 'though it'll be a squeeze. I'll probably only stick me 'ead round the door and then go 'ome. Tell you what, Martha, I'll call on you later with a slice o' the cake.'

Something in Ena's tone advised Martha to accept this offer as being the best she could hope for. She made her excuses and left them alone.

After she'd gone Albert asked, 'Did you mean that, about not stoppin' long?'

'Well,' said Ena, 'I'll only be in the way. It makes no odds if I'm there or not.'

'Yes, it does,' said Albert, awkwardly. 'It makes a difference to me.'

Ena kept her eyes straight ahead, not daring to dart a look in Albert's direction. 'What do you mean?' she finally asked.

Albert stopped walking. The rest of the guests had gone up Viaduct Street and there was some distance now between them and the pair who stood beneath the gas lamp on the corner of Weavers' Row. 'I mean...' stuttered Albert '...I mean that I enjoy your company, Ena. I can't tell you 'ow much yer letters mean to me. I read them over and over. I even know some by 'eart. It means so much to me that you write.'

Ena felt embarrassed by the earnest young man's words but she didn't want him to stop. 'I enjoy your letters too,' she said.

'Do you think–' Albert broke off and

looked at the receding line of guests. 'Maybe we could be more than friends?' he said in a rush.

He mistook Ena's gasp for one of horror, and felt angry with himself for daring to put his feelings into words. 'I'm sorry,' he said.

'There's no need,' she said. 'It's just a surprise. I didn't think you felt that way.'

'I do,' he said. 'Very much... I'm not good wi' words.'

'You don't seem to be doin' so badly,' Ena said.

'What do you say, then?' asked Albert, hopefully.

Ena grasped Albert's hand. 'I'm very touched by the suggestion, Albert, I am truly, but I can't promise myself to another man until this war's over. After Phil, I couldn't bear to lose another man. Do you understand?'

Albert understood completely. She was letting him down lightly. It had been stupid of him to think that a girl like Ena would consider him as anything but a friend. He felt foolish.

He backed off slightly and Ena, reading his eyes, realised he'd got the wrong impression. She felt frustrated: how could she make him see she meant what she said? She

324

had thought the future was going to be clear with Phil, that he'd return from war and they'd marry in the Mission, as Dinky and Madge just had, then live happily ever after. But it hadn't worked out like that. If a bullet claimed Albert ... well, she couldn't go through all that again. She just couldn't.

Ena left the wedding reception early, but she forgot Martha's cake and went straight home instead of calling on her friend. She felt uncomfortable in Albert's presence now and felt the need to be alone for a while before he was due to arrive for his tea. As she pushed open the front door she hoped that the rest of the family would be out. She needed a cup of tea and a lie-down in her bedroom with nothing to listen to but her heartbeat, nothing to think about but her own breathing.

''Ello, love,' said Mary, popping her head round the scullery door. 'Fancy a nice cup of tea?'

Ena smiled: Mary could always be relied upon to know what she needed. She flopped into a chair and, despite herself, started to talk. It was often the way. When she felt she needed to be alone more than anything, Mary's presence brought the reassurance she sought and it was the easiest thing in the world to tell her what weighed so heavily on her mind. 'I've upset Albert,' she began, and then recounted to her mother all that had passed between them, of how she did have strong feelings for him but didn't want to run the risk of being hurt again. Of how hurt he'd seemed, and how he'd withdrawn into himself, and how wretched she felt. 'It's not fair,' she said.

'Nobody ever said it would be fair,' Mary observed.

'What?' asked Ena.

'Life.'

Suddenly Ena spotted a spray of red flowers in Mary's glass vase, won for her by Thomas at a fair ten years previously. 'Where did they come from?' she asked, surprised.

'I went out for a walk,' Mary said, 'and they were growing by your granny's grave so I picked them.'

Mary longed to hug her daughter close and promise it would all be all right, but she had always tried not to mislead her daughters and she knew only too well that it wouldn't be all right. It never was.

CHAPTER ELEVEN

June 1918

'They say it'll be all over by Christmas,' said Ivy Makepiece, as she stood in the queue at Tommy Foyle's shop.

'That's what they said in 1914,' the shop-keeper said, with a laugh.

Ivy fixed him with a glare. In her mind shopkeepers and publicans lived to serve, not comment. She sniffed and watched him carefully as he weighed out the four ounces of sugar she had requested.

Standing behind Ivy, Sarah Buck broke wind, then looked apologetically around the shop. A large woman, used to picking at food between meals, rationing and in-creased prices had forced her on to a diet of cabbage soup and the odour that came with it was never far from her.

Ivy wrinkled her nose. 'You need to see someone about that,' she said, in disgust. 'It's not natural.'

Keen to move the conversation away from

327

herself, Sarah leapt at the opportunity to tap into one of Ivy's favoured topics. 'I see Gertie 'Ewitt's bin caught red-handed.'

Ivy's face broke into a delighted grin. 'Yes,' she said with glee. 'Mr Edwards caught 'er shovin' a plaice down her drawers and called the bobbies. She'll go down for certain this time.'

Gladys Arkwright, also in the queue, tutted disapprovingly.

'Got somethin' to say?' demanded Ivy.

'Only that I don't think we should be crowing over the misfortunes of others.'

'Misfortunes my arse,' said Ivy, causing Gladys to flinch. 'Gertie 'Ewitt's nowt but a low-life thief and deserves all she gets.'

'Times are hard, Mrs Makepiece–' began Gladys.

'Don't give me that,' snarled Ivy. 'You've never known it 'ard! You've never 'ad to scrimp to put food on the table, you wi' yer rent paid and yer fancy tea parties. You don't live in the same world as the rest of us, and I'll tell you straight, I've never stooped to thievin' to feed my kids. Gertie 'Ewitt can go 'ang for all I care.'

Sarah nodded in agreement. 'She's brought shame to Coronation Street,' she said sanctimoniously, forgetting all the times Jim Corbishley had thrown her out of the Rover's for being roaring drunk.

Half an hour later Ivy's words still rang in Gladys's ears as she set about preparing her dinner of cold ham and salad. She'd always tried hard to serve the community and it wasn't her fault that she had independent means, and that she wasn't charged rent for living in the vestry. Heaven knows, she worked hard enough for her board, sweeping the hall every morning, setting up for meetings and, on occasion, playing the harmonium. It certainly wasn't a labour of love. Try as she might, however, she couldn't shake Ivy's condemnation out of her mind.

Ena Schofield made the most of the fine summer weather by travelling on the open top deck of the number sixteen tram as often as possible. Only one had an open deck and it was considered an honour among the conductresses to be assigned to it. Ena's unblemished record of punctuality, along with a letter received at the depot from an elderly woman commending her kindness in retrieving a dropped penny from beneath a seat, led to her being awarded the coveted post during the hottest week of June. As the tram rolled up and down Rosamund Street, Ena leant against the guard rail, her face turned towards the sun. When the tram came to a halt outside the Catholic Men's Social Club, a slight woman, heavily pregnant, stumbled as she attempted to climb on. Seeing her plight, Ena raced down the stairs to help her. 'Are you all right?' she asked, as she bent down to help her on. Then she recognized her. 'Madge!'

Madge Low looked up into Ena's concerned face and her face broke into a smile. 'Ena, thank goodness it's you! I'd 'ave felt a right fool if it 'ad been anyone else. I caught me foot in me skirt climbin' up.'

Ena led her to the nearest free seat. Madge sank into it gratefully and automatically stroked her stomach. Ena gasped at the size of the bulge.

Madge laughed. 'I know. I'm huge. It's a good job Dinky was away in the trenches in the months before we wed otherwise folk would say I 'ad to get wed.'

'How far gone are you now?' asked Ena.

'Seven months.'

Ena straightened and rang the bell twice for the driver to continue on his way. She returned to Madge's side and, making sure no one was watching, refused the farthing she was offered. 'You shouldn't 'ave to pay to scrape yer knees,' she said, with a twinkle in her eyes.

Madge thanked her and shifted in discomfort on the seat. 'It's too hot to be carryin' so much weight around,' she said. 'I felt I was goin' to pass out yesterday.'

'Are you still workin' at Earnshaw's?' asked Ena.

'Oh, aye, I've another seven weeks to go there, and we need the money.'

Ena shook her head. Much as she envied Madge's married and pregnant state, she'd hate to be living alone, pregnant, uncertain when her husband was coming home. *If* he was coming home. She peered along the tram towards the next stop. As no one was waiting to board and no passengers seemed about to disembark she called, 'Fitton's Corner.' When no one stirred, she rang the bell three times, which told the driver not to bother stopping.

'You're lucky,' said Madge, ''avin' such a good job.'

'Aye,' said Ena happily. 'I am.'

If Madge's life at No. 1 Coronation Street was lonely, at least it wasn't as pressured as those of the inhabitants of the house next door. As Ivy Makepiece had predicted, Gertie Hewitt was sent to prison for the theft of one fish from Edwards' fishmonger's. She left behind, at No.3, twenty-year-old Flo, who struggled to cope with her half-sister, nine-year-old Molly. Flo didn't have the time or energy to lavish attention on Molly in the way Gertie had done, and resented the child's easy life. When Flo had been nine she'd been set to work as a part-timer at Hardcastle's mill, running in and out collecting discarded bobbins from beneath the roaring looms. However, Gertie had promised that Molly should be apprenticed to a sewing room where she'd learn a proper trade befitting a young woman. Flo had rightly taken offence at the implication that her own job, running three looms at Earnshaw's, was not a fit one. Still, Flo mused, she couldn't blame Gertie for wanting the best for her daughter. She felt certain that if their positions were swapped she'd feel the same and now, with Gertie sent down for three months, it fell to Flo to step in as Molly's surrogate mother.

Molly found the new arrangement objectionable as she no longer had someone at her beck and call: Flo refused to tailor her social life to suit her sister. She had been independent from an early age and saw no reason why she should play nursemaid day and night. As a result Molly returned from school each day to an empty house and was given instructions by her half-sister to start preparations for the evening tea. At first she resented the change and sulkily refused to co-operate but one hearty slap from Flo was enough to persuade her to comply.

Today, though, the Hewitt household was light with anticipation. After four years away, serving his king and country, Corporal Thomas Hewitt was coming home on leave, invalided out and ordered to rest until a bullet wound in his leg had cleared up. The letter he'd written giving warning of his arrival had only come the day before, and Flo and Molly had been rushing about in preparation for their hero's homecoming.

Madge waited while Ena handed in her ticket machine and takings, and clocked out, then linked arms with her for the short walk down past Swindley's Emporium and Edwards' fishmonger's home.

Since attending Madge and Dinky's wedding Ena had been a regular visitor to No.1 Coronation Street, helping Madge to decorate the tiny house and make it cosy for Dinky's homecoming, whenever that would be. Ena had been forced to shrug off the premonition she had had that Dinky would never see the lovely little home Madge had made for him. Such thoughts didn't help anyone.

Now Madge invited Ena in to show her the tiny bonnet and shawl her mother had knitted for the baby. Ena instantly wished that she was a knitter too: she'd have loved to make the baby something. Still, she thought, her own mother liked nothing better than to spend evenings clicking away and would thrill to the idea of producing something for Madge's baby.

'There's somethin' I've been meanin' to ask you, Ena,' said Madge, as they strolled down Rosamund Street.

'What's that?' asked Ena. The mixture of good company and fine weather was making her feel lightheaded.

'Well ... I've written to Dinky and suggested that when we 'ave the little 'un christened you might be Godmother.'

Ena stopped walking and hugged her friend. 'That's the nicest thing anyone's ever asked of me,' she cried.

'I couldn't 'ave anyone but you, Ena.

334

You've bin a brick to me these past few months. So you agree then, you will be Godmother?'

'Oh, yes, I'd be honoured,' said Ena.

Suddenly Madge cried out and clutched her stomach.

'Whatever's the matter?' asked Ena.

'Just a pain. Little 'un's probably kickin' me or summat.' Madge tried to sound calm but the sharp shooting pain had disturbed her and she wished the journey home could be cut short. She quickened her pace.

As the pair hurried around the corner of Coronation Street by the Rover's Return, they passed a young soldier standing on the pavement regarding the street as if recollecting a bygone age. Ena did little more than glance in his direction as they passed. She noticed he had a moustache and that his arm bore the two stripes of a corporal but otherwise paid him no heed as she hurried Madge into No. 1.

Molly had been looking out of the bay window of No. 3 for over half an hour. Then, with a squeal, she recognised the familiar and instantly comforting form of Thomas limping towards her. With a cry of 'He's here! He's here!' she ran from the front parlour and threw open the front door.

In the kitchen, Flo ripped off her apron, threw it into a chair and hurried out to the hall to join in the welcome. Thomas was home at last after four years.

Thomas dropped his kit to the pavement and threw open his arms as Molly darted out of the house and flung her whole body hard against him. She weighed more than he had anticipated and he staggered. 'You're back!' she cried, over and over.

He held her close to him and, looking beyond her, felt his heart leap as Flo rushed towards him. With the child still clinging around his neck, Thomas opened his arms and embraced his sister. She fell into his arms, crushing Molly between them.

'Let's get inside,' he said softly, 'before they start sellin' tickets.'

'Let 'em,' said Flo. 'I don't care, I'm just that 'appy to 'ave you back.'

Molly grabbed Thomas's kitbag and set off towards No. 3 with it. It was too heavy for her to carry so she ended up dragging it along the pavement.

Flo hugged Thomas again, then went after Molly. As they turned to go into the house she noticed a solitary figure standing on the other side of the street, watching their every move. Even the sight of Ivy Makepiece couldn't dampen Flo's spirits and she shouted out, 'Our Thomas is back, Mrs Makepiece. Back for good. Isn't it wonderful?'

The words, delivered in joy, hit Ivy hard, reminding her that her own son Ralph would never return from the war, invalided or not. She spat into the gutter and yelled, 'Nowt wonderful in a 'Ewitt comin' back to its lair. Rats do it all the time.'

Inside No. 3, Molly had pinned a banner to the back of one of the kitchen chairs. It read 'Welcome Home, Tom' in red and blue crayon, and in each corner she had drawn a Union Jack.

As he limped into the house Thomas stumbled against the chair and muttered in pain. As he did so his hand tore the banner.

Flo looked at her brother anxiously. 'Does it 'urt an awful lot?' she asked.

'Aye,' he said. 'It comes and goes.'

'Never mind,' said Flo. 'You're 'ome now.'

Next door, at No. 1, Madge Low was in tears as she clutched her stomach and doubled over in pain.

Ena felt at a loss. She had no idea of how she could help her friend.

As she felt a wet sensation running down her leg Madge gave a cry. She pulled up her skirt and discovered her leg was stained red. She glanced up to Ena and was assaulted again by a violent pain.

Ena acted instinctively. She lowered Madge into a chair by the range then darted out of the house, trying frantically to remember at which house Sarah Buck, the local midwife, lived. She pounded at the door of No. 9 Coronation Street and almost fell into the hall when Sarah pulled it open.

'You've got to come,' shouted Ena. 'Summat's not right!'

While Flo put the finishing touches to the celebratory stew she and Molly had prepared for Thomas's return he sneaked out into the backyard to smoke a Woodbine. Since TB had claimed five members of the Hewitt clan, including Thomas's parents, smoke had been banished from the house for fear of starting Molly coughing. To Thomas and Flo, who had lived through the hacking of their dying relatives, a cough was the worse sound in the world.

Thomas stood in the gateway of No. 3, his back to the whitewashed backyard, looking down the ginnel along which he had run so often as a child, shooting makeshift arrows from a wooden bowl that his cousin Archie had left behind after a rare visit to the poorer family members. As he stared down towards the gate, which led to the Corner Shop, Thomas realised suddenly that he wasn't alone. He was staring at a young woman. A beautiful young woman.

'Who do you think you're gawpin' at?' she demanded, strolling confidently down the ginnel towards him.

Thomas blushed. 'Sorry,' he said. 'I were just rememberin' me youth.'

'Oh, aye?' She stopped close by him and looked him up and down.

'I live 'ere,' he said, almost apologetically.

'Oh, aye?'

'Thomas 'Ewitt,' he said, taking the butt end of the Woodbine out of his mouth, throwing it on to the cobbles and grinding it beneath his boot.

'I remember you,' said the woman, with a sneer.

Thomas stared at her, hoping for a flicker of recognition, but couldn't identify her from his past life, which seemed so long ago now, like a distant dream. For four years now he'd huddled in the trenches, deafened by machine-gun fire and shell blasts. Before that, he had lived in another world. Now here he was, making idle chatter with a pretty girl, while other men – brothers, comrades – still withstood the barrage on the other side of the Channel. None of it made sense and there seemed no point in trying to make sense of it.

'I'm Mary Makepiece, from No. 11,' said the woman, her hand ready to strike back if he raised a hand to her. Makepieces and Hewitts were always hitting each other.

'Oh, yes,' said Thomas. 'You've changed.'

'Oh, aye?' said Mary threateningly.

'In a good way,' Thomas said hastily. 'You look...'

Mary eyed him awkwardly. Suddenly she felt uncomfortable and shifted under his gaze, but she did not move away from him. She had to admit that he was better-looking than he had been the last time she'd seen him.

'I shouldn't be talkin' to you,' she said finally.

'Why's that?' he asked, frowning.

'You're a 'Ewitt. We don't talk to 'Ewitts.'

'Ah, yes,' said Thomas. 'The great feud. What was it about? I forget.'

The question shocked Mary into realising she hadn't the faintest idea why her family were at daggers drawn with the Hewitts. They just always had been. 'I dunno,' she said.

Thomas grinned. 'If we don't know what we're fightin' for, there don't seem much point in fightin',' he said simply. 'At the front we're fightin' to advance the front line and we all know what we're fightin' for. If we didn't we might just as well go 'ome.'

'You 'ave come 'ome,' she said.

'I've bin invalided out for a bit,' he said, 'till my leg fixes up. Shan't take long,' he said, almost apologetically.

The back door to No. 3 opened and Flo called, telling Thomas that his tea was ready. He smiled at Mary and inclined his head to her. ''Appen I'll see you again,' he said.

''Appen you will.'

Ten minutes later, back inside No. 11, Mary Makepiece casually brought up the subject of the hated Hewitts and asked her mother why they were the sworn enemy. 'I dunno,' said Ivy impatiently 'Cos they're 'Ewitts!'

Ena mopped Madge's brow as her friend contorted in agony.

'What's 'appenin' to me?' Madge cried.

'I don't know,' said Ena, holding her hand

tightly and casting an anxious glance down to where Sarah Buck stood, biting her lip and watching Madge with concern. 'Mrs Buck...' she began.

'Shurrup, I'm thinkin'!' Sarah barked.

Ena had very little experience of birth but knew instinctively that all was not going to plan. For a start Madge was only seven months pregnant, and the bloody lake in which she lay in her bed was not a good omen.

'She needs a doctor,' said Sarah.

'I've no money,' said Madge in alarm.

'You've started early and I can't do much about it,' said Sarah. 'You need a doctor.'

Ena's mind ran to her own savings, safe at home under her mattress, and wondered how much Madge would need for professional help. 'Where's nearest doctor?' she asked.

Sarah shrugged, 'I've never 'ad need of one. I dunno.'

'Then who *would* know?' cried Ena.

'Don't leave me, Ena,' gasped Madge. 'I need you wi' me.'

'You need a doctor, Madge. Summat's wrong.'

Madge started to cry. 'It 'urts so much.'

Sarah backed away from her in alarm.

'Please, Mrs Buck,' begged Ena, 'do something!'

Sarah racked her memory. She had presided over difficult births before, but this was the worst she had witnessed.

'Fetch me boilin' water,' she snapped at Ena, 'and more towels. Fetch 'em from my 'ouse if need be.'

Ena nodded, released her hand from Madge's grip, and ran to her task.

Despite the hot weather, the chicken stew went down well at the Hewitt's home, but as she cleared away the plates, Flo wished Gertie could be at the table with them, enjoying the feast as much as the rest of the family.

As if he had read her mind Thomas suddenly announced that he would like to visit his stepmother at the first opportunity. Flo nodded, and rose to carry the plates into the scullery. As she stood up she didn't notice that Molly too had got up from the table and the two collided, sending the dishes crashing to the floor.

'You clumsy stupid girl!' shouted Flo, and Molly promptly burst into loud wails.

'Shut up!' cried Thomas, his hands flying to his ears, and leapt up, sending his chair crashing down behind him. The noise added to the din inside his head and tears were in his eyes as he scanned the room for cover. Finding none he darted into the scullery, clawed at the back door handle and rushed outside. Molly stared after him, shaking with fright.

After her initial shock at his behaviour, Flo followed Thomas out of the house, in time to see him run into the outside water closet. He slammed the door tight shut behind him, sat on the lavatory seat and drew his legs up to his chest, his head buried in his folded arms.

When Flo pushed open the wooden door she found him whimpering into his shirt-sleeves. 'Whatever's to do?' she asked gently, putting out a hand to comfort him.

At her touch Thomas pulled away. 'I'm all right, I just need some time.'

'Summat's wrong,' said Flo.

'It was the noise, that's all.'

She squatted on the floor of the closet. Tentatively she put out a hand and gently stroked his arm. 'I want to 'elp,' she said.

'You can't,' he said. 'No one can.'

'Let me try, Tom. You always used to 'elp me when we were youngsters and I want to 'elp you now.'

Thomas raised his tear-stained face and stared at his sister. His mind was clouded with noises and images but the sight of her was comforting. 'It's the noise. I 'ate noise,' he said.

'Cos of the war?' she asked.

He nodded. 'You've no idea what it's like,' he said simply 'The roar of it, the din... You never 'ave a moment to yerself. If they're not shellin' us some bugger's shoutin' orders at us.' He gulped and looked down at his leg. 'When I got this bullet I were lucky. Lucky I was shot at and not shelled. My sergeant, he had both his legs blown off. We were cuttin' a gap in the Boche wire and they shelled us good and 'ard. When the smoke cleared we saw 'im on the wire, wi' 'is legs off. We couldn't get to 'im cos they had the position covered so 'e 'ad to stay 'angin' there til 'e died.'

Flo shuddered and wrapped her arm around him.

'And it's still goin' on and when my leg's mended they'll send me back to it all so the Jerries can 'ave another go at finishin' me off.'

Flo cuddled him close to her, rocking him. 'I shan't let them take you back,' she said. 'I shan't.'

Despite himself, Thomas clung to his sister and wept into her shoulder.

Alerted by Ena during her search for towels, Gladys Arkwright had been stunned to hear of the drama taking place across Coronation Street, but she was impressed by the way Ena put her whole self into doing what she could to help her friend. After giving her all the towels she had to hand, Gladys grasped Ena's arm and blurted out, 'You know real life, don't you, Ena?'

Ena was puzzled by the question but nodded. 'Aye,' she said. 'I do.'

After she had fled back to Madge's, Gladys did the only thing she could: she dropped to her knees and prayed.

That night, the regulars gathered at the Rover's Return, unaware of what was going on next door. Thomas had managed to lay his ghosts to rest long enough to join them. It wasn't so much the drink he craved but the company of men. It was all very well being at home with his family but he missed the comradeship and could relax in the smoky atmosphere of the Public bar. He was treated to a free pint of Best bitter by Jim Corbishley and the others slapped him on the back and offered to set up the next ones for him.

Thomas raised his beer to his lips, gulped some, smacked his lips and beamed at Jim. 'That's a corker of a pint and no mistake.'

'Bet you never tasted anythin' so good in them trenches,' said Jim.

'Aye, that's the truth. We don't 'ave beer, you know, but the sergeant keeps a bottle of rum. We all take a swig of it every day to keep our spirits up.'

'Rum?' Jim pulled a face. 'Give me ale any day.'

'Aye,' agreed Ned Buck. 'Ale for soldiers, navy lads drink rum.'

Thomas nodded but was distracted from the conversation by the arrival at the bar of Mary Makepiece. 'Me mam's sent me for a couple of bottles of pale ale,' she told Jim.

'She's turned into a bonny lass,' mumbled Fred Piggott to Ned.

'She has that.'

Draining his glass, Thomas caught her eye and nodded at her. She inclined her head towards him in a gesture she could deny later if word of it got back to her mother.

'Yer ma not feelin' up to an outin'?' asked Jim.

'It's bath night,' said Mary. 'She can't be

bothered wi' goin' out after bath night.'

'Would you like a drink?' blurted Thomas, before his brain could catch up with his tongue.

'Aye, go on. A pale ale,' said Mary.

Fred raised an eyebrow at Jim across the bar.

'What's the toast?' Mary asked mischievously.

'We're just welcomin' young Thomas back to the fold. It were right crafty o' 'im to get a bullet in the leg, weren't it?' said Ned, with a chuckle.

'Oh, aye,' said Mary. 'Dead crafty.' She raised her glass and took a big gulp.

'By 'eck, lass, you sup like yer mam,' said Jim.

Mary finished her drink, smiled her thanks at Thomas then, with the two bottles, told Jim to slate the money up for repayment at the end of the week before she flounced out of the bar. Thomas's eyes followed her.

Ned nudged Fred Piggott. 'You'd best shut yer mouth, son, or you'll be catchin' flies in it,' he said to Thomas.

'What?' asked Thomas, bewildered.

'You – stood there wi' yer mouth 'angin' open and yer tongue down to your boots.'

'Give over,' said Thomas, flushing.

The men laughed at his discomfort and returned to their beer.

Returning home to No. 11 Coronation Street with her mother's ale, Mary was in good spirits. She'd been bought a drink by a handsome lad in uniform, and there weren't many of those in Coronation Street these days.

Her youngest brother, Will, was in the bathtub in front of the range when she let herself into the house and put the bottles on the table. To annoy him she peered over the blanket wall that protected his modesty and laughed. 'There's nowt to write 'ome about yet, is there?' she said playfully.

'Mam!' screamed Will. 'Tell our Mary!'

Ivy came bustling into the room carrying a bundle of mending. 'Can't you leave the poor lad alone just for five minutes?'

'I can leave 'im alone for ever,' said Mary.

Ivy looked at her accusingly. 'You've bin drinkin'.'

Mary laughed. 'What if I 'ave? I went to the Rover's, not the Mission 'All.'

'Where've you got the money to buy ale?' demanded Ivy. 'You'd best not 'ave chalked it up wi' my bottles!'

'Did I 'eck,' said Mary. 'If you must know a gentleman bought me a drink.'

'A gentleman? In Coronation Street? 'E must've bin lost,' Ivy expostulated.

'It were Thomas 'Ewitt,' said Mary, caught off-guard by her mother's seeming good humour. She smiled to herself, and didn't see the slap coming until it was too late. She gasped and clutched her face, a big red mark spreading across her cheek. 'What was that for?' she demanded.

'You don't accept drinks from 'Ewitts!' shouted Ivy. 'Not now, not never!'

It was two o'clock in the morning when the distress of the previous evening and the night finally caused Ena to break down. She sat on the horsehair sofa in Glady's cosy vestry and clung to her friend as tears choked her. Gladys was crying too. 'It's so harsh,' she said.

'Why does God let things like this happen?' demanded Ena. 'Why?'

'I don't know, love, you're not the first to ask the question and you won't be the last.'

Madge's baby, a son, had been born dead three hours previously, and Madge, exhausted and haemorrhaging, had followed him out of the world less than an hour later.

No. 1 Coronation Street was now set in quiet darkness, with Sarah Buck having called in her undertaker husband Ned to deal with the bodies. She had sought solace in the gin bottle.

'She 'ad so much to live for,' choked Ena. 'A lovely 'ome, an 'usband, new baby, it's just not right.'

'I know, love,' said Gladys, stroking a stray hair away from Ena's brow.

'I'll 'ave to write to Dinky in the mornin', then go and see 'er mother. She'll want to know everythin' that 'appened. If only I'd gone to get a doctor, but she wouldn't let me leave her.'

'You were her friend, Ena. I see that now as one of your gifts.'

'What are you talkin' about?' asked Ena, sniffing back her tears.

'The Gifts of the Spirit. You have the gift of making friends, and you do it so easily. You seem to go through life adopting people, taking their burdens upon your own shoulders.'

'I don't,' objected Ena. She didn't see herself in that way at all: she was just a girl who took an interest in other people.

'It's not a bad thing,' said Gladys. 'Just the opposite, in fact. It's a precious gift to have and not many have it. You need to nurture it.'

Ena wanted to say, 'You're talking daft,' but she respected Gladys and knew that she would only say what she truly believed. She fell silent.

'Have you considered what you want to do when the war's over? Do you think you'll stay working the trams?' asked Gladys.

Ena had not thought about it at all and said so.

'Well, I've an idea,' said Gladys, wiping the tears from her eyes. 'It was something Mrs Makepiece said to me yesterday that got me thinking. I'm in need of a helper here, not just someone to dust and clean and lay out chairs, but a helper in the community.'

Ena looked at her quizzically 'I don't follow.'

'What is a church, Ena?' asked Gladys. 'Is it just a building or is it the people inside it?'

'It's the people,' said Ena firmly.

'Yes, and the Mission of Glad Tidings is nothing without those who worship inside it and live outside it. It strikes me that even though you live in Inkerman Street you know more about the lives of folk on Coronation Street than I could ever hope to.'

'I'm not a busybody!' said Ena in indignation.

'I never said you were,' said Gladys. 'But you think about it. I want help in reaching out to folk, letting them see the Mission is more than a building. I want you to be at the heart of the Mission. I've already talked to the Supervisor and he's all for it. The pay wouldn't be all that great but–'

Ena cut her friend short. 'Wait a minute, you're goin' too fast for me. Slow it down and start over.'

Gladys sighed as she watched another lock of hair fall into Ena's eyes. She pushed it aside. 'A hair-net is what you need, my girl.'

CHAPTER TWELVE

November 1918

The news raced through the kitchens of Coronation Street. The Corbishleys were moving. Men like Ned Buck were alarmed, until they were reassured that the Rover's wouldn't be closed down, just transferred to another landlord. Then many of the regulars pictured themselves moving behind the bar to act as mine host and fleece the working men of their hard-earned pennies. Jim Corbishley found the idea of any of his regulars taking on the responsibility of the pub hysterical. He was aware that a small body of them, Ned Buck and Fred Piggott amongst them, watched his every move behind the bar as he pulled beer pumps and opened bottles. He knew what they were thinking: that anyone could master such a trade. They gave no thought to balancing books, the keeping of the ale, the turfing out of aggressive drunks at the end of the night. He gave a hollow laugh when he considered that, more often than not, *they* were the drunks.

The Corbishleys' decision to leave the pub had been made after Nellie, now fully recovered from her near-death experience, had announced that she couldn't bear to remain in the Street and watch all the young men filing in through the pub doors, knowing that her own Charlie would never be one of them. As newspapers carried reports of British troops breaking through German lines and the Allies advancing through Belgium and France, the writing seemed to be on the wall for the Kaiser and Nellie wanted to act fast. She persuaded Jim that they deserved a break from being at the beck and call of the public and offered to move to his native village, Little Hayfield, where his brothers lived. She calculated that they had enough saved to rent a decent-sized cottage, with a couple of rooms left over to take in boarders if they so wished. Jim wasn't keen until she said, 'Just think, Jim, we could even have a little orchard.'

For years Jim had planted apple pips in bits of earth and attempted to grow a tree in the Rover's backyard but the closest he'd come to success was a twig that a drayman had stepped on. The thought of fruit trees gave Jim the push Nellie had hoped for.

Pearl had become hysterical when the news of the Corbishleys' departure had reached her and only calmed down when Nellie assured her that wherever she and Jim went they would always need a house-keeper. Having relied on Pearl for house-work and cooking for eight years there was no way that Nellie was going back to rolling pastry and making jam. Pearl, like Jim, was won over.

The residents of Coronation Street had their first look at the new landlord of the Rover's on the afternoon of 10 November. The brewery had planned the handing-over ceremony a couple of weeks before and it was a happy coincidence that the end of the war had left everyone in carnival spirits. The Corbishleys were due to leave the premises just after closing, giving them time to catch the train to their new life. Nellie was eager to shake the dust of Coronation Street from her heels but Jim was sad to bid the old place goodbye.

The woman who was going to take Nellie's place was Mary Diggins, a forty-three-year-old woman with no children and a passion for the music hall. She was short and plump and Pearl warmed to her immediately: Mary reminded her of a Toby jug her aunt had kept on her Welsh dresser. Mary annoyed Nellie by seeming to take great delight in the pub and its nooks and crannies – what Nellie referred to as 'gloryholes that collect dust' Mary saw as interesting features.

Nellie felt certain Mary wouldn't last two minutes attending to the demands of thirsty customers. She looked ripe for gossiping and taking too much of an interest in the lives of her customers. In Nellie's book a good landlady served beer, pocketed the profits and left the chatting to her husband. Nellie thought Mary's redeeming quality was her husband George, a big strapping fellow who was a retired police sergeant with a neat bushy moustache. Here was a man with whom Nellie felt comfortable; strong and able, a hearty man who enjoyed the company of men but also made women feel noticed. Jim Corbishley had never been like that, Nellie thought dejectedly.

Guy Ridley presided over the handing-over ceremony. He was one of the bosses at the brewery, a man who closely resembled a beer barrel. He was short and performed the ceremony standing on a chair taken from the Snug, but even then he didn't tower over heads as he had hoped to.

'Gentlemen ... and ladies,' he said, 'It gives me great pleasure, on behalf of the brewery, to thank James Corbishley for his sterling work over these past sixteen years. Sixteen years that haven't been the easiest of times for him or, indeed, for any of us. In recognition of his loyal service to Newton and Ridley, I am proud to present to him this beautiful timepiece, which, I am sure, will adorn his new bed-and-breakfast establishment in Little Hayfield.' He handed over a carriage clock. Jim hastily passed it to Nellie, who looked at it in disgust. Sixteen years, and all they had to show for it was a tiny clock.

'Before I officially hand over the pub to the new landlord, I should like to announce another significant change.'

There was a murmur among the gathered residents. As a body and as individuals, the residents of Coronation Street were not fond of change.

''E'll be puttin' prices up,' muttered Ivy Makepiece.

Hearing Ivy, Guy laughed hollowly and said, 'I can assure you that the prices won't be changing. No, the only thing changing will be the name of the establishment.'

That news didn't go down well with the gathered crowd and at once they started to voice their disapproval. Ridley raised his hands for silence. 'Let me clarify,' he said, 'the name is going to alter slightly. Some of you may remember that the pub is named the Rover's Return to commemorate the repatriation of my own dear son Patrick, after the Boer War. It was Patrick's own idea that the pub should be known as the Rovers Return, without an apostrophe, to celebrate the return of all your gallant heroes following this dreadful conflict.' He paused for applause but none was forthcoming from the confused crowd. Ivy Makepiece spoke for them all: 'What's an apostrophe?'

The Corbishleys' leaving party at the newly named Rovers Return Inn was attended by all their neighbours. Even Gladys Arkwright was persuaded to step over the threshold of the pub and to partake of a lemonade, bringing Ena along with her for the experience.

The two women sat together nervously just inside the pub doorway, each casting furtive glances towards the door whenever it opened, just in case the Mission superintendent should come a-calling.

'It don't seem right,' said Ena in hushed tones.

'I know,' said Gladys, 'but it seemed childish to turn down the invitation. I've known the Corbishleys since 1902 and they've always been welcome at my house. In fact, Nellie Corbishley used to be a regular attender until her spot of bother. It's only a lemonade.'

'Sure you don't want summat stronger?' asked Fred Piggott amicably.

'No, thank you. Miss Schofield and I have both signed the Pledge,' said Gladys.

'Oh, so 'ave I,' said Fred.

'When?' demanded Gladys, staring at his pint pot.

'Each Whit week, whenever there's a trip to Blackpool or Southport. I sign Pledge to get me free ticket on chara and then when I get 'ome I lapse. It's a terrible thing, lapsin'. I just ain't got the stayin' power.'

Gladys turned up her nose in disgust and was ready to retort when Ena placed a restraining hand on her arm. It wasn't worth rising to the bait.

In the Snug, Ivy Makepiece stared into the Public bar with a glint in her eye. On

361

another day the glint would have been aimed at Gladys and her little helper but today she homed in on another coupling that hit closer to home. Huddled together by the dartboard, with their backs to the cellar door, Thomas Hewitt and her daughter Mary were making hay together. Ivy couldn't tell what Thomas was saying because his back was turned towards her but years spent working in noisy mills had taught Ivy how to lip read and she could clearly read Mary saying, 'You'd best stop, me mam's lookin'.' Ivy's eyes narrowed and she drained her pale ale.

Now Mary watched her mother warily. She didn't want a scene in a crowded pub. Since her declaration that she and Thomas were courting, the old girl had done all she could to prevent them seeing each other, as had Gertie Hewitt, fresh from her spell in prison. Thomas's leg was no better so he hadn't returned to France. In fact, he had prolonged his injury by putting too much pressure on his leg so that he continued to be written off as sick. He still suffered terrible nightmares, and daydreams when his head was overwhelmed with the crump of shells bursting overhead. But he was learning to live with it.

Mary put her hand on Thomas's and squeezed it. 'Let's not make me mam mad,' she said. 'She's not worth the bother.'

'Aye,' said Thomas, annoyed. 'So far as I'm concerned, yer mam and our Gertie can go 'ang themselves. It's us that matter. The future, not the past.'

Mary looked up into his eyes and smiled. She was falling in love and the headiness of the situation made her giddy.

But not as giddy as the blow to her head. She cried out, and Thomas spun round to face Ivy before she had a chance to lower her hand. 'You miserable old cow!' he cried in Ivy's face.

'Stay away from my daughter, you toe-rag,' cried Ivy.

'We're just chattin', Mam,' whimpered Mary, clutching the side of her face. Ivy always dealt a mean swing.

'You'll not chat wi' a 'Ewitt!' screeched Ivy.

'Oh, belt up, you old bag,' spat Thomas, pushing Ivy away from him in disgust.

Ivy looked at him in horror. 'He struck me!' she cried to her neighbours. 'Did you see 'im lash out at me.'

'Aye,' said Ned Buck, 'and if you don't leave them alone I'll lash out at you too.'

Ivy stared at her neighbour in fury. ''Ow dare you–' she started.

'Oh, belt up and let the youngsters 'ave their pleasure.'

'Like your Alice?' asked Ivy. ''Avin' 'er pleasure in the back alley wi' Fred Piggott's lad?'

'You old bitch!' screamed Sarah Buck, launching herself at Ivy's back. She grabbed her hair and pulled the smaller woman sharply backwards. As Ivy went down Mary gave a screech and cried, 'Get off my mam!' then leapt upon Sarah Buck.

As chairs toppled over and Thomas attempted to prise Mary off Sarah's back, Gladys and Ena looked on in astonishment. If this was a common event in a public house they knew they were well out of it.

The cheers of the men and the women's screams were cut short by the splash of cold water. Jim Corbishley, standing beside the bar in his best suit, his cases ready in the back, put down his pail and said, 'That's the last time I do that.' He nodded at George Diggins, who stood staring at the heap of wet women, and said, 'It's the only way to separate them. Dogs and women, they're all the same.'

Gladys gathered up her coat and gloves

and pushed back her chair. She and Ena stood together in the pub doorway putting on their outside clothes and were jostled when the door opened and two men barged in.

'Do you mind?' cried Ena, as a door handle was rammed into the small of her back.

'I'm sorry,' said the younger of the men, then drew breath sharply. 'Ena?'

'Alfred?'

Ena's heart leapt as she looked at Alfred Sharples, framed in the pub doorway. The older man, she now saw, was his father, the conman.

'What you doin' in a pub?' he asked.

'What are you doin' in Weatherfield?' she asked.

'Where's your wife?' asked Gladys pointedly.

Much to Gladys's chagrin, Ena refused to go straight home with her and instead agreed to talk to Alfred. His disgruntled father seemed to share Gladys's views on the proposed conversation and set off purposefully to the bar, leaving Alfred to suggest that he and Ena took a walk.

Ena's mind buzzed with the disbelief that

she was actually walking down Coronation Street with a man she had once loved who had hurt her badly. She felt she should have run screaming from him rather than agreeing to give him her time. 'You've some nerve, I'll give you that,' she said finally.

'Please, Ena,' he said, 'you've no idea how wretched I've felt since I last saw you.'

'I've no doubt,' said Ena sharply, 'but, then, you were used to lying and pretending, weren't you? I was probably just one of many you lied to.' She was angry.

'I should 'ave told you I was married,' he said simply. 'I'm sorry I didn't but I didn't feel like I was married.'

'Was?' said Ena scathingly. 'I take it you still *are* married. I must be stupid walkin' down 'ere wi' a married man.'

'I'm no longer married,' said Alfred. 'I'm a widower. And, in reality, I never was truly married. Not in the truest sense of the word.'

Ena frowned, 'I don't understand.'

Alfred sighed and stopped walking. He stood outside Tommy Foyle's Corner Shop, beneath the gas lamp that illuminated the tins of fruit and canned meats in the window display. 'You see, a few years ago my father ran up some gambling debts and he couldn't repay them. This was before the war and we lived and worked together up Bury way. The chap he owed money to was struggling. You remember 'ow it was before the war. Some 'ad plenty and the rest of us 'ad nowt. This chap, he demanded me dad paid 'is debts, sayin' 'e'd tek us to court if Dad didn't pay up. Dad would 'ave gone to prison for sure, and 'e'd 'ave died there. That's why 'e came up with 'is plan. You see, this man 'ad eight children, most of them too young to earn their keep, so Dad suggested that I married this chap's eldest daughter so 'e didn't 'ave the worry of feedin' 'er no more. The chap agreed and I 'ad to go along wi' the plan, cos I didn't want me pa to go to prison. I were nowt more than a lad meself and I went along wi' it.'

Ena stared at Alfred in disbelief. It sounded like a plot from one of the Charles Dickens books Gladys kept on her shelf.

'So we got wed and me dad 'ad 'is debts cleared. She moved in wi' us and that was that. Only thing was, I never took to 'er and, well, to put it as nice as I can the marriage were never a proper one. We were man and wife in name only and now she's died of influenza. There's a lot of it about.'

'Aye,' said Ena, her mind racing. If his

story was true, and she figured no one could make up such a tale, then Alfred wasn't the Crippen she'd believed him to be.

'I were away fightin' most of the time, I only came back that time I met you, wi' me bad leg. That mended and I went back to fight. I'm only back now on leave because of my wife bein' taken. Compassionate, they call it. We buried 'er this afternoon, and all I wanted to do was rush round to see you. You could 'ave knocked me down wi' a feather when I saw you in the pub.'

'It were a celebration,' said Ena vaguely.

'I believe in fate, me,' said Alfred. 'Do you?'

'I dunno.'

'I believe things 'appen for a reason and I don't see why I should waste this chance to say what's on me mind. Ena ... will you marry me?'

Ena opened her mouth and stared at Alfred in the half-light of the dark street. Her arms flapped against her sides: she was unsure what to say or what to do.

There was an air of expectancy on the morning of Monday 11 November. The newspapers dared to speculate on the near end of the war. In Weatherfield residents

368

relied on the oldest form of communication
– word of mouth – to spread the news.

'I don't believe it,' said Alice Schofield, at
the breakfast table, 'I think it'll go on for
another two years at least.'

'But supposing it *is* true,' said Ena
excitedly. 'Supposing we go to bed tonight
in a world without war.'

'Nay, lass,' said Thomas sadly, 'there'll
always be wars.'

'So long as there's men fool enough to
fight 'em,' added his wife wisely.

Ena sighed into her porridge. 'Just think
'ow wonderful it would be,' she said
wistfully.

Alice snorted. 'You can tell our Ena's in
love again,' she said.

Ena blushed and turned sharply to her
sister. 'Who are you to say if someone's in
love or not?'

'You've seen that married fella again,
haven't you?' said Alice snidely.

Thomas lowered his spoon and stared at
Ena. 'Is this true? Are you seein' a married
fella?'

Mary was as quick as ever to calm her
family. Rising, she started to clear the breakfast things and said, 'He's not married, he's
a widower, and if Ena wants to see im then

that's 'er look-out.'

Thomas frowned. 'Who is this fella? Do I know 'im?'

'No,' said Mary, in a way that Thomas knew meant, 'Let that be an end to it.'

He sighed. He had always thought that girls would be easier than boys. With boys you had to watch over them, stop them getting into scrapes and making fools of themselves when sniffing too much of the barmaid's apron. However, it had turned out that girls, with their affairs of the heart, were twice as much trouble. Thomas glanced at his daughters and softened. If they had been boys neither would be sitting at the table: they'd be holding guns in a trench somewhere. Either that or lying in a foreign grave like so many decent British lads.

'If you must know,' said Ena, ''is name is Alfred Sharples. And it's a name you may 'ave to get used to.'

Mary eyed her daughter cautiously. 'Why's that, then?'

'Because,' said Ena, taking a deep breath, ''e's asked me to marry 'im.'

'Marry 'im?' shouted Alice. Fury rose inside her. It really was too much. Ena had had two proposals and she was the younger sister.

370

'And what did you say to 'im?' asked Mary calmly.

'I told 'im I'd think on,' said Ena.

'Aye, you did right,' said Mary.

'You need to think on and carry on thinkin' on,' said Thomas, 'if you're takin' on a man who's bin wed before. 'E'll be set in 'is ways. Old fella, is 'e?'

Ena laughed. ''E's same age as our Alice and I don't think 'e's set in 'is ways at all.'

'And 'ave you,' said Mary, 'thought on?'

'Aye.'

'Well?' said Thomas impatiently. 'Are you gonna wed the lad?'

'Oh, I can't make up my mind,' said Ena, 'which is why I've thought of what I've thought of.'

'You've lost me,' said Thomas.

'If the war ends today I'll marry 'im,' said Ena. 'If it doesn't I won't.'

Mary smiled. 'It's as good a way as any to decide,' she said, and laughed.

Thomas, caught up by his wife's infectious laugh, threw back his head and guffawed. Her parents' good humour caused a broad grin to break across Ena's face and she joined in. Only Alice sat isolated from the merriment. She stared at her family as if they had turned into lunatics.

At nine o'clock, Albert Tatlock clambered off a train. He had not had time to send a telegram or letter to the Schofields to inform them that he was on leave again. Instead, he arrived in Manchester with no fuss and no one to greet him. It was as well because he didn't want a fuss. He was aware of the euphoria at home but gave it little heed. He'd come from the trenches and the war was still in evidence there. Still, it was a curious time to be given leave but he needed respite from fighting.

Of course, Dinky had turned it down, preferring to stay on and fight than face the ghosts of his loved ones in Coronation Street. That was, in part, why Albert was intending to spend his leave in Weatherfield, rather than with his brother and his aunt. Since Madge Low's untimely death, No. 1 Coronation Street had remained empty. Dinky still held the rent book and tenancy agreement but had neither the heart nor inclination to return to the house where he had spent just one night of marital bliss. He had instructed Albert to act as his agent, and deal with the house and its contents as he saw fit. It was only on the boat back to England that Albert had decided how best to put the house to use. He would live in it himself, with his own bride.

At nine forty-five, Ena drew her scarf close to her face and blew into her hands. Ideally she would have liked to be wearing gloves or mittens but from experience knew that, even with her small fingers, it was impossible to operate the ticket machine when they were covered. She stamped her feet on the guard board of the tram and wished her driver would get a move on. Once the vehicle was in motion she was free to huddle in a warm corner.

Her thoughts, when not calculating the fare from Gypsy Corner to St Mary's, were occupied with Alfred and the sudden way in which he had blurted out his proposal. It hadn't surprised her. What *had* surprised her had been her encounter with the first wife those couple of years ago. Up to then she had seen herself drifting happily into marriage with Mr Sharples. She had felt secure in their future as a couple. Since then she'd continued to puzzle over the existence of a wife, having seen herself so clearly walking down the aisle with Alfred. No, his proposal didn't surprise her, and neither did the calm she felt now. Still, she mused, it was a good thing that his wife had turned up, as their relationship had been tested. She'd proved to herself, if it had needed proving, that she wasn't really interested in anyone else. If she had been, she'd have been walking out with Albert Tatlock by now.

Thinking of Albert, Ena bit her lip. She hadn't written to him in a while and was too aware that when she did next she'd have to mention Alfred. She knew Albert would take the news badly. Still, if the war ended soon there'd be no need to write as he'd be coming home.

At ten fifteen, Gladys Arkwright passed the collection plate down the rows of wooden chairs. The brief Monday-morning service was drawing to a close and, as always, she kept a close eye on the plate as it passed from hand to hand. All too often coins had disappeared from it rather than being added. At the end of the row, Ivy Makepiece handed it to Gladys. In the past ten years Gladys couldn't bring to mind one instance when Ivy had placed a coin on it.

Ivy continued singing the hymn of thanksgiving through her fat lip, a testament to her fight the previous evening. She grimaced as she tried to form the words. Behind her back Gladys allowed herself an uncharitable smirk.

At ten thirty, Thomas Schofield sneaked out of Hardcastle's mill to join his regular smoke-mates behind the loading bay at the rear of the mill, facing Coronation Street. As one of his chums was his foreman Thomas rested easy in the knowledge he wasn't committing an offence that would lead to his dismissal. 'Do you reckon it'll be over soon then?' he asked the foreman.

The other man spat out a loose fleck of tobacco.

'Don't mek much difference if it is or it isn't,' he said. 'Looms still gotta be operated, ain't they?'

'Aye,' said Thomas dejectedly.

At ten fifty, Alfred Sharples let himself out of his father's house by the graveyard, and started to walk briskly towards Rosamund Street. He knew that the number-sixteen tram, with Ena on it, would be trundling into the depot in five minutes' time and that she'd have a seven-minute turn-around break. Seven minutes wasn't long but even if he just caught a glance of her he might be able to work out which way her mind was working. Would she be his or not?

At eleven o'clock the world went mad. For those living around the parish church of St Mary's, Weatherfield, it started with the peal of the church bells that had remained silent for four years. They burst into life as the vicar heard the clang from neighbouring St Paul's. In the next parish, the vicar of St Peter's heard it and ran to his own belfry. One by one the churches of Weatherfield and the surrounding districts announced that something had happened. What that something was remained a mystery until the desk sergeant at Tile Street police station sent his bobbies out on their bicycles, ringing their own bells and proclaiming: 'The war is over!'

Word spread faster than spilt milk, as factory- and mill-workers, dockers, miners, housewives, children and shopkeepers passed on the news. The wonderful news.

Walking to the tram depot, Alfred Sharples was alarmed when workers from Earnshaw's mill suddenly broke out of the building and on to the pavement. 'What's to do?' he cried. 'Is there a fire?'

'War's over! War's over!'

Alfred stumbled into the crowd as they took over the street wanting to celebrate with loved ones and friends.

Albert Tatlock's tram disembarked at the Rosamund Street depot just as the news reached the workers in the building. Drivers and conductors threw their caps in the air and cheered with joy. A woman grabbed Albert and kissed his cheek. 'Isn't it wonderful?' she yelled. 'War's over!'

Thomas Schofield ran from Hardcastle's, not waiting for the foreman to pass on the management's ruling that work was suspended. He ran straight home, with only one thought on his mind. He barged down Inkerman Street and pushed his way into No. 14, where Mary stood open-mouthed in the middle of preparing the Monday lunch. 'What's to do?' she cried in alarm. 'Is it our Ena?'

'Nay, lass,' cried Thomas. 'It's the war. It's over!'

Mary dropped her baking tray full of potatoes and watched one roll beneath the kitchen table.

Gladys Arkwright sank to her knees in the

middle of the Mission hall and opened her arms to praise the Almighty.

Drinking in the Rovers Return, Fred Piggott and Ned Buck raised a glass each in memory of their sons.

Alone in her bed at No. 13 Coronation Street, Emma Piggott, taken ill that morning with the influenza that was sweeping the nation, heard the cheers and cries outside. She heard someone calling, 'War's over, Mr Foyle,' and her lips started to tremble. Their war might be over, but hers never would be. Her precious sons would never return.

Ivy Makepiece walloped her young son, Will, round the head. 'Don't tell lies!'

'I'm not lyin',' shouted Will. 'War's over!'

Watching her grandfather strangling chickens on Plank Lane market, Minnie Carlton broke into a broad smile and beamed at her friend Martha Hartley. 'If war's over my Armistead'll be comin' 'ome. We can get wed and I'll be Minnie Caldwell.'

Martha grimaced. 'Do we 'ave to stand and watch this? It's fair turnin' me stomach.' She gave a squeal and pointed at a chicken's body with its legs still moving although its neck was broken.

Minnie's grandfather laughed and thrust a chicken's head at Martha. Frightening women was one of the few pleasures left to him.

Thomas Hewitt and Mary Makepiece were lying in each other's arms on a hill overlooking Rochdale when the news reached them. They'd saved up for two weeks for the day's trip. It was a rare chance to be alone together. Tram, then train, and then a walk to the nearest hill, gazing down over the sooty landscape. She nestled into him and he pressed himself against her. Two lovers on the brink of a new world.

Ena heard the news as she stepped down from her tram and stood on the forecourt. The first time she had stood on peacetime English soil in four years. It was heady stuff. As her passengers ran off, seeking out their homes, she stood dazed in the midst of the depot.

'Ena?'

She turned, and wasn't surprised to see Albert standing there in his uniform. She started to laugh. It made perfect sense that right now Albert would be in the depot. He looked at her, concerned, as laughter convulsed her. She realised that she must look as though she was having a hysterical fit. She put out a hand towards him and said, 'It's all right, lad, I'm just adjustin' to the news.'

'Aye,' he said, 'it teks some gerrin' used to.'

'Ena!'

She turned at the sound of her name to see Alfred running up to her from the depot doorway. 'You've 'eard?' he asked, scanning her face.

'Aye, isn't it wonderful?' Suddenly the depot began to spin, and trams came at her, faces blurred together. Ena hit the concrete floor with a thud.

She came to lying on one of the seats of her own tram. Between them Alfred and Albert had carried her to safety, as people ran around the depot like headless chickens at Plank Lane market. It was as if a giant had released a crate of white mice on to the floor, as they darted in different directions, looking for a bolt-hole.

Ena groaned and opened her eyes. At first she couldn't remember where she was and then she heard the two men talking and remembered.

'I'm Albert Tatlock,' said one.

'Alfred Sharples,' said the other.

'I'm a friend of Ena's.'

'So am I.'

'Oh.'

'I see you two 'ave met,' Ena said, and looked around her, feeling foolish for fainting. 'What are you doin' in Weatherfield?' she asked Albert.

'I'm on leave,' he said.

'So am I,' said Alfred.

'Coincidence,' said Albert.

'Fate,' said Alfred.

'You'll 'ave to forgive me,' Ena said, 'only I just remembered what I'd told meself this mornin'.'

'Oh, aye?' said Albert.

'Yes.' She smiled. 'That's the answer by the way ... yes.'

Albert looked in confusion from Ena to Alfred. Then he didn't need to ask what the question had been. He could see it written on their faces. Suddenly he felt foolish. Foolish to be present at such a time and foolish to have thought that maybe ... just maybe...

Outside the Rosamund Street tram depot

the world was a mad place, but inside the number-sixteen tram the fragmented pieces of Ena's world were falling into place. She gazed into the eyes of the man she loved, took in his uniform, and heard the deep sigh of her friend, the man she had grown to know through his letters during the harshest of times. A man she could call a true friend.

'Albert makes a smashin' best man,' she said to Alfred, with a twinkle in her eye.

The publishers hope that this book has given you enjoyable reading. Large Print Books are especially designed to be as easy to see and hold as possible. If you wish a complete list of our books please ask at your local library or write directly to:

Magna Large Print Books
Magna House, Long Preston,
Skipton, North Yorkshire.
BD23 4ND

This Large Print Book, for people
who cannot read normal print,
is published under the auspices of

THE ULVERSCROFT FOUNDATION

... we hope you have enjoyed this book.
Please think for a moment about those
who have worse eyesight than you ...
and are unable to even read or enjoy
Large Print without great difficulty.

You can help them by sending a
donation, large or small, to:

**The Ulverscroft Foundation,
1, The Green, Bradgate Road,
Anstey, Leicestershire, LE7 7FU,
England.**
or request a copy of our brochure for
more details.

The Foundation will use all donations
to assist those people who are visually
impaired and need special attention
with medical research, diagnosis
and treatment.

Thank you very much for your help.